BELLE AMI

VENGEANCE

TIP OF THE SPEAR
THRILLER SERIES

BELLE AMI

VENGEANCE

TIP OF THE SPEAR
THRILLER SERIES

www.belleamiauthor.com

Published Internationally by Tema N. Merback
Calabasas, CA USA
belleamiauthor.com
Copyright © 2020 Tema N. Merback

Previously published as Vengeance © 2018 by The Hartwood Publishing Group, LLC

Revised and Re-Released by Tema N. Merback © 2020

Exclusive cover © 2020 Fiona Jayde Media
Interior design by Tamara Cribley, The Deliberate Page

PRINT ISBN 978-1-7322071-7-2
EBOOK ISBN 978-1-7322071-6-5

I dedicate this book to every woman and child who has endured abuse, rape, slavery, and human trafficking.

*The best men are not consistent in good—why
should the worst men be consistent in evil?*

– Wilkie Collins, *The Woman in White*

"Destroy the seed of evil, or it will grow up to your ruin."

– Aesop

CHAPTER 1

Midtown Manhattan, New York
September 11th
7:00 p.m.

Some firsts are unpredictable.

Some expected.

And some are down-right zingers.

But Layla Rose Hassani's firsts were nothing short of cliff-hangers.

Kidnapped in Dubai, thrown into an Iranian prison, attacked and brutalized, betrayed and abandoned—all "firsts" that even four years later still gave Layla nightmares. But one "first" changed her life forever.

The first time Layla met Cyrus Hassani.

He swooped in and rescued her from an Iranian prison, saved her more times than she could count, and almost died while getting her out of Iran. Layla fell in love with Cyrus during that perilous escape. He was the most irresistible man in the world—and her very own Superman.

Cyrus was the first man she'd made love with—and without a doubt—he was the only man Layla would ever love. The gift for all she'd endured in Iran was four years of a happy marriage and the blessing of their precocious four-year-old daughter Cerise.

But even with so much love and happiness, Layla's fears rippled beneath the calm surface of her life. Cyrus's past as a deep-cover agent in Iran working for Israel's Mossad, along with her own past as a survivor of that brutal kidnapping, meant they had to be cautious. The very danger that had brought her and Cyrus together could tear into their lives once more and rip them apart

Newsflash: Beware the jinx.

She thought about spitting on her hands like her grandmother, Dina, often did. If the superstitious gesture would ensure her good fortune, then damn she was on board.

But would it alleviate her secret fear?

How long before I spin out of control and end up in a ditch with an expired AAA card?

Her prayer?

You can have your cake and eat it too. A successful marriage and career are yours for the asking.

But no matter how many things went right, she still feared losing Cyrus and their daughter Cerise.

She was fortunate, indeed, that the past four years had been full of love, laughter, and learning. That foundation of strength had enabled Layla to add another first to her list. Her first internationally curated art exhibition.

Layla turned in a slow circle, gazing around the sprawling gallery of the Museum of Modern Art, bedecked with bold, brilliantly colored paintings on loan from the Tel Aviv Museum of Art.

She smiled at Zachary Biggs, the diminutive dynamo, otherwise known as MOMA's special exhibit's director. "I can't thank you enough for believing in me, Zac. You've given me a fabulous first…a 'pinch me' moment I'll never forget."

"You earned it, Layla." Zachary's blue eyes twinkled from behind his red, round-framed glasses almost as big as his head. "You've shown what a pro you are. This is a creation you can be proud of."

"Thank you," she said as they began to walk through the exhibit. "Without you, I couldn't have done it."

"I doubt that." Zachary stopped to admire Picasso's *Torso of a Woman*. "I agree with the notion that the curator of an art exhibition is like a movie director, and the installation process itself is akin to making a movie. If so, this show is your directorial debut. I knew the first time we met, you were a talent."

Layla's cheeks flushed at the older man's praise. "I'm honored by your faith in me, Zachary."

"Mounting successful shows at MOMA is my job," Zachary said, waving his hands with a conductor's flourish. "Nurturing talent is my passion. So, what's next for the rising star curator of the Tel Aviv Museum?"

Layla studied the cubist-style painting with Zachary. "Do you recall that in 1953 a seventy-two-year-old Picasso painted this last portrait of Francoise Gilot, his lover of seven years? This was the last of eight paintings and marked the end of their tumultuous love affair. Gilot left Vallauris, their home, shortly after that with their two children and settled in Paris."

Zachary nodded. "Picasso was a genius but not exactly a model partner and father."

Layla's thoughts drifted to her own genius, who was back home in Israel, taking care of their work of art, Cerise. Her Superman could definitely be controlling, but it was only because he worried about their safety. "I do stress about the demands of career and the toll it takes on a family. I've loved being back in the States. Putting on this show is one of the best things I've ever done, but right now, all I can think about is returning home to Cyrus and Cerise. Three weeks away is a long time. I'm glad I'm flying back tomorrow."

"It's a shame they couldn't join you in New York for the opening. It would have been a lovely interlude."

"Yes, but unfortunately, Cyrus wasn't able to take time away from work." *That's an understatement.* Her Superman husband was currently at the top of Iran's hit list. When he saved Layla and got her out of Iran, he also broke his deep cover—and as far as the IRI was concerned, committed treason. The once rising star of Iranian intelligence now had a target on his back—kill without question. Thank goodness when he first joined Mossad as a university student in Paris, he'd gotten his Jewish mother and sister out of the country. When the regime overthrew the Shah in 1979, Cyrus's parents had undergone terrible suffering. His mother had been arrested, raped, and tortured for civil activism. Pregnant with her rapist's child, she was finally released from prison and returned home to her husband, Aram, and Cyrus, who was only six-years-old.

Cyrus's father, who loved his wife deeply, helped her heal and showered love upon the baby girl who was born eight months later. But the repressive regime continued to batter his parents. His father—a successful architect—lost his practice and the family's wealth. Suffering a heart attack, he retreated to their home, a changed man, and eventually committed suicide.

Cyrus discovered the body.

Heart-broken but determined, Cyrus went away to Paris to study nuclear physics at the University of Paris. When a Mossad agent approached him about joining the ranks, Cyrus readily accepted. The country of his father's childhood had changed, and so had Cyrus.

Tears sprang to Layla's eyes whenever she thought about what her husband and his family had gone through.

It would be a long time before he would be able to travel outside of Israel.

Underneath the over-sized red glasses, Zachary's face resembled a Sharpei dog. Folds, wrinkles, and jowls headed south. "I was worried the protestors on the streets were going to kill the show."

"I was concerned about that too," Layla agreed.

"Sometimes, the first amendment is a pesky thing." Folds, jowls, and wrinkles rearranged themselves into a smile. "Fortunately, it doesn't take a genius to see the BDS and anti-Israel protesters are anti-Semitic and racists."

Zac was right about the protestors, their motives were questionable. Layla glanced at her watch. "Sorry Zac, I'm late for my dinner appointment. I'm afraid I have to run."

He held out his hand. "It's been a pleasure working with you, Layla."

She hugged him. "Thank you, Zachary. Working with you has been a dream come true."

They walked to a bank of elevators. "Is your security detail waiting downstairs?" Zachary asked as he pushed the down button.

"No, I released them for the night." She shook her head. "Those poor guys did a double shift because the other team was called away on short notice for some VIP. I felt awful for them and told them the gallery would arrange my escort. But to be honest, the restaurant is only a few doors down and the consul general will make sure I get safely back to my hotel."

"Are you sure? I'd be happy to have a guard walk you over."

"No, I'll be fine."

The elevator dinged. Layla got in. "Come see us in Israel."

"Will do. Safe journey, Layla."

The elevator arrived on the first floor, and she hurried through the nearly deserted lobby. Her heels clicked on the honed green slate floor, echoing in the large foyer. She appreciated Zachary's concern for her safety and thanked her lucky stars Cyrus didn't know she was walking the streets of Manhattan without security. The frenzied pace of the last few weeks had provided little opportunity for her to reclaim that free spirit she'd enjoyed before marrying a top spy.

She saw no reason why she couldn't walk the four minutes to the restaurant. Tomorrow her watchdogs would see her safely delivered, from the hotel door to the departure gate, for her flight back to Israel.

Fingers crossed—Cyrus will never find out about my little act of rebellion.

She bit back a giggle, feeling like a teenager skipping school, as the museum security guard stood ready to unlock the door for her. She smiled and waited as he did the honors. Nodding good evening, she stepped out onto West 53rd Street.

A warm September evening greeted her, she was glad she'd decided on the cream linen pantsuit and left her trench coat back at the hotel. Having been closeted all day in the museum, she took a deep breath. She glanced up at the banners hanging from streetlights and read, "Masterpieces of Israel."

What a rush. It's like seeing your name in neon lights.

She headed southeast on West 53rd toward 5th Avenue, a confident bounce to her step.

Midtown Sunday night traffic was light. Five minutes later, she passed under the signature white awning and red-lettered signage of the famed French restaurant, Ma Maison. Inside, the scent of flowers transported her to the French countryside. Beyond the reception area, she caught a glimpse of the floral arrangements in towering displays of color on rows of tables that cut through the dining room.

The maître-d' greeted her. "Good evening, Madame."

"Good evening. I'm meeting Avi Zaken for dinner."

"Of course, follow me, please. The consul general is waiting."

Layla followed the man as he deftly navigated the room. The soft, golden glow of chandelier light caressed the faces of the elegantly attired diners. Laughter and conversation blended with the dulcet voice of a French chanteuse singing "La Vie En Rose."

A white-haired gentleman wearing a pin-stripe Saville Row suit got up from the corner table with a warm smile on his face. "Layla, dear." He kissed both of her cheeks. "Congratulations on your triumph. Your father and Cyrus must be bursting with pride. I can tell you, everyone back home is exceedingly proud of your accomplishment."

"Thank you, Avi," Layla said, beaming.

He waited while the maître d' seated her in the upholstered, curved, red banquette. Avi took his seat, tanned face, glowing with admiration. "I'm delighted we could find the time for a meal together. My dinner dates are usually politicians or diplomats—this is a welcome change." He winked. "I much prefer sharing a meal with the most beautiful woman in New York."

"Avi, charming as ever, I see."

"No, my dear, just an honest, overworked government employee. Tell me, have you enjoyed being home in the US?"

"I have, but it's been such a whirlwind trip. I've hardly had a moment to myself. I've loved being back in the US, but the truth is I can't wait to get back to Cyrus and Cerise. Three weeks is too long to be separated from them."

"Ah, the love of a mother and a young marriage, just as it should be. What a beautiful couple you two make."

Their white-jacketed waiter interrupted, pouring Layla a flute of champagne.

Avi nodded his thanks to the server and raised his glass. "To you, my dear, and your family. *L'chaim.*"

"*L'chaim.*" Layla sipped, the bubbles tickling her nose. She took a moment and looked around the room.

"Avi, this restaurant is fantastic. What a treat to dine in such a beautiful place. Thank you for this invitation. It's the perfect end to a perfect trip."

"One of my favorites in New York, the last bastion of classic French cuisine and elegant dining. I don't get here often, but we're celebrating, are we not? Wait until you taste the food. The Dover sole is unforgettable."

"Cyrus is going to freak when I tell him. My husband is a wonder in the kitchen. Cerise and I are lucky. I'm afraid my cooking talents are far from gourmet." She lifted her brows and smiled self-deprecatingly. "I wish Cyrus could be here with us tonight. The ambiance and cuisine would be his ticket to heaven."

"It's a shame he couldn't accompany you..." Avi's voice plummeted to a whisper. "I'm afraid, even after five years, it's too dangerous for him to leave Israel."

"Do you think the Iranians will ever forget about him? I want so much for us to travel throughout North America and Europe."

"My dear, be happy you were able to dissuade him, and he permitted you to come here at all. I heard from the prime minister he put up a big stink, demanding increased security for you. I'm afraid it's unlikely the Iranians have forgotten an operative who betrayed their secrets. He's an unsung hero in Israel, but those in the know are grateful for his service. I think it's best he remains just where he is. A rising star at Mossad, doing whatever it takes to neutralize Iran's nuclear threat."

"Speaking of my husband's need to neutralize threats, please don't tell him I blew off my security and walked to the restaurant without my watchdogs."

Avi's face was a study in control. "That security team is clearly not Mossad. I should be chastising you, my dear, but since you arrived in one piece and are as dazzling as a ten-carat diamond to these old eyes, I'll withhold my lecture and agree to keep your secret. However, I do intend to reprimand those lazy good-for-nothings for letting you out of their sight."

Layla burst into laughter. "Please, Avi, don't be too harsh on them. In all fairness, I insisted they take the evening off. As far as your ancient stature, we all know you're as spry and adept as ever. They don't call you the silver-tongued diplomat for nothing."

"That, my dear, is a media sobriquet, an exaggeration."

"I'd say it's more of a well-earned designation. One thing is for sure—when I tell Cyrus about tonight, he's going to be jealous not only of the Dover sole but also of the man who wined and dined me."

Avi raised his hands in mock fear. "Then we'd best not tell him. I've no intention or need to incur the wrath of such a skilled adversary. I may be single and divorced, but I'm harmless. Please tell him dinner with me, excited you as much as dining with your father. Speaking of your father, how is Dr. Wallace?"

"Busy as ever between the laboratory and his doctoral candidates."

"Our country is grateful to have him on our side."

"It's hard to believe Israel is now our home. Dad's adjusted better than I thought he would. After my mother's death, I didn't think I'd ever see him happy again. Of course, Cerise has a lot to do with that. She keeps him laughing."

"Grandchildren are the greatest of blessings. And there's the added pleasure of being able to hand them back to their parents when you've had your fill."

Layla chuckled. "I'm lucky that Cerise has her Grandpa Aleck and her great-grandparents, Dina and Morris."

Avi raised his glass again. "To your continued good fortune, my dear."

Layla clinked her champagne flute to his. "You too, Avi, to your good health, and may you continue to represent Israel so ably."

"Thank you, my dear. But I must say, your husband is the lucky one. If he decides to seek another career, he'd have a bright future in politics with his admirable abilities *and* his secret weapon."

"Secret weapon?"

"*You*, my dear! With you by his side, Cyrus could go very far."

She shook her head. "Politics? I've never given it a thought, and neither has Cyrus." It occurred to her Avi's suggestion might hold merit…especially if it meant her husband's welfare. If Cyrus were an elected official, he would become a public figure. That might deter the Iranians from acting on any death threat against Cyrus since any attempts on his life would have major international implications. "Perhaps you've hit on something. I can't imagine anyone being able to resist my husband's charm." She sipped her champagne, hiding a smile as she pictured her blunt and forthright husband pandering to world leaders.

After dinner, while Avi settled the bill, Layla excused herself to go to the ladies' room. Washing her hands, she glanced in the mirror and noticed a young woman pushing a wheelchair into the elegant restroom. The large woman sitting in the wheelchair was bent forward, her face hidden in the folds of a scarf.

Layla smiled at the young woman who pushed the chair. "Don't worry, take your time."

In accented English, the woman thanked her as she tried to help the invalid rise. She struggled to lift the unsteady woman.

"Here, let me help you." Layla kneeled to assist and gasped as she felt a sharp prick in her leg. "Ouch!" She looked down and saw the glint of a hypodermic needle. Before she could even open her mouth to scream, her entire body spasmed.

Oh, God. What's happening to me?

Her legs gave out beneath her. She sank to the floor, her ability to control her muscles gone.

I'm paralyzed!

She tried with every ounce of strength in her being to wrap her lips around one word: *HELP!*

But all that came out of her mouth was a gurgling sound.

The two women worked as a team as they hauled Layla up and dumped her into the chair. The woman who'd pretended to be incapacitated crouched in front of her, unwound the scarf from her head, and grinned. Layla's eyes bulged with terror as she desperately willed herself to scream...

Hit! Kick! Claw his eyes out!

The man smirked and reached underneath the wheelchair. When he rose, he held a briefcase. After entering a code, the briefcase snapped open. Carefully he activated a switch, and the contents lit up and began to hum. He gave a satisfied nod to his accomplice and locked the case. Then he pulled a roll of duct tape from beneath the chair.

Rigid with terror, Layla watched him tape the briefcase behind a Demilune cabinet situated against the wall.

Layla's body may have been frozen, but her mind whirled into high gear as she realized they meant to blow up the restaurant and kill everyone there, including Avi.

I have to stop it!

In a frantic effort to resist, she tried to move her fingers and hands, but no part of her body responded. She groaned in anger as they effortlessly wrapped her in the scarf and blanket.

How could she have been so stupid to blow off her security? To risk everything without a thought to the danger? Her husband was a target, which made her a target.

I'm going to die, and I brought it on myself.

All she could do was watch as the terrorist removed the long black cover he'd been wearing. Underneath, he wore slacks, a shirt, and a tie. He grabbed a sports jacket from beneath the wheelchair and slipped it on.

With the transformation complete, he nodded to his accomplice. She peeked out the door and waved him out. A minute later, the woman wheeled Layla out.

Layla's bright hair was covered in the scarf and blanket. Anyone seeing her would believe she was an elderly invalid. She tried to scream a warning as they rolled past Avi, but her body was no longer hers. Avi was scrolling through his smartphone and didn't even look up. Every fiber of her being willed herself to scream, but all that emerged from her throat were muted hisses. Between the buzz of the chatting patrons and the music humming around the restaurant, no one could hear her pathetic cries for help.

My God! I will never see Cyrus or Cerise again. I will never see my family again...

An elemental agony gripped her soul, but she was unable to shed tears because of the drug flowing through her veins.

At the entrance to the restaurant, the man with the shoulder-length dark hair waited, holding the door open. Her terror-filled cries echoed only in her mind. She managed a slight tremble, and the wheelchair infinitesimally shook, which only registered in the maître d's eyes as pity. He quickly looked away and bid them a polite goodnight.

Outside, a black SUV idled at the curb. The doors swung open, and a man with curly dark hair jumped out. The two men lifted Layla out of the wheelchair, strapping her into the back seat of the vehicle. The woman who'd pushed the wheelchair slid in beside her. The driver hopped back into the front, while the long-haired man who'd pretended to be the invalid left the wheelchair on the sidewalk and took the front passenger seat. The driver zoomed off, much to Layla's despair.

Her heart pounded, fear strangled her. She struggled to regain control of her body—she needed to fight the drug that immobilized her. If she had any hope of being rescued, she needed to stay vigilant. Even the smallest detail might mean the difference between life and death. She did her best to keep as alert as possible, paying attention to every detail.

The vehicle raced away and left Ma Maison behind with a screech of rubber on pavement. The long-haired man in the front seat turned. He pulled a cell phone out of his pocket and punched the keypad. His finger hovered a moment, and he glanced at his accomplices. They nodded their approval, and he pressed a number. A few seconds later, a series of deafening explosions reached Layla's ears, followed by the blare of fire alarms, police sirens, and screams of terror.

Through the dark tinted windows, Layla caught glimpses of the shocked faces of people on the street as they turned to watch the fiery storm that had erupted. It was chaos—people running as fast as possible away from the blast.

Layla closed her eyes for a moment as the horror sank in.

Oh, God! Today is September 11th!

Her kidnappers had chosen the anniversary of the worst terrorist attack on US soil to execute their vile deed.

Inside the car, the kidnappers hooted in glee, their excited conversation sounded congratulatory. It was madness.

Hundreds of people are dead and dying, and they're doing a happy dance.

She recognized the language. *Farsi. They're Iranian.* Fear of a different kind crept up her spine.

Kidnapped, I'm kidnapped. These monsters just blew up the restaurant and murdered innocent people, and I'm the cause.

Guilt tore through her.

Oh, God! Avi and all those poor people.

Could she have done something to prevent this? If only she'd brought her guards. They would have accompanied her to the washroom. Could they have stopped the terrorists? But the terrorists had no doubt prepared for any eventuality, including her security detail. They probably would have efficiently subdued them with the same drug they'd injected into her. Her bodyguards would have been dragged into a bathroom stall and ended up as part of the body count. Ironically, her desire for some time to herself on that brief walk had saved two lives.

She swallowed the lump in her scratchy throat. It felt like someone had dragged rusty nails down her gullet. Even the debilitative drug couldn't prevent the tears now blurring her vision…

My sweet Cerise, Mama loves you. Forgive me, my angel. Forgive me.

She shook with the heartrending sobs that only a mother could feel knowing her daughter would grow up without her.

She'll have the same kind of childhood I did. Without the love and care of a mother to guide her.

At least Cerise would have Cyrus to protect her.

Cyrus!

Her very soul fractured in agony.

My darling Cyrus. My Superman. We had four beautiful years together. Please don't slip back into that darkness. For Cerise's sake and for mine.

I love you. I love you both until the end of time...

No!

A voice screamed inside her head.

For God's sake! Fight! Fight for Cerise and Cyrus. Fight for yourself.

You survived torture, near-rape, and brutality before. You can survive this.

With every fiber of her being, she fought to move. Shocked, she was able to lift her arm.

The drug must be wearing off.

Glancing at the door beside her, she realized it was unlocked.

Could she do it? Could she fling open the door and roll out? She'd only ever seen it done in the movies.

The traffic was light now, she might just manage it without getting hit by an oncoming car.

Her arms and legs began to tingle as the feeling returned. Adrenaline pumped through her veins, giving her added momentum.

I'll only have one shot at this.

Her breath caught as the car slowed down, and the right blinker flicked on.

Do it now!

Letting out a roar of rage, she elbowed the woman beside her and reached for the door handle to fling herself out.

For a second, she thought she would make it, but her movements were too jerky and awkward. The next moment, the locks immediately shot down, and the car sped up. The driver flicked on the radio and blasted rock music.

Layla groaned in frustration. The woman spat out curse words at her in Farsi. The bitch pulled another hypodermic needle from her bag.

"No!!!"

Layla's screams were drowned out by the loud music as she fought off the woman with the needle.

The man in the front turned around and backhanded Layla in the face. Dazed, she fell back against the seat. She moaned as the familiar prick of the needle, punctured her skin.

The effect was immediate.

Her body slumped over.

And a black curtain came down over her eyes.

CHAPTER 2

Washington, D.C.
September 11th
10:45 p.m.

The persistent ring of a cell phone wrenched David Weiss awake. His body was still entangled in the sheets with Cass's cheek pressed against his chest. His eyes still heavy from sleep, he reached blindly for the phone. "Hello," he rasped.

"Where the hell is Agent Saladino?"

Shit, we're fucked.

David looked at the phone, cringing when he saw the initials, JC. "Hold on, sir. I'll get her."

"Is that you, Agent Weiss? Why are you answering Cassandra's phone?"

He struggled to find a reply. "Uh, I'm sorry, sir. I thought it was mine. We were just going over some casework, and Cass went to make some coffee. Both our phones were on the table, and I grabbed it by accident." He tried to make light of the odd hour, filling the pause with a chuckle. "You know how she is? She's in work mode twenty-four-seven." He wondered if the director would buy his cock-and-bull story.

"Working this late? Agent Weiss, you need to put your foot down, or she'll wear you out. Both of you need to learn to relax when you're not on duty. Not that you're going to be seeing any downtime anytime soon. Get Cassandra now. We've got a problem, and I want you both on it."

David covered the phone with his hand as he nudged Cass.

"Who is it?" she yawned, stretching like a sleek cat.

"It's the director," he whispered. "I screwed up. I thought it was my phone, but it was yours."

Cass bolted upright and grabbed the phone from his hand. "Yes, sir, what's up?" Cass listened. "Yes, sir, coffee. It won't happen again." She scrunched her eyes closed, this time for what David thought to be a long time. "We'll leave immediately, sir. I'll call you when we're in the air." She hung up.

"So, what's up?"

Cass ran her hands through her hair. "A restaurant's been blown up in Manhattan. The initial report states over a hundred casualties. On 9-11, again." She met his gaze, her eyes aflame with anger. "It looks like a terrorist attack. J.C. wants us on the case ASAP. You have a packed suitcase here, don't you?"

"Yeah, one here and one at my place."

"Good. A helicopter will be waiting on the roof at headquarters in forty-five minutes."

"Cass, do you think the director suspects us?"

Cass dressed as she spoke. "I don't know. He's pretty savvy, but we've been a pretty successful team, and the director will always do what's best for the agency. Right now, his mind is on one thing only. An attack on US soil that should have been stopped. Somehow we failed, not just us but every anti-terrorist agency in the homeland and abroad." She shook her head. "Another soft target. All of those innocent lives gone in an instant. All the bad guys we stop, and it's never enough. One gets through, and a hundred people die."

"We'll get them, babe." He kissed her temple.

"I know. It's just that the bad guys only have to be right once, but we have to be right all of the time."

"Sometimes, bad things happen, no matter how hard we try."

She wrapped her arms around him, hugging him tightly. "I'll never accept that. I won't rest until we get them."

"Ditto, partner. Together we're unstoppable."

She smiled. "We'd better get a move on, or we're going to be unstoppable and late."

CHAPTER 3

Tel Aviv, Israel
September 12th
5:00 a.m.

"Cyrus, I'm sorry to call with such devastating news."

Cyrus shot up in bed, immediately reaching for Layla and feeling nothing except cool sheets.

A chill crept up his spine.

He swallowed hard. "Yes?"

"I just got a call from New York. There's been an attack." It was Rafi Cohen, the director of Mossad's North America desk.

A pounding began in his chest as if a regiment of infantry stampeded over his heart. "What happened?"

"A bomb exploded in a restaurant…near the Museum of Modern Art. Probably a hundred or more people have been killed. Avi Zaken was there. We assume he's dead."

"Oh, my God, they got the consul general. Layla's going to be devastated. She's very fond of Avi."

"About Layla." Rafi's voice softened. "We checked with the consulate. Layla was scheduled to have dinner with Avi…I'm so sorry, Cyrus."

Cyrus's heart stopped. He couldn't breathe. He held the phone in a death grip. "How do we know she was in the restaurant?" he barked. "Have you checked with her security detail? Maybe she was late. She's always running late. Maybe she canceled at the last minute because she was tired from the opening. Maybe they ended up going to another restaurant. For God sakes! Maybe there's been a mistake."

"Layla released her security detail earlier in the day—"

"Why would she?" He closed his eyes. "Shit. Shit. Shit, that sounds like Layla." He fought to steady his voice. "What else?"

15

"The FBI's tracking down museum security and surveillance footage inside the museum and on the street. I can't tell you for certain if she was in the restaurant, but in all likelihood, she was there." Rafi's voice cracked. "I'm so sorry Cyrus—"

"It's not true," he whispered.

"Cyrus, it's all over the news. The FBI's calling it a terrorist attack on the anniversary of 9-11," Raffi said.

He wanted to scream. He wanted to punch a hole through a wall. He wanted to crawl into the fetal position and die.

"What about Aleck—Layla's father— has anyone notified him? I can't—I mean—I can't talk to him right now."

"Dodi's calling him."

The prime minister. Good.

"We've already requested inclusion in the case," Raffi continued. "The prime minister is up in arms. He's adamant this attack will not go unanswered. He's called for an emergency meeting at the Office, but given the circumstances…if you feel you can't—"

"I'll be there soon." Cyrus hung up and stared at his cell phone, it fell from his fingers and landed on the bed, bouncing once before it settled on the mattress.

She can't be gone. She can't be gone. She can't be gone…

He reached for Layla's pillow and pulled it into his chest, inhaling her scent.

Layla. Dead. Layla. Dead. Layla. Dead.

He roared with grief. He howled, keening like a wild beast.

My fault. My fault. My fault.

The words burned into his brain like a firestorm leaving nothing but ashes.

I'm the target. It's me they wanted. Oh, dear God, why didn't I stop her from going?

He wanted to kill someone—something—anything that might stop the pain. He thought about the Jericho pistol in his drawer. He wanted to hold the shiny, black, instrument of death to the head of her killers. He wanted to pull the trigger. He wanted to see blood gush, brains splatter—he wanted revenge. He closed his eyes and pictured the turquoise blue of Layla's eyes. He began to shake like a man with a pneumatic fever. He stuffed the pillow in his mouth and screamed and screamed and screamed.

"Daddy! Daddy!"

The patter of small bare feet on hardwood reached his ears.

Cerise!

He stumbled out of bed and ran into the master bath, splashing his face with cold water.

"Daddy, where are you?"

"In here—" his voice cracked. "In here, *metuka.*"

The door flew open. A small child, her bed-messed, auburn hair clung to her damp scalp. She ran into the room, flinging herself into his arms. "Daddy, I heard a monster yelling," she sobbed, tears glistened on her cheeks. "I'm scared, *Abba.* I miss Mommy."

"Ssh, Ceri, ssh. It's okay, my darling, *Abba's* here. There's no monster, I promise. No monster." He held his daughter close. His hand smoothed her hair as he comforted, "It's okay, baby, Daddy's got you." He walked around the room, cuddling her close, whispering soothing words in her ear.

Cerise pulled back and laid her chubby little hand against his cheek. Her Nile green eyes, identical to his, gazed at him with trust. "Thank you, Abba."

His heart was being torn apart. "You're welcome."

Guilt sliced through him, the pain worse than the blade which had nearly killed him five years before in Iran. Layla had always called him her Superman.

Some Superman, I am.

When Layla had been kidnapped in Dubai five years ago and held hostage in Iran, he'd risked everything to save her. He'd nearly died protecting her. His recovery had been long, excruciating. In his foolish pride afterward, he'd rejected her efforts to see him, thinking she'd be better off without him. He'd thought himself unworthy of her love.

A year later, a miracle brought them back together. He was given a second chance. He held the proof of their love in his arms. Cerise had fallen asleep, he lay her on the bed, smoothing her damp curls back from her forehead. Spying a delicate red-gold thread of hair on Layla's pillow next to Cerise, he touched the silky strand. His eyes blurred with tears once more as he bent down and kissed the crown of Cerise's head.

He picked up his cell phone and called Layla's grandparents.

He needed to plan.

CHAPTER 4

Mossad Headquarters
Gilat Junction, North of Tel Aviv, Israel
September 12th
7:00 a.m.

It was a perfect blue sky morning, but Cyrus's heart was full of blackness.

He parked his car and walked through the security checkpoints, entering the secret hexagonal building that housed Mossad. He was directed to a private conference room where he was greeted by the drawn faces of the officials. Every department head had been ordered to an emergency meeting with the prime minister.

Cyrus poured himself a cup of coffee. He needed to hold something in his hand. He needed to keep his mind occupied because otherwise, he'd go mad. A hand gave his shoulder a firm squeeze. He turned and met the eyes of the prime minister.

"Cyrus, words can't express my sorrow for you and Cerise," Dodi said in a low voice, heavy with emotion. "I promise you I will do whatever it takes to bring those responsible to justice."

"Thank you, sir." He ignored the noose of guilt that grew tighter around his neck—ignored the constriction of his chest—ignored the pounding of drums in his head—ignored the crash of cymbals in his ears.

Function. He told himself. *Function.*

"I took the liberty of calling Aleck myself. I made the same promise to him."

Cyrus dropped his eyes, ashamed he hadn't called his father-in-law. "I haven't spoken to him yet. I didn't know what to say—How is he?"

"Devastated. The loss of a daughter, impossible to endure. But he's a pragmatist, a man of science. He'll find his way through with the help of friends and family. Thank God for the child."

"This is all my fault."

"None of this is your fault. The truth is, Avi may have been the target. Layla may have been collateral damage.

Collateral damage.

Cyrus shuddered. It made him sick to listen to those words. It made him sick to hear the prime minister use the past tense when speaking of Layla.

A few hours, a few days, a fucking lifetime, there's no way I'll ever get used to it.

"I don't think the attack had to do with Avi."

"How do you know?"

Cyrus looked the prime minister in the eye. "I just know. I think they were trying to get to me."

"We'll know more soon. Where is Cerise."

"I took her to Layla's grandparents."

"Yes, I remember, the Holocaust survivors who fought in the War of Independence."

"I thought Cerise would help them bear the pain. They've lost so much already. I don't know how they'll get past this."

"Death is not something you never get used to. Survivors are better at it than most of us." The prime minister scanned the room. "I think we should begin." He patted Cyrus on his shoulder. "I plan to include you in every aspect of this investigation if it's what you want?"

Vengeance will be mine…

"That's exactly what I want, sir."

The prime minister turned to the occupants of the room. "Let's begin, gentlemen."

Cyrus knew, or knew of, every man in the room: Noam Levi, the director of Mossad, Uri Klein, the head of operations planning and coordination, and Rafi Cohen, the director of the North America desk. Cyrus's boss, Lieb Dahan, the head of the Atomic desk whose focus was Iran and the Arab nations was also there. They exchanged a nod. Thrown in were a couple of government ministers whose expertise was intel and counterintelligence.

At the end of the oval table sat one man Cyrus had never seen him before but instinctively knew who he was. The man's shaggy hair, beard, and glasses had the air of an absent-minded professor type, but his height and muscular build gave him away as a member of *Metsada*, special operations. The same top-secret branch of Mossad that Cyrus had worked for when he was a deep-cover mole in Iran. Israel's most lethal death squad lived in the shadows. Their personas were ever-changing along with their disguises.

Cyrus had been one of them for ten years until a slip of a red-haired young woman had changed everything.

Layla.

He couldn't believe the love of his life was gone. Five years ago, he'd broken his deep cover to save her. Cyrus had been deep undercover for ten years as a top Iranian security agent when in truth, he'd been working as an agent for Israel. Cyrus had been born and raised in Iran, his father had been Iranian, but his mother was Jewish. Cyrus's parents had both suffered at the hands of the Iranian regime. His mother had been arrested, jailed, raped, and brutalized in prison when she'd participated in a rally while his father, a prominent architect, had been stripped of his wealth and achievements after the fall of the Shah. Years later, a broken man, Cyrus's father committed suicide. Cyrus's anger and hatred of the Iranian regime burned inside him. When he'd gone away to university in Paris at the age of 18, only months after his father's suicide, he was approached by an agent for Mossad and recruited. Undergoing rigorous training, Cyrus had burned with hatred over the suffering of his family and had channeled that into fighting Iran's nuclear threat from the inside. Ten years he worked deep undercover until a pretty red-headed American girl named Layla Wallace had been kidnapped in Dubai while on holiday with her boyfriend.

Cyrus still saw red when he thought about her so-called boyfriend. The boy's wealthy Saudi father paid the exorbitant ransom for his son but had left Layla to rot in prison. She wouldn't have lasted long enough to rot, she would most likely have been dead within a week from the notorious brutality in the Iranian prison system. Cyrus had gotten to her just in time. Just as the brute guard, Mohammad Marzban, had hauled her into a secluded part of the prison to rape her.

Cyrus's heart clenched. He didn't realize it at the time, but looking back, he'd fallen in love with Layla at first sight, when he had been ordered by his superior Jalal Rahimi, deputy minister of Oghab2, MOIS's counterintelligence directorate to remove her from Evin Prison where she'd been taken after the kidnapping. The Iranians had guessed she had a powerful connection—her father, Aleck Wallace. Aleck was a renowned nuclear physicist, born in Scotland, he'd immigrated to the US where he settled with his Israeli wife, Rebecca. After Rebecca passed away from cancer when Layla was a teen, Aleck had raised his daughter with all the love he could give her.

When Aleck had been informed by the FBI about the kidnapping, he knew what he had to do. He realized the FBI was not acting fast enough, so he contacted his former Harvard college roommate, who was now the prime minister of Israel. Despite their life-long friendship, Aleck and Dodi were different at their core. Aleck would have sacrificed everything to save his daughter, including leaving his home in Boston and his adopted country, the United States, for Israel. Escorted by a Mossad agent to Tel Aviv, Aleck was taken to Mossad headquarters, where Dodi had amassed a special ops team to extract Layla. The key to the team had been Cyrus himself. His orders from Mossad had been to get Layla out of Iran. If he couldn't get her out, his orders had been to kill her so that the Iranians could not use her as a bargaining chip to get to Aleck. Those orders had come from the top—from Dodi himself. Cyrus had disregarded the orders and would have gone rogue if it had come down to it. Layla or Aleck never knew about those orders. Cyrus had never told her or Aleck. If Aleck ever found out, he would probably leave Israel and take his specialized research in nuclear physics with him. But Cyrus could understand Dodi's reasons, Israel's very existence would have been threatened if Aleck was forced to work with the Iranians. Millions of lives would have been at risk.

"The FBI has secured the scene, and a team of Israeli explosive experts are on their way to assist," the prime minister began. "I expect it will take less than thirty-six hours to process the site." He looked at Cyrus, his voice softening. "DNA evidence should reveal who the victims are and, if we're lucky, it will point to who was responsible.

"I'd like to hear briefly from each of you," he went on in a stronger tone, "and then I suggest we adjourn until we receive more information from the FBI and our team of experts. I want you all to work together on this, sharing everything between departments. We must function as one unit if we're going to be successful. Once we've identified who did this, we'll plan our retribution. This attack will not go unanswered."

Cyrus listened to the various leaders deliver their initial reactions and what information had been gleaned so far. He wasn't surprised the man from *Metsada* didn't speak. It was a secret division of Mossad, completely autonomous, its existence barely acknowledged by anyone in government. The man sat among them like a ghost. No one addressed him. However, Cyrus knew when the time came, and words became superfluous, the "long arm of Israeli justice" would be called upon to fulfill their mission statement: "Whatever we can't kill, we close down." Whoever had attacked Israel would be eliminated, and their operational command would be shut down. It didn't matter where on earth they hid, *Metsada* would not rest until justice was served.

Revenge was all Cyrus could think about. The only thing that mattered. He had every intention of being the man who pulled the trigger. He would kill them all, whoever had taken Layla from him. He pulled out a business card from his wallet and wrote a quote on the back. A Bible quote from Deuteronomy: *"Show no pity: life for life, eye for eye, tooth for tooth, hand for hand, foot for foot."* *Revenge shall be mine. You owe me.*

On his way out of the room, he slipped the card in the Metsada agent's pocket.

CHAPTER 5

A pile of ash.

Ma Maison—the once elegant restaurant where movers and shakers in New York city converged to meet, eat, and celebrate—had been reduced to smoldering rubble.

FBI agents Cass Saladino and David Weiss arrived by helicopter to supervise the investigative team. They landed amid the dozens of police and fire department vehicles. The NYPD and NYFD had cordoned off a two-block radius around the explosion site. Firefighters manned ladders still dousing what was left of the building with water. On the street, the coroner, firemen, and building safety inspectors stood waiting for the okay to enter. The blast had ignited a firestorm fueled and intensified by the stoves, ovens, and gas lines. No one was getting inside the building anytime soon. They could only wait for a declaration of safety. There was no hope of finding any survivors, just the grisly task of collecting remains and evidence.

The Federal Bureau of Investigations, along with our law enforcement partners, declare the explosion at Ma Maison to be a terrorist attack. Further updates will be provided as necessary. Due to the nature of the attack, the FBI will not be releasing any details that might hinder the investigation. Our primary focus at present is to find the perpetrators of this heinous act and prevent any further attacks. The safety of American citizens and our homeland is our primary concern.

Cass's statement was released and carried by every media outlet in the USA and abroad. Then like the investigator she was, she turned her attention to unraveling the facts surrounding the worst attack on US soil since 9-11.

Hundreds of people had been in the vicinity, either on the street or in neighboring buildings, when the bomb exploded. The injured were rushed to area hospitals while Cass and David took the lead in questioning bystanders who had been uninjured or mildly injured and being tended in one of the emergency medical tents set up by EMS and first responders. One man and his wife had been blown into the entrance of a building farther down the street. Miraculously the man had minor cuts, and his wife, though shaken, was unharmed.

Cass checked her notes: John and Abbey Durand. Fifty-five and fifty-two, respectively. He was approximately six feet, short, medium brown hair, receding hairline, glasses, wearing a grey suit. She was approximately five-six with a dyed blonde bob, slender and stylish, wearing a red wrap-around dress tattered and blackened from the explosion and debris. A blanket was draped around her shoulders. Both real estate agents. "John Durand? Anything you may have seen will be helpful to us."

"My wife, Abbey, and I were on our way to Ma Maison for dinner," he said, gripping his wife's hand. We couldn't get a cab—we were late."

"We were celebrating our twenty-fifth wedding anniversary," Mrs. Durand added, wiping her eyes with a crumpled tissue. "No kids but two Shih Tzus."

Mr. Durand glanced at his wife's teary face, his own eyes swimming with tears. "If we'd been on time...."

Cass looked at David. How many times had they heard the same comment from other survivors? Cass had always struggled with the concept of fate. Why were some people killed and others not? Was it fate, or was it just a random set of circumstances? "I know you've been through a terrible shock," Cass continued, "but do you remember what you saw just before the explosion?"

Mr. Durand closed his eyes in concentration. "As we walked down 52nd Street toward the restaurant, a black SUV with tinted windows, pulled away from Ma Maison and raced toward us at a dangerous speed, about seventy miles an hour." Mr. Durand opened his eyes. "I remember saying to Abbey how crazy that was, and then less than a minute later, everything exploded."

"Do you recall the make of the vehicle?"

"A Chevy Tahoe. Decked out with all the bells and whistles," Mr. Durand opened his eyes. "My brother-in-law just got one after landing a big contract at work. I went with him to the dealership. I can still see that car, the way it barreled down the street…and then the explosion. It was horrible—"

David interjected, "Did you see the license plate?"

John shook his head. "No, we couldn't because of the speed of the vehicle."

"New York plates?" David dug in.

"I think so, but I can't say for certain."

"John, tell them about the wheelchair," Mrs. Durand interrupted.

Both David and Cass asked at the same time. "What wheelchair?"

"Oh, yes, that's right. Abbey and I had been worried they wouldn't hold our reservation because we were so late. We were focused on the entrance of the restaurant as we were rushing down the street. A woman exited pushing a wheelchair with another woman sitting in it—"

"There was a man behind her. And then another man got out of the SUV. The two men lifted the old woman from the wheelchair and placed her in the SUV," Mrs. Durand said.

"The same SUV that raced down the street at us, just before the explosion," John added.

"And I thought it odd that they'd left the woman's wheelchair on the sidewalk. I mean, who does that? Why would you leave someone's wheelchair?" Mrs. Durand asked.

"Abbey's great aunt is in a wheelchair, and those are really expensive," Mr. Durand added.

"We were going to push the wheelchair back into the restaurant, but then—" Mrs. Durand's hand covered her mouth as a sob escaped her. Her husband wrapped his arm around her.

Cass signaled to an agent who came running. "Jim, find out if they've found a wheelchair. I want it processed immediately."

"Did you see what the person in the wheelchair looked like?" David asked. "How do you know it was an elderly woman?"

They both looked at each other, shaking their heads. "We don't know," Mr. Durand replied. "We couldn't see her too well. I guess we just assumed she was old. We were too far away, and she was all wrapped up in a dark blanket and wore a headscarf."

"Do you mean like a scarf someone going through chemo might wear?" Cass asked. "Or a hijab?"

"A hijab," Mrs. Durand answered. "I worked for ten years as a TSA officer before going into real estate. I know just about every kind of clothing there is."

Cass nodded, her lips curving up in a slight smile. "Did the woman look like she was awake? Conscious?"

"No, she didn't move any part of her body. She looked kind of slumped over," she said. "I guess she could have been paralyzed."

David scratched a few notes into his notebook. From the corner of her eye, Cass read the phrase: *Possibly paralyzed or drugged.*

"Can you describe the people in the SUV?" David asked Mr. Durand.

"Um…"

"Honey, my husband knows cars. I know people!" Mrs. Durand interjected. "The two men had black hair. One had long hair to his shoulders, and the other had short curly hair. The long-haired one was tall, over six feet. Striking looking guy, handsome. He was built too. Muscular. The guy with the curly hair couldn't have been more than five-nine, muscular too, but not as impressive as the tall one," she said with a lift of her brows. "And the woman with them had black hair too. She was about my height, five-six but overweight. Not very pretty. They looked Middle Eastern. Like I said, twenty years in the TSA. Don't get me in trouble for profiling, but we couldn't help it. After 9-11, we were all on high alert."

"No, ma'am." Cass didn't look at David. She knew if she did, there'd be a smug look of 'I told you so' on his face. They'd discussed this a thousand times. Political correctness and the public's fear of being labeled or accused of being anti-this or anti-that prevented people from coming forward with valuable information that, in hindsight, might have prevented a crime. He was right.

Mrs. Durand was quite chatty. "Unfortunately, or fortunately, otherwise we might not be here to tell you anything, we were too far away for me to give you details as to eye color. Oh, by the way, they were beautifully dressed. Definitely high-end duds. European labels. You know what I mean, honey." She winked at Cass.

"Thank you, Mr. and Mrs. Durand, you've been a big help," Cass said. "We'll contact you if we have more questions later." She waved another agent over and told him to release them and get them a ride to their hotel.

She and David walked back to the command post. Cass couldn't help but comment. "Quite a character that Mrs. Durand, don't you think?"

"Hilarious, she should be in the FBI. I nearly lost it when she made the profiling comment."

"Interesting about the wheelchair. There could be prints, DNA, who knows?"

"You know this doesn't pass the smell test. It's beginning to feel like there's something else going on here."

She shrugged. "We'll know more once we've identified the victims."

Cass's cell phone rang. The initials JC vibrated on her screen. "Yes, sir." She waited. "We welcome any help the Israeli evidence analysts can offer. Oh, and we've discovered some interesting information." She quickly filled him in on what they'd learned. She paused. "No, I don't think the engineers are going to let us into the building until tomorrow, maybe not until tomorrow night. The evidence is spread over a large area. They must have used a lot of explosives to cause this kind of devastation. Definitely a seasoned bomb maker."

"Yes, sir. I'll keep you informed…I'll let the Israelis know." She hung up.

David's eyebrow raised in question. "What's this got to do with the Israelis?"

"The director just told me the Israeli consul general was dining at the restaurant with a woman, an American, who lives in Israel. She's the curator of a cooperative art exhibition at MOMA between Israel and the US. Get this. Her husband works for the Israeli government in intelligence. Where, or in what capacity, we're still waiting to hear. He's suggested they may have been the targets."

"We need to get into the building." David frowned toward the team of engineers who stood helmeted, waiting to inspect the building.

"Well, I'm not risking your sweet ass, or mine, until it's safe."

"Ditto, boss." He smiled and bent to whisper in her ear. "You know how far I'd go to protect your sweet ass."

The double entendre was not lost on her.

CHAPTER 6

Lancaster, Pennsylvania
September 12th
9:00 a.m.

Layla woke with a start, soaked in sweat, gasping for air. *Where am I?* Her head spun from the drugs. Her eyes wouldn't focus. The horror of her last moments before the injection came back. *Ma Maison. The explosion. Avi.* She clamped her eyes shut, trying to drive out the gruesome images of death and destruction. Tears rolled down her cheeks. She tried to wipe her face, but her hand jerked. She was handcuffed to the bed frame.

She managed to dry her eyes, and her vision cleared. She looked around. Square room. Whitewashed walls. A plastic chair. One window. She listened but could hear no voices. No sound of traffic. No human movement. Her mouth was dry, her lips chapped. She needed water. She needed to go to the bathroom.

She was frightened. Confused. *How is it possible I've been kidnapped again?* She needed to find out. She called out, "Hello, is anybody there? Anyone? I need help."

Even though she'd called out for help, the sound of footsteps panicked her. Someone was coming. She held her breath as she listened to the key turn in the lock. The door opened, and a man entered the room. The man who'd been dressed as a woman in the bathroom. The man who'd activated the bomb. She recoiled from the rifle pointed at her.

"What do you want infidel?" he said in accented English. His gaze strafed her body, riddling her with bullets of contempt.

"I…I, please, I need water, I need to go to the bathroom."

The way he looked at her made her skin crawl. Hatred and lust warred for supremacy in his eyes. She recognized the hat he wore, a green beret with an emblem embroidered on it.

Bravely she asked, "You're Iranian, aren't you?"

The man's frown deepened. "We ask the questions."

"Please, what possible use can I be to you? I'm an art curator. I have nothing to do with politics, or whatever it is you want."

The thin line of his lips curled into a vicious sneer. "Cyrus Hassani? Dr. Aleck Wallace?"

Layla blanched. "I'm sorry, you've made a mistake I…I have no idea whom you're talking about."

"Don't be an idiot. You're an amateur and a terrible liar. We know who you are. Your husband is a traitor, and your father has become an unacceptable threat. We are aware he's working on a project that threatens the IRI. Your husband must be punished, and your father must be stopped."

The IRI…? "The Islamic Republic of Iran," she whispered as she recalled the name. A wave of nausea seized her. *Please, God, I hope I'm still in the US and not in Iran.* Horrific memories of beatings and near-rape flashed through her mind. "I won't help you."

The man's smile was scornful, dismissive. "We don't need your help. We only need you. You're the bait."

The truth of his statement made her gasp. They kidnapped her to set a trap for Cyrus and her father. She needed to stop talking. She needed to think. "Please, I'm thirsty, and I have to go to the bathroom."

"In good time, your needs will be met."

The door flew open, and the short, curly-haired man from the SUV entered. "I see our prisoner is awake. Good. We need to make a video for YouTube." The way he looked at her made her want to scrub her skin raw.

"All that red hair should be riveting on video."

The man with the rifle spoke. "If you cooperate, things might go easier on you."

"What…what do you mean by co-operating?" Layla's eyes swept back and forth between the two.

Curly head reached into his back pocket and removed a sheet of paper. "You will read this, and we will film you. The release of this video on the Internet should grab the attention of the Americans and the Israelis."

"Ali is going to take good care of you. He's a very persuasive man, very skilled."

The blood drained from her face. *Is he threatening me with rape?*

He unhooked a ring of keys from his belt loop and released the handcuff, binding her to the bed frame. Layla rubbed her wrist.

He turned and addressed the other man. "Ali, I'll be back in a minute with the video camera." Laughing, he teased, "Behave yourself, brother. There will be plenty of time later to satisfy your needs."

Layla sat in the chair, her eyes downcast, desperate not to invite additional scrutiny from Ali. They were brothers, but Layla couldn't see the resemblance, other than they were both dark and swarthy. Ali began to circle the chair, his rifle aimed at her. He lifted her hair with the muzzle, his breath quickened. Layla shuddered from the touch of the cold steel against her neck. "Please, stop," she begged.

"Why?"

"Because you make me uncomfortable. You're scaring me."

"Don't be afraid. I'm not going to hurt you. If you let me, I might be able to help you."

"Why would you help me?" She forced herself to look at him.

"An exchange might be possible."

"I don't know what you're talking about. I have nothing to give you."

"You're very lovely. Surely that is of some value."

Without considering the risk, she erupted. "I would never let you touch me!"

He shrugged, smiling. "As you wish. I can assure you I would never resort to rape. There's no reason when all you need is to be convinced of the benefits."

"Convinced of the benefits? You're living in a fantasy."

His grin displayed a gleaming white row of teeth. *The bastard is enjoying this. Torturing me turns him on.*

"It would be foolish for you to die when a few hours of pleasure would grant you freedom. You might consider that once we've dealt with your husband and your father, you might be set free to return to your child."

Oh, God, my baby! Cerise. A cold chill swept through her. Powerless. She felt completely and utterly impotent. He watched her, his eyes riveted on her face as if he could read her thoughts.

The other man returned, and Ali backed away from Layla. Curly-head set the camera up on a tripod and adjusted the lens. "Go ahead and start reading."

Layla scanned the words on the page and shook her head no. "I won't. I won't read this. You can kill me, but I won't read this." Defiantly she let the paper fall to the floor.

Ali and curly head looked at each other knowingly. "Oh, but I think you will. Show her the video on your iPhone, brother."

Ali handed the assault rifle to his brother. He took his iPhone from his pocket and opened an app. Holding the iPhone in front of Layla, he hit the play arrow. Layla caught her breath. Her eyes blurred with tears as she watched her grandparents exiting their home in Tel Aviv. Between them, holding each of their hands was a giggling Cerise. Her beautiful, auburn-headed child looked up and asked, "*Savta* and *Saba*, can we get ice-cream after the park, please?" Layla's hand pressed against her mouth as she tried to keep herself from sobbing. Her grandparents continued walking with her daughter down the street toward the park, completely unaware they were being tailed and filmed.

Ali clicked off the video. He opened another app that displayed photos of Cerise sliding down a slide and being pushed on a swing by her great-grandmother. The last pictures were of Cerise and her great-grandparents sitting outside at a nearby ice-cream parlor.

Layla began to shake as though she had the flu. *My God! They could order their killings with just one text or phone call.* "H-how close were they that they w-were able to record their conversation?"

"Electronic surveillance equipment with a bionic ear synced with video can receive and record from great distances," Ali said. "However, in this case, they weren't very far away."

"Give me the paper." She swallowed the bile that burned her throat.

The two men donned balaclavas and stood on either side of her, deadly bookends pointing rifles at her. Shaking from head to toe, she stared into the camera and read in a quavering voice.

"My name is Layla Wallace Hassani, and I am married to Cyrus Hassani, a traitor to the Islamic Republic of Iran. My father, Aleck Wallace, is a nuclear physicist helping the infidel Israeli occupiers build weapons that threaten to annihilate the Islamic Republic of Iran and bring war to the Middle East.

Because of their crimes, I was kidnapped. I'm being held prisoner on the Great Satan America's soil. Because of its support of the Little Satan Israel, a bomb was detonated in a restaurant in the cesspool known as New York City. Hundreds of people were killed, including Avi Zaken, the consul general for Little Satan Israel. There is no place on Earth, nowhere safe that the long arm of Islamic justice cannot reach. America has shown itself to be weak and corrupt, an easy target. This is Allah's justice, and in his name, it was done.

Turn over both Cyrus Hassani and Aleck Wallace to the Quds Force in Syria for trial and sentencing, and I will be released to raise my daughter.

We will fight in the name of Allah until every infidel is driven from the Middle East. We will never rest until Israel is forced from the Holy Land, and Palestine is free of the occupiers.

If you fail to heed this warning, I will be executed by the sword of Allah, blessed be his name, sharp is his sword, which will never grow dull. This bombing is only the first of a series of disasters which will be inflicted upon you should your leaders fail to follow our directives. We have the means, and we will not be stopped."

Layla raised her eyes to the camera. *Forgive me, Cyrus. Forgive me, Father.* Silently she mouthed, "Save Cerise."

Fear fueled her resistance. Love fueled her bravery. She would do whatever it took to keep her daughter safe.

CHAPTER 7

Tel Aviv, Israel
September 12th
6:00 p.m.

He could breathe. He could walk. He was still functioning, but his soul was ashes.

Cyrus approached the door of Layla's grandparent's home. At any other time, he would have been happy to spend an evening alone with his child. But this was not like any other day—this was the day after his world had come crashing down.

His work in intelligence had taught him that starting backward through a process of elimination was sometimes better. Removal of the least likely threats allowed him to focus on the more likely perpetrator—Iran. Believing he was the target of Iran's reprisal, he pinned his efforts on the Quds Force and its affiliate, Hezbollah. Targeting Layla was a bullet intended for him. He'd poured over pages of intel, both HUMINT and SIGINT intelligence, trying to find anything confirming Layla had survived the bombing. He'd worked all day hoping for traction but had ended up only spinning his wheels.

Now he was drained, and his defenses were down. He vacillated between the fragile hope Layla was still alive and the devastation of losing her forever.

A gentle breeze blowing from the Mediterranean rustled the leaves of the bougainvillea that wove up the trellis. The fading light cast shadows at either end of the porch. Approaching the door, he closed his eyes, willing himself to project something other than sorrow to his child.

The door flew open, and his daughter rushed past her great-grandparents' legs, like a butterfly in flight. He knelt and opened his arms, love swelling in his chest.

"Daddy!" Cerise, like her father, was a linguistic savant, the three languages of her parents seamlessly blending in her mind, mixing and arbitrarily voiced.

"How is the love of my life doing? Did you have a good time with *Savta* and *Saba*?"

Her green eyes reprimanded him. "Daddy, I'm not the love of your life, Mommy is. You always say that to her. Both of us can't be the love of your life."

Cyrus fought brimming tears. *Layla dead. Layla dead. Layla dead.* The words pounded in his mind. But his heart, his heart refused to accept them.

"Of course, you're right, Cerise. I should know better than to try and fool someone as wise as you. But isn't it possible for one man to love two women equally?"

Cerise's chubby little hand cupped her chin in contemplation. "You are right, *Abba*." Her delighted grin enveloped him. "You may love two women so long as one of them is Mommy, and the other is me."

"And what if we give you a sister?" The pain of voicing aloud his and Layla's hope cut like a knife. He was acting out a charade for his daughter. Trying to convince himself that if expressed aloud, he could keep Layla alive and make their future real.

Cerise rested her head against Cyrus's, her arms wrapped around his neck. "Oh, *Abba*, then you will love three women." A moment passed before she pulled back, her twinkling eyes meeting his. "I'm not sure, *Abba*. Can you handle three girls?"

Cyrus chuckled and kissed the top of her precocious head. Nothing could dampen the love he felt for his child. He rose and took her hand, walking toward the woman who'd witnessed and survived more horrors than any human being should ever know. Dina Freiberg Rose, Layla's grandmother, stood waiting, her hooded eyes scrutinized him, questioning.

Dina had loved and lost so many family members and friends during the Holocaust that Cyrus often found it hard to meet her gaze. She seemed to be able to read everyone's thoughts with just one sharp look. When they got inside, Dina walked into the kitchen, where she motioned for him to sit down at the table.

"I really should get Cerise home, Dina, you must be exhausted after a full day and night of caring for a four-year-old. Where's Morris?"

"Morris is playing cards at a neighbor's house. I insisted he get out of here for a few hours. Sit, Cyrus. I want to talk to you. Cerise has eaten, and you look like you could use a good meal."

Cyrus slouched, his shoulders bent. Dina's piercing gaze could melt a polar ice cap. Her scrutiny reminded him that he was the cause of one more tragedy that had struck the family.

"Cerise, my darling, come into the living room and I'll turn on the TV. I want to give your *abba* some of the chicken soup I made."

Without hesitation, Cerise obeyed her great-grandmother. Taking her hand, she looked lovingly at the older woman, her green eyes full of trust. Her parting comment to him was a testament to her adoration of the old woman. "Oh, Daddy, *Savta* makes the best chicken soup in the world. Wait until you taste her matzo balls, they are so yummy."

Cyrus was in awe of the deep and abiding love between the old woman, who'd seen too much of evil, and the innocent child who'd seen none. Dina returned, her slippers slapping against her heels as she walked. When she reached the pot simmering on the stove, she stirred, filling the air with the aroma of chicken, vegetables, and spices. His daughter's singsong voice tickled his ears as she sang along with the characters on the children's program.

"Times like this, Cyrus, require a strength many don't possess. When I saw my parents, my sister, and two brothers shot in the street by the Nazis, their blood pooling, their lives over in an instant, I didn't think I could go on. I thought witnessing my family's murder was the worst thing that could ever happen to me."

Cyrus stared at Dina's rigidly straight spine, speechless.

"I was wrong, of course. Work camps and then the concentration camps taught me there were degrees of horror. They also taught me how to bear the unbearable. When I was liberated at Bergen-Belsen, all I wanted was to live in safety, in peace." She ladled soup and three matzo balls into a bowl and set the bowl in front of Cyrus.

She pulled out the chair across from him and sat, clasping her veined hands together. His eyes stared at her intertwined fingers, bumpy knuckles, papery skin that revealed deep purple veins. Hands that had toiled through the war, they'd held both life and death. The strongest hands he'd ever seen.

"Fighting for the birth of Israel, for a secure homeland gave me a reason to live. I found no peace in Israel, but I found something worth dying for. In the Irgun, I met Morris, a Polish survivor who'd suffered unspeakable horrors. We fought a war. We won a war. Life carried on. God blessed us with Rebecca, and then he saw fit to take her from us." She took a tissue from the pocket of her flowered apron and wiped her eyes.

Layla had told him the story of her mother, Rebecca. He knew she'd studied at Harvard, where she befriended two fellow students. She married Aleck Wallace, who became a nuclear physicist and professor. The other roommate she'd keep up a correspondence with until the day she died of uterine cancer. He went on to become the prime minister of Israel.

Cyrus had a hard time imagining how Dina and Morris could live with so much loss. *Tough as iron.* He'd seen the same will of steel in other survivors. His mother had the same sort of strength.

"You look terrible, Cyrus."

He didn't know what to say. "I…I lost my wife. How do you expect me to look?"

"How are you going to save my granddaughter if you don't take care of yourself? Cerise needs you to be strong. Eat," she ordered.

The fragrance of the clear chicken broth stirred a hunger he hadn't felt since the news…he couldn't even think the word to himself. His whole body stiffened at the thought, rebelling. Bile rose in his throat as he forced himself to acknowledge what might be the truth—*Layla dead—Layla dead—Layla dead.*

Anger thundered through him. It pulsed in his temples so strongly he thought he might explode. He tried to suppress it, but the anger poured from him, hot, burning, like molten lava. "Dina, you of all people should let me wallow in my sorrow. She's gone, Dina, Layla, your granddaughter, my wife, the mother of my child is gone!"

Dina studied him. "Anger is good, *liebling*. It's proof you're alive."

He instantly deflated. Dina failed to be roused by his harsh words. All his insecurities re-surfaced. He was never good enough for Layla. A double agent. Half-Jewish and working for Mossad—but Iranian. The enemy.

He imagined that after the loss of her entire family in the Holocaust and then the loss of her only child, Dina had pinned her hopes and dreams on Layla. Layla, who'd grown up thousands of miles away in America, had only developed a special relationship with her grandmother when she'd returned to Israel after her kidnapping in Dubai.

Dina knows the truth. She knows I broke Layla's heart.

While protecting Layla's life, he'd almost lost his. Getting her out of Iran had been a harrowing journey. He'd been seriously injured in a fight, stabbed in the stomach. After months of surgeries and therapy, he'd refused to see Layla. He thought she would be better off without him. He was a broken man, but that didn't excuse anything. He should have known, and he should have realized she needed him. She'd gone through the pregnancy alone. And then he waltzed back into her life, and she forgave him. He was broken inside, and she healed him. She and Cerise. But how do you heal a broken man who's lost the only woman he could ever love?

Dina had every right to hate him. Every right to wish he'd stayed away. If he had, then maybe Layla would be alive today.

Looking into the old woman's piercing blue eyes, he wondered if she knew he was to blame for Layla's death.

"It's my fault. I'm the reason Layla is dead." His voice was as hollow as a ghosts.

Dina's eyes narrowed, ever so slightly, but she said nothing.

Neither he nor Layla had ever revealed the truth of Cyrus's past. In Israel, they were safe, at least that's what they'd believed. But keeping his past a secret hadn't kept Layla safe.

His fingers spread wide on the table, pressing down on the worn linen tablecloth to keep his body from shaking from guilt and shame. "You see, in Iran, I worked for the Israeli government. I did things. Terrible things, to keep Israel safe. I can't prove it—yet—but this could be retaliation against me." His voice ground down to a whisper, "They wanted to hurt me. Do you understand? It's my fault. Once we have proof…"

"She's not dead." Dina's eyes held his unblinking. "I feel it. I feel her. I have always known when death is at my door. He's not here." Her thin, wrinkled lips formed a grim line.

Has grief stolen her mind? But as he stared into the depths of those wise old eyes, the tiniest bit of light crept into the cracks of his broken heart. He placed his hand over her bony wrist. "I'm sorry, truly sorry. I loved her more than anything in my life. She was my heart and soul. I need you to know she was everything to me. She knew every hour of every day how much I loved her. I can't bear the thought of you thinking otherwise. I can't bear the thought of you hating me."

Dina burst into laughter. Laughter, so deep that tears formed in her eyes. She dabbed her eyes with the tissue she'd shoved back in the pocket of her housecoat. "Why would I hate you, Cyrus? Why would I hate the man who brought such joy to my granddaughter? The man who created the child who is the crown jewel of my old age. You must be *meshuga*, crazy." She grabbed his hand in a hawk-like grip and pulled him close. All he could see were her blue eyes, ancient, but the same blue as his wife's.

41

"Layla's love for you is endless. It filled her whole being. You were her other half. My granddaughter was very clear, like me, about her needs and what she wanted from this life. She never doubted you were the one for her. Once she set her sights on you, you were toast. Now eat the soup. Layla and I need you to be strong. Soon you are going to have to find my granddaughter and bring her back to me."

Cyrus shook his head. *This woman is crazy.* But he knew better than to argue with an old woman who claimed to possess powers he could never understand. It was enough Dina believed in him, believed he would rescue Layla just as he had in Iran. Her belief stirred something in his soul. Yes, he was a spy—methodical—logical. But he was also a man who loved a woman. Miracles were possible when a person loved. Layla's love had saved him, and now, if she was alive, he would save her. He prayed the old woman had a gift of vision, and the ability to see into the future.

He ate the golden soup and fortified himself in hopes of that possibility. If Dina was right, he would find Layla. Save her. Bring her home. He would bring her home to the two old people beneath this roof. Home to the daughter, who still did not know what she'd lost. Home to the father who'd devoted his life to her. Home to the man who was dead without her.

CHAPTER 8

September 13th
5:00 a.m.

He awoke, soaked with sweat. He'd dreamt of making love to her. Of that first time in Iran when he couldn't deny his love for her any longer. His body ached with the sensual memory of holding Layla. Every muscle was sore as if he'd just been in a fight to the death. The alarm clock read five a.m. He was too tired, and it was too early to face the day. He kicked off the damp sheets as he tried to harness his strength to face another day.

By the time he'd gotten Cerise home, bathed her, tucked her in, and kissed her goodnight, he'd had just enough energy to crawl into bed. His day of examining every bit of intel and data about the bombing had yielded little. Separating his personal devastation from his professional objectivity had taken its toll. The images of death and destruction strewn across his desk ate into his soul. The photos of body parts of the once-living, the torn and tattered clothing worn by them, reduced their lives to insignificance. At one time, he could examine such images and be able to maintain his emotional distance. But after Layla and Cerise, he was no longer immune to the impact of such suffering. These were fathers, mothers, brothers, sisters, grandparents, decent people who didn't deserve to have their lives snuffed out in an instant.

Innocents targeted by cowards.

But even those horrific images couldn't stop the tide of weariness washing over him. And so he'd fallen asleep into blessed oblivion as soon as his head hit the pillow.

And now awake once more, his grief hit him like a punch to the solar plexus, stealing his breath. What wouldn't he give to hold his wife in his arms again. He closed his eyes and imagined her face the way she looked when he made love to her, but all he could see was the way she looked when she was afraid. He shuddered at his inability to reconnect to the dream or to her.

The emptiness of his world returned to him. A torrent of emotion ripped through him, the pain of his heart being torn in two. He lay there, a grown man, trying to reconcile himself to the loss of his beautiful wife, the love of his life, and he cried. He cried for himself, for Aleck, Cerise, and for the two old people who had lost brothers, sisters, parents, a daughter, and now, God forbid, a granddaughter. His heart seized, rebelling from the emotional pain. He remembered they'd been trying to have another child. The thought of not only Layla's loss but also that of that potential child scalded him, burning him like the fires of Hell, testing his sanity. He lay unable to move until the first rays of sunlight drove the shadows and his demons from the room.

Morning came, and with it, the reality of another day. Like an actor on a stage, he did his best to behave normally with Cerise as he prepared her for preschool.

Mindlessly, he chopped vegetables. The mundane activity simulated normalcy. They laughed over a breakfast of *shakshouka*, eggs poached in a tomato and vegetable sauce, and a chopped salad of finely diced tomato, onion, cucumber, and bell peppers. He listened to his fire-headed daughter reprimand him several times when he did something in a manner differ-ent from Mommy. It took all his strength to hold back the tears, stabbing his eyes when Cerise confided she liked his cooking better than *Ima's*. If Layla was dead, he couldn't imagine how he'd find the words to explain to his daughter that her mother was gone forever. Instead, he focused on the charade, forced himself to laugh as the joy oozed from her like nectar from a hibiscus flower.

"*Abba*, when is *Ima* coming home? I miss her?"

"Soon, baby girl, Mommy will be home soon. I know she misses you just as much as you miss her."

"But she hasn't called in so long."

"It's only been two days, baby. You know she's very busy with the art opening." Lying to Cerise felt like a bayonet thrust into his stomach. He could barely swallow his food. He looked at his watch. "Come on, Cerise, get a move on. We're going to be late. Go brush your teeth and get your backpack. I don't want to have to listen to teacher Miriam lecture me on being late." He held his hands to his heart, mimicking fear. "She scares me."

Cerise's giggles erupted in a scale of notes resembling bells. "Don't worry, *Abba*, teacher Miriam will forgive you." She ran toward the bathroom, her thick auburn curls bouncing about her head.

Cyrus took a deep breath, silently praying this day would pass without any of Layla's DNA being discovered at the bomb site.

He dropped Cerise off at preschool, reminding her that her great-grandmother would pick her up afterward. Before he'd gotten back into the Kia, his cell phone began to ring. He fumbled with the phone, answering as the door slammed shut. "*Ken*," he said, starting the engine.

"Can we meet?" He didn't recognize the voice—*No caller ID*.

"When?" *The card worked. Metsada*.

"Now, if you'd like?"

Cyrus knew better than to question the man on an unsecured line. "Sure. Where?"

"Edna in Ramat HaSharon, it's not too far from 'The Institute.' Persian cuisine, you'll like it."

"Fine. I'll be there in twenty minutes."

Click.

Cyrus pulled into the parking lot and hopped out of the car. The closed sign was up on the restaurant door. He peered through the glass window and pounded. From inside, a beefy guy wearing an apron approached and unlocked the door. "Sorry, sir, we don't open until eleven-thirty."

Cyrus looked at his watch, which read nine a.m. "I'm supposed to meet someone here. Now." He looked around the parking lot. There were no other cars.

"Who are you supposed to meet?"

Cyrus narrowed his eyes at the man. "What difference does it make?"

The man shook his head. "No difference to me. Go around back to the table with an umbrella. You can wait for your mystery man there."

"What, wait for two and a half hours?"

The larger than life fellow just shut and locked the door without a reply.

What the hell. May as well give it a few minutes. He walked around back and sat down at the only table with an umbrella and lit a cigarette.

"Those things will kill you."

Knocking the table over, Cyrus jumped, simultaneously turning and pulling his Jericho from its holster. He pointed the gun at the stranger.

The man, sported bleached blond, spiked hair, and wore an earring and dark sunglasses. He'd snuck up behind Cyrus and stood, his arms crossed over his chest with a smirking grin on his face. He wore a Hawaiian shirt with pineapples on it and beige Bermuda shorts that revealed thick, tanned, muscular calves.

"You scared the shit out of me."

"I'd say you're either rusty or sloppy."

Cyrus relaxed his trigger finger and holstered the pistol. "A little of both. I spend too much time sitting at a desk." He reached out his hand, not bothering to ask the man his name. The rules of the game dictated no names or at least not real ones.

They shook hands, and both bent to right the table, taking a seat opposite the other. Cyrus studied the man's face. "I know you—we've met before, haven't we?"

"No, we've never met."

"Correction, we didn't actually meet, but you're the guy who wore the disguise at the emergency meeting with Dodi. Dark glasses, wig, Metsada, right? I put the card in your pocket."

A smile rose from his generous lips, which revealed a row of sparkling white teeth. "What you wrote on your card was an interesting way to introduce yourself. Call me, Aryeh."

"The lion, the king of beasts." He scrutinized Aryeh. "The name fits. You, of course, know everything about me. So, tell me why I'm here."

The back door of the restaurant opened, and both men's hands instinctively flew to their weapons. The heavyset chef backed out of the door carrying a tray laden with food. He set the tray down and placed two frost covered highball glasses of what looked to be lemonade.

"Aryeh, I brought out your favorites." He covered the table with small bites of what must be specialties of the house. Cyrus's eyes widened, the thought of food sickened him.

Aryeh's grin spread across his face. "Wait till you taste this. Being Iranian, you'll appreciate this spread." Rhapsodizing, he pointed to each dish. "Hummus as silky and creamy as butter. *Paner o sabzi—o gherdoo*, a feta cheese, herb and walnut dip—so good you'll think your mother made it. *Tzatziki*, a yogurt, cucumber and mint dip that's an aphrodisiac." He lifted the lid of a crock, and aromatic steam rose into the air. "*Khorakeh goosht*, a fragrant beef stew which could tempt a fricking vegetarian. Not to mention, the fucking best *dolmeh bademjan*, stuffed eggplant, outside of Tehran. But this," he brought his fingers to his lips, sending a kiss to heaven. "This is the piece de resistance. The *khoresht fesenjan*, a pomegranate and walnut stew better than sex with a supermodel."

Aryeh clapped the big man on the shoulder. "Thank you, Eran, you know there's nothing I miss more than your cooking. It's what I dream about when business takes me away from Israel."

"Enjoy, brother. I have to get ready for the lunch crowd, or I'd join you."

Aryeh wasted no time filling up his plate and dug in. He moaned with pleasure. "Fantastic."

If I don't start eating, I'll be good to no one. Cyrus filled a plate and forced himself to take a few bites.

Aryeh tore off a piece of warm pita bread, dunked it in the hummus, and stuffed the whole piece in his mouth. "When I'm away, I dream about this hummus." After a reasonable length of non-stop eating, Aryeh patted his stomach with satisfaction. "I have some news for you, Cyrus." He wiped his mouth.

Cyrus laid down his fork, all interest in the feast lost. "Is it about my wife, Layla?"

Aryeh studied him carefully as he spoke, and Cyrus knew he was assessing his actions and reactions. Scrutinizing whether he was as good as his reputation. "Your wife's alive. She didn't die in the bombing." He paused, letting the words sink in. "She was kidnapped."

Layla's alive. Layla's alive. Layla's alive…

Cyrus wanted to sob out his relief. He wanted to yell with joy. He wanted to drive back to the pre-school and hold his daughter tight. He wanted to tell her that Mommy would be home soon, that he was going to get her and bring her home. He wanted to call Aleck and Dina and Morris and tell them the amazing news. But, he stopped himself from doing all those things. Instead, he took a deep breath as his heart resumed its normal rhythm. "How do you know? Why haven't I heard from The Institute?"

"Because they don't know yet."

This fucking guy isn't going to tell me jack-shit unless I beg. "Damn it, Aryeh. You have to tell me what the hell you've learned and where you got the intel."

"I have a friend in the FBI. She called me with the DNA results as soon as she received them. They found your wife's DNA in a wheelchair outside the restaurant. Hair follicle. She wasn't inside during the explosion. My contact interviewed two witnesses who saw a woman loaded into an SUV. Whoever kidnapped her must have drugged and disguised her, probably in the bathroom. Simple as pie, they wheeled her out without raising any suspicion."

47

"How well do you know this FBI agent? How good is she?"

He grinned. "She's a hot little redhead, top-notch. We had a short-lived fling. She's a total pro. No bullshit. Your wife's alive, but we haven't a clue as to where she's been taken or why. We suspect this is part of a larger plan. The consul general is dead—a clear message to Israel that they can assassinate whomever they choose no matter where. Of course, American soil being the most unlikely and impossible place to exact punishment. They're probably rejoicing in outgunning us for once." Aryeh picked up his glass and downed the lemonade. "Layla represents another problem altogether. This is payback for your treason to Iran. Her father is another possible target. Nuclear physicists who help Israel are on their hit list."

"So, what's your theory?"

"Our theory is they intend to kill you and blackmail Aleck. It seems clear they're hoping you'll leave the sanctuary of Israel and make yourself an easy target. It smells of Hezbollah—perhaps a joint Iranian/Hezbollah effort. It happened on the anniversary of 9-11—another major bombing in America might scare the bejesus out of the US and encourage a significant pullback in its support for Israel. They'll claim Israel masterminded the whole bombing to stir up trouble." He paused and slathered another piece of pita with hummus and a generous helping of *tzatziki* and popped it in his mouth.

The relief of knowing she was alive had pumped endorphins through Cyrus's body as if he'd just gotten a massive dose of serotonin, but his joy quickly turned to worry. Cyrus lit a cigarette. Layla had gotten him to quit years ago, but the stress was getting to him. He needed to think. Later, when she was back in his arms, he'd stop. Gladly, he'd do anything she asked.

Layla was alive, but she was in the hands of sociopaths, who wouldn't hesitate to kill her when her usefulness was over. Both Mossad and Metsada would consider him too close to the situation—a hindrance to the team. They would try to stop him from going. They might even order him to stay in Israel.

Like hell, I will.

"Aryeh, I'm prefacing my request to you with these three words, *You owe me*. I'm the man for this operation. I refuse to sit here in Israel while someone else tries to save Layla. I need to go. I need to find her. And I want the distinct pleasure of destroying those bastards who not only took my wife but also murdered Avi. I want to be on the team."

"Cyrus, you of all people should know a team must function with one mind." Aryeh, sat forward, tapping his finger on the table. "It takes months and sometimes years to create such a well-oiled machine. You're out of practice. It would take too long to bring you up to speed. We don't have that kind of time. I'm sorry, but I can't risk my agents, and I can't risk your life. Sorry, you're too close to the situation. Besides, you have a child to think of."

Cerise. I have to make sure she's safe. I also have to do what I'm good at. No one understands the Iranians better than me—not even Metsada. Mossad had created him and trained him, but he had insider knowledge of Iran's Oghab2, having worked undercover in Iran for almost ten years. He'd never failed in a mission before, and he wouldn't fail now. Not when so much was at stake. Saving Layla. Bringing her home. "Aryeh, you must reconsider. You need me for this operation."

"Sorry, no can do," Aryeh repeated.

Cyrus clenched his hands into fists. He was at the edge, ready to explode. "Then I'll just have to go around you and Metsada and do this with Mossad. If Mossad refuses, I'll go it alone. I can flush these animals out from whatever rock they're hiding under."

Aryeh shrugged. "I can't stop you from doing what you have to do. You know Metsada works autonomously. I won't stop you, and you certainly won't stop us. No one will stop the long arm of Israeli justice. You know the dance."

"Tell me something—you never intended to let me work with the team, so why did you arrange this meeting and tell me about Layla being alive? I would have heard soon enough."

"I thought it was the least I could do, given what you said on your business card. Besides, I wanted to see the legend in person."

"And you find the so-called legend wanting?"

"Not at all. However, having weighed the risks, I'm just not comfortable putting our team's ass on the line. Maybe if we'd had more time."

Cyrus stood and held out his hand to Aryeh. "Thanks for lunch. *L'hitraot*, until we meet again."

"Cyrus, we'll find Layla. I promise you—you'll have your vengeance."

"Thanks, but I plan on finding her first and taking care of things my way."

"I know you're a man of action. I would expect no less. But consider that your actions could place your family in danger. Perhaps, it would be wise to see them temporarily relocated to a safe house."

Aryeh's words of warning gave him pause. When he'd signed on with Mossad, his one stipulation was that they get his mother and sister out of Iran. Mossad had orchestrated an elaborate ruse to fake the deaths of his mother and sister in order to re-locate them safely to Israel under new identities. They had been living on a kibbutz for more than fifteen years. He'd visited them undercover several times over the past five years. He wanted to bring them out of hiding, but it was still too dangerous, besides they'd made a life for themselves on the kibbutz and they were happy there. For the moment, Cerise, Dina, and Morris were vulnerable. Aleck was a stubborn man and would refuse to go into hiding. "Their safety is my first priority. I'll see to it."

I need a safe location. Somewhere no one would think to look for them. Once I know they're untouchable, nothing on earth will stop me.

Hold on, baby. Your Superman is coming.

CHAPTER 9

Lancaster, PA
September 13th
9:00 a.m.

I'm waiting for you, my Superman. Please find me…

Layla lay on the bare mattress curled in a fetal position. The room with its nailed shut window was airless. Her hair was damp and matted to her head. She hadn't washed in two days, hadn't left her bed except under supervision to go to the bathroom. She felt dirty and depressed. She forced herself to eat the food Ali brought her only because she had to keep up her strength. Every passing minute, every hour of every day she stayed alive meant she had a chance of seeing Cyrus and Cerise again. In her heart, she knew Cyrus would come for her. It was only a matter of time.

The hard click of a key turning the lock alerted her. She watched the knob turn and shrank back when she saw the AR-15 assault rifle Ali carried.

"Why do you do that?" he asked.

"Do what?"

"Look as if I'm going to kill you."

"Isn't that your intention? You bombed a restaurant in Manhattan, killing hundreds of people. And you've taken me hostage to lure my husband into a trap. Every time you walk into this room, you point that rifle at me. That's why I have this look on my face."

"I'm not going to hurt you." He swung the gun to his back. "Is this better?" His eyes traveled over her face and then trailed down her body.

She hated that. Hated that she was a prisoner. Hated that he could waltz in whenever he wanted and stare at her. Hated that she lived in fear of being raped at any moment and then killed without a moment's thought. "Nothing you do makes me feel better."

"Maybe if you got to know me—"

"I know enough," she said, cutting him off.

"Maybe if you knew my reasons, knew who I was, who I am."

"It doesn't matter who you were or why you are the way you are. The only thing that matters is who you are now—a terrorist. A killer."

Anger flashed in his eyes. She'd landed a blow, but it was no victory. *I'm on dangerous ground. I need to be careful. He has all the power.*

Layla eyed him warily as he sat in the plastic chair beside the bed.

"My name is Ali Zandi," he began in a surprisingly calm voice. "The man with the curly hair is my brother, Omar. We grew up in Shiraz, Iran. Our father was a citrus farmer. We were poor but happy. Hopeful of the future. My father was a stern taskmaster, sometimes brutal. My mother was like a piece of paper with nothing written on it. Submissive. She loved us, but we never really knew her. She died when I was fifteen. My father remarried a short time later. The woman was strong, nothing like my mother. More like you, tough as nails, she kicked our asses."

"How can you tell I'm strong?"

"I'm very good at seeing into people's hearts." His smile seemed sincere—another surprise.

What was he playing at? *If you could see what's in my heart, you wouldn't be pleased. You'd know that if given the opportunity, I will kill you.* She dropped her eyes and plucked at her blanket, lest he could read into her thoughts. Better to appear docile.

"My father expected Omar and me to improve our family's fortunes. He dreamed of a future where the name Zandi would be known and admired. A name that would command respect. Omar was never a student, but I was. Omar joined the army, and I qualified for admittance to Shiraz University of Applied Science and Technology, where I earned a degree in chemical engineering."

"Why are you telling me this?"

"I want you to understand."

"Why?"

"So you will know I'm not your enemy."

"But you are."

He shook his head. "After graduation, I was recruited by the IRGC. I received military training. By that time, Omar was in the Quds Force. He worked as an aide to Major General Qasem Solatani. He requested and arranged my transfer to the Quds unit."

Her brows shot up to attention. She knew who Solatani was, knew he was a longtime target on Israel's kill list. Solatani was the architect of the

Russian-Iranian alliance, a friend of Putin. Khamenei called him a "living martyr." He was Israel's worst enemy, and the most cunning. He'd sworn never to rest until Israel was annihilated.

Ali smiled proudly. "I see you've heard of our revered general.

"Solatani is a murderer."

"Watch how you speak of my dearest friend."

She felt the color drain from her face. *He's a madman.* She eyed his gun—if only she could get her hands on it.

Ali followed her gaze and chuckled. "I wouldn't if I were you. Think of your child. If you and Cyrus die, Cerise will be an orphan."

She dug her fingernails into her hands to keep from screaming in terror at the thought. Their names on his lips made the bile rise in her throat.

"You're familiar with only one side, your husband's side of the story. He's a traitor to his country. You should know there is always another side."

There was no confusion in her mind as to the differences between the two men. Cyrus, too had been groomed to play a significant role in the IRGC hierarchy. However, the similarities ended there. Cyrus's family had suffered at the hands of the Iranian regime. He'd been recruited by Mossad to be a mole. Ali lived in the service of those who wished to destroy Israel and all who resided within her borders. Cyrus lived to preserve lives. His life's work was to prevent a nuclear war. The two men could not have been more different. One a murderer willing to kill innocent men, women, and children, the other who sought to save lives and kill only when necessary.

"What did my husband do to you?" She needed to know how much he knew, what their intentions were.

Ali slapped his leg, his whole body erupting in laughter. "Let's see…" he said after the laughter faded away. "The traitor, Cyrus Hassani, compromised our nuclear program. He delivered crucial information, which resulted in the assassination of scientists who were working on essential research. Your husband also provided a thumb drive containing the Stuxnet virus to a contractor who unknowingly infected the computers at Natanz, causing the centrifuges to spin out of control and self-destruct. Cyrus was a very effective spy. The list goes on, shall I continue?"

"No, it won't be necessary. I understand why you hate me."

He stared at her as if surprised at her accusation.

"I don't hate you, and you are not my enemy. Why should I hate you, you are a woman caught up in a battle you have nothing to do with?"

Brazenly, she challenged him. "You set off the bomb at the restaurant. I saw you do it. I'm a witness to your crime. You'll never let me live or leave here."

"Why not? I don't expect to survive this mission. All of us, my brother included, are ready to die here. We have sworn to die for the will of Allah."

"I don't understand, what could possibly be worth dying for? You're young, attractive, and intelligent. You have your whole life ahead of you. Why murder a restaurant full of innocent people? For what? Revenge? Israel would gladly live in peace with Iran, Hezbollah, Hamas, the entire Muslim world, but instead of choosing peace, you die daily, killing us and killing each other. Tell me for what? Tell me, what kind of God demands death from you?"

"You can never understand what we've suffered at the hands of the Western world."

"I understand perfectly. What I don't understand is how blowing up innocent people will ever achieve your goals. Your God is a monster if he demands this of you. What other atrocities are you planning?"

He trembled with fury. His fists clenched and unclenched. She cringed, expecting him to hit her.

He took a deep breath, and his expression returned to one of politeness, friendly even. "Would you like to take a shower? I know it must be terrible not to be able to wash."

"By myself?"

He smiled sheepishly. "Of course, by yourself."

Afraid to show too much enthusiasm, she nodded. "That would be nice."

He pulled the keys from his pocket. When he released the handcuff from her wrist, he stepped back, motioning toward the door. "Please don't try anything, I'm right behind you. Don't give me a reason to hurt you."

"No worries. Right now, I'd kill for a shower."

He rewarded her with a grin. "I like your American saying. No worries. It's very descriptive."

When they reached the end of the hallway, she peered into the bathroom. The shower tub had a plastic curtain enclosing it, a toilet, and a sink with a mirror above it. Ali had planned this. There were towels and clothes folded on a step stool.

"There's toothpaste, a toothbrush, and a brush in the medicine cabinet. I'll be waiting right outside the door."

"Thank you, Ali."

He nodded, his face reflecting satisfaction at her gratitude.

She couldn't remember the last time she'd enjoyed a shower more. The water was hot, and the soap smelled like vanilla. She shampooed her hair twice just in case she didn't get another chance. The hot water drowned out any sound, and the shower curtain was closed, so she didn't hear or see Ali slip into the bathroom. When she shut the water off and pulled back the curtain, she gasped. "You bastard! What the fuck are you doing here? You lied to me." She grabbed the towel and quickly wrapped it around herself. Her anger mounted and threatened to bubble to the surface like a geyser erupting in a spout of steam. "Get out! Now!"

Ali's hands were up in a sign of surrender. "Calm down. I'm not going to hurt you. I swear. I'll wait outside." He grabbed her dirty clothes and was gone.

She leaned over the sink. The way he'd looked at her naked body made her sick. Her despair was so great that she could barely stand. She sat on the edge of the tub and held her head in her hands. How am I going to survive this? Her eyes blurred with tears. This was way worse than Tehran. In Tehran, Cyrus had arrived in the nick of time, saving her from the sociopath Mohammad. He became her rock from that day on. Now she was under the control of another sociopath, but one who had a different approach. A man who was trying to gain her sympathy. A man who clearly had designs on her.

She dressed hurriedly in the pair of jeans and T-shirt he'd left. He'd taken her bra and panties, so she had to go without underwear. The clothes were tight. She pulled and tried to stretch them as much as she could. She exited the bathroom and saw him standing just outside the door. His eyes roved over her again.

"Look, I'm sorry about walking in on you, but you were in the shower for so long. I had to find out what was going on."

"Stop ogling me—it's pissing me off. And stop with the lies. You wanted to see me, and now you have. What you are is a pervert."

He shrugged, continuing to stare at the T-shirt that clung to her breasts.

She crossed her arms over her chest and glared at him until he finally looked away.

"Would you like to sit outside? You have been cooped up for two days—you must miss the sunshine."

He disgusted her, but the thought of being outside, smelling the fresh air, and seeing the sky was a carrot she couldn't resist. Even so, she couldn't help lashing out at him. "That would be nice after your crude behavior."

The smirk on his face made her itch to slap him. *Or better yet, bash him over the head with a hammer.*

"Let's go," he said, holding the rifle firmly in his grasp. "I warn you. There's nowhere for you to run. We're miles from town, and it's unlikely you're going to outrun a bullet." He patted the AR-15. "I'm a sharpshooter, don't think I won't use this. Come on." He motioned with the muzzle for her to retrace her steps down the hallway.

When she reached the door of her room, she turned to ask, "Where to?"

"Keep going and turn left down the next hallway. The door is there."

She opened the screen door and stepped onto a porch. She took a deep breath and let it out slowly. Across the graveled entry was a metal silo attached to a large red Amish barn. Beside it, a fenced vegetable garden where the last plantings before winter were freshly tilled. Beyond the white fences was an orchard of apple trees and beyond the orchard miles of cultivated farmland that spanned as far as the eye could see. Ali was right—there was nowhere for her to go. She had no idea where she was, except the obvious, she was in the countryside.

It was a beautiful day with puffy white clouds rolling across a robin's egg blue sky. Strands of her wet hair lifted in the breeze. From the corner of her eye, she caught Ali studying her. She sensed his desire to touch her. She tried to ignore his blatant stare, concentrating on anything that might give her a clue as to her location. The trees hadn't begun their seasonal change of color, which meant she could be in Ohio, Pennsylvania, New Jersey, Delaware, or Maryland. Glancing at the red barn again, she settled on *Pennsylvania, Amish country. It makes sense they'd pick a place where the locals respect privacy, theirs, and everyone else's.*

"Would you like to take a walk around, get some exercise? It'll be good for you to work up an appetite, you're too skinny."

Good, hopefully, I'm not attractive to you then. She struggled to be amiable. She wasn't going to learn a thing from Ali if she was constantly snarky. "I'd like that. Where are we anyway?"

He chuckled. "You don't really think I'm going to tell you, do you?"

She frowned. "No, I guess not."

They spent the afternoon walking through the fields. By the time they returned to the house, the sun sat low in the sky. Before entering the house, Layla took a last wistful look, relishing the serenity of the landscape. A flock of geese flying south in V formation to their winter refuge, noisily honked. Large tears made their way down her cheeks. She tried to steal some comfort from the beauty of nature.

"Where is everyone?"

"They're all preparing for our next operation. It isn't anything you need to concern yourself with. I pulled the lucky straw. I get to be your babysitter."

Ali followed her back to the room. Her prison. He handcuffed her to the bed.

"You must be hungry. I'll get you some dinner."

She closed her eyes and said through stiff lips. "Thank you for today. I appreciate it…It was…kind of you."

He stopped at the door, his face in shadow. "Perhaps you will think better of me in the future."

If only he'd met her as a young man in Iran, his life might have been different.

Ali couldn't get the vision of Layla's naked beauty out of his mind. In the kitchen, he dropped a tab of acid into a glass of pomegranate juice. Then he pulled a baggy out of his pocket and added the dirty white crystalline grains of Ecstasy to the concoction and stirred until the two hallucinogens had dissolved. He'd pictured her nude so many times, but seeing her in all her glory was something to behold. He couldn't go to his grave without having her.

Allah would forgive him for this one indiscretion. The drug combination would make her a willing participant and induce her to experience a pleasure she'd never felt before. Chances are she wouldn't even remember whatever occurred between them. A part of him hated that she would have no cognizance of it.

He picked up the tray of food he'd prepared for her and glanced out the window. Black clouds laden with moisture had darkened the sky. He smiled, imagining the dramatic accompaniment of thunder and lightning to his planned lovemaking with Layla.

She ate her meal alone, savoring the pomegranate juice Ali had brought her. He was right about one thing; the fresh air had awakened her appetite. She ate everything and drank all of her juice, even asking for a refill. After they'd said good night and Ali had left, locking the door behind him, she lay thinking about what had passed between them. He was wrong if he thought she could warm up to him. She knew it was to her advantage to pretend. In some bizarre way, Ali might be a blessing. Certainly, her confinement was less brutal because of him. And perhaps she could glean some information from him. Something that might help her escape. She tried to go over everything that had happened that day. Tried to remember everything he'd told her. She needed to keep her wits about her. But her eyelids felt so heavy that she soon gave herself up to sleep.

A clap of thunder jolted her awake. Lightning lit the room with bursts of white light. Layla's head was spinning, her body drenched in sweat. Her senses amplified by a consuming fever. She twisted, pulling at the handcuff, her wrist raw from her efforts.

She screamed as another boom of thunder rumbled outside. She cried out for Cyrus. Her breath came in short bursts. "Cyrus!"

The door opened, and a man rushed into the room, gathering her up in his arms. She tried to focus on his face, but everything was a blur. He pressed his lips to her ear, whispering, "*Aziz am*, what's wrong? What can I do?"

Cyrus.

Hearing her husband's endearment, she relaxed into the strong arms holding her. His cheek was cool against hers. "Cyrus, you're here, you've come to take me home. Oh, my darling, I've been waiting for you."

He laid her back on the bed and unlocked the handcuffs, then gathered her back into his arms.

Reaching up, her hands encircled his neck. "My love! I've missed you so much. You promised to keep me safe. And you have. Thank God you're here."

So much heat. She was on fire. Like the first stage of a rocket when it hits the Earth's atmosphere. She raised her head and ran her lips and tongue down his neck. He drew in a breath, and his body trembled beneath her lips.

A kaleidoscope of colors flashed before her eyes. Dizzy, she pressed them closed. She was overwhelmed by need. Want. Every part of her body burned with desire. "Cyrus…" she moaned. She needed to feel him inside of her, to douse the flames consuming her. An insatiable hunger—as if nothing could satisfy the sensations that surged like electricity through her.

Outside the storm raged, the wind threatened to rip the shutters off the house. As if amplified by a loudspeaker, the rain sounded like fists beating against the roof. She shivered against him—Goosebumps swelling on her skin.

He moaned, his fingers tangled in her hair as his lips claimed hers. She ran her hands down his chest to his groin, gasping with pleasure at his hardness. "Oh, Cyrus…I've missed you so much. I've missed our lovemaking. I want to make another baby with you."

He growled and pushed her away. "No, Layla, don't touch me."

His rejection sliced like a knife into her gut. "Cyrus, don't you love me anymore?" she sobbed.

"I can't do this, Layla. It's not how I wanted it to be…"

She couldn't make her eyes focus. His face was a blur, and her brain wasn't processing correctly. A white pellucid light filled the room. It blinded her. Seconds later, a crash of thunder shook the house. She quivered like a leaf. She couldn't focus or see clearly. She didn't understand what was happening to her body, or why her husband wouldn't make love to her. "Cyrus, please hold me. I'm frightened. Something's terribly wrong with me."

Strong arms gathered her up. He ran his hands up and down her back, calming her. He kissed her temple and whispered. "It's okay, *eshgham*. Don't be afraid. Nothing is going to happen to you." He rocked her in his arms.

Her cries had brought him rushing to her room. He'd stood beside the bed, his eyes riveted on her, his heart pounding wildly in his chest.

"You are the most beautiful woman I've ever seen."

She lay back, pulling him down beside her. "I love it when you tell me I'm beautiful."

He pressed his hardness against her belly. More than anything, he wanted to make love to her. "I want you to enjoy this."

"When haven't I enjoyed our lovemaking? It's been so long," she moaned. "Don't stop until I scream your name. I love you, Cyrus."

Her kisses licked his body like flames, sizzling on his skin.

Cyrus! Cyrus! Cyrus!

His body froze at the mention of the traitor's name. It wouldn't be his name she screamed, and he couldn't bear the thought. His intention when he gave her the drugs was to have a willing lover. In his mind, what he'd planned wasn't rape. But when she called him Cyrus, his body shut down, and jealousy consumed him. He knew what he was feeling was irrational.

Do it. Fuck her.

And what was the difference? She thought he was her husband. At least he could get rid of this irrational need.

He'd never known anyone like her. And he couldn't imagine dying without having loved her.

I can't!

He wanted her to love him, the way she loved Hassani. No. He wanted her to love him more.

I won't. I can't make love to her, knowing she thinks I'm her fucking husband.

He'd been following her for so long. Watching her. Reading about her life, her career, her love of art. Her devotion to her daughter and father and grandparents. Her adoration of her husband. Ali had watched the footage from the safe house in Iran—Hassani had taken her out of Evin Prison and brought her to the safe house in Tehran. Of course, Hassani had fallen in love with her. How could he not? She was beautiful and brave, and she'd made Hassani smile and laugh with her outrageous comments. Ali had half-fallen in love with her himself just by watching those videos.

Layla trembled in his arms, calling out Cyrus's name over and over again as though it were a mantra. Ali drew her close and soothed her quivering body.

Without a clue, she'd turned his world upside down.

His yearning for Layla's devotion had somehow eradicated the oath of martyrdom he'd sworn.

Everyone he'd ever known was driven by hatred, everything he and his brother did in this life was based on a driving need for revenge. But like a snake shedding its skin, Ali was peeling back his lifelong beliefs. What he was beginning to feel must not be touched by anything vile or corrupt. He must find a way into her heart. He told himself it was possible. She could love him, if not forever, at least for the short time left to him.

He held her in his arms and prayed Allah would give his blessing and grant him this one wish. She'd expressed a desire to have another child. *Why not my child?* The sweetness of that notion made his heart thunder in his chest. Tonight, he would pray for forgiveness for having drugged her, and he would hold her through the night until the drugs wore off.

Tomorrow he would find a way into her heart.

CHAPTER 10

Tel Aviv, Israel
September 14th
7:00 a.m.

Three weeks had passed since Layla had left for New York and the MOMA opening. Three days had passed since her kidnapping. Cyrus fought to keep his child's world sane by sticking to their weekday routine. He dropped Cerise off at her great-grandparents' house in the morning before he went to work. This day appeared to be no different than any other. He looked in the rearview mirror. The child's hair was a tangled mop, and he regretted not doing a better job of getting a brush through her curls.

"Cerise, please let great-grandma Dina brush your hair. Teacher Miriam is going to be mad at Daddy again, for not doing his job."

The angelic face frowned at him. "Don't worry, *Abba*, teacher Miriam won't know because Grandma will brush it, she uses magic, and it doesn't hurt."

Cyrus didn't know how to answer but decided it was better for her to believe in magic than to argue with a four-year-old. He got out of the car and opened the rear passenger door; lifting Cerise out of the car seat, he set her down. He took her hand, and they walked to the front door of the house.

"Your grandma's magic is a good thing. Listen, honey. I want you to do whatever *Saba* and *Savta* tell you to do. I think they're taking you on an adventure, a magical trip."

Cerise's brows drew together in a question mark. "Are you coming with us?"

Before he knocked on the door, he crouched down to eye level with Cerise and kissed the tip of her nose. "No, angel, not right away. I have something to take care of first, but I'll join you as soon as I can."

"Is Mommy going to come too?"

"I hope so." Cyrus knew the less he said, the better.

Satisfied, the child nodded her head. "Okay, Daddy. Where are we going?"

"It's a surprise."

Cerise clapped her hands. "I love surprises, but I want Mommy to see the surprise."

"She will, baby, and we'll have a party when Mommy gets home. Now, give daddy a big kiss because I'm going to miss you." Lifting her face, Cerise shut her eyes and pursed her lips.

Cyrus held her cheeks and kissed her, trying to stop the tears that threatened to undo him. He stood and knocked on the door. Dina answered, and Cerise ran past her into the house, calling hello to her great-grandfather. Cyrus bent to kiss the old woman's wrinkled cheek and whispered, "Everything's set."

Dina said nothing, ignoring his information. "What time do you think you'll be here to pick Cerise up?"

"Probably late. I have a dinner meeting." *The woman would have made a great Mossad agent.*

"Don't worry about a thing—we'll see you when you get here."

He nodded. "Great. Dina, see if you can get a brush through her hair, she says it doesn't hurt when you do it because you use magic."

Dina chuckled. "I will brush her hair."

He turned and waved goodbye as she shut the door. His inclination was to look around and see if there were any suspicious people in the neighborhood or any vehicles he hadn't noticed before, but he knew it was better to follow the established routine and behave normally. He forced himself not to look back at the house as he drove away.

Cyrus nursed a cup of coffee at the Starbucks across the street from Cerise's pre-school. He'd parked two blocks away and entered the coffee shop from the back. He found a table with a view of the street, but far enough away from customers to allow privacy. He held a satellite phone and monitored the dispatches between the extraction team. Looking at his watch, he noted the time. Seven-forty-five a.m. Right on schedule. He watched as Dina and Cerise walked up the street and entered the pre-school.

"The package has just arrived at the post office. Over."

"Is the delivery truck in place and ready to roll?" Cyrus's hushed voice registered barely above a whisper.

"Roger. No sign outside of the package yet, but the horse is saddled and ready to ride. Scratch that, here we go, we have a visual on the package, and it's being led to the horse." A minute passed. *"Package secured. Giddy-up, we have a go."*

Cyrus heard the screech of tires over the phone. "Papa's on his way." He strode quickly to the rear exit of the café and ran to his car. He started the engine, hit the gas, and raced away.

He rendezvoused with the black SUV at the onramp to Highway 1, linking Tel Aviv and Jerusalem. They headed southeast toward the Shapirim Interchange and Ben Gurion International Airport. The windows of the SUV were blackened, and he couldn't see in, but he knew Cerise and Dina were inside. Morris had taken a cab and would meet them at the private jet terminal.

Whisked through security at the gate, the caravan drove onto the tarmac and the waiting Gulfstream G280. Two Mossad agents jumped out of the SUV and scanned the area before opening the rear passenger doors and helping Dina and Cerise out. Cyrus picked up his wide-eyed daughter and kissed her.

"Daddy!" She squealed excitedly. "Am I going on this airplane?"

"Yes, *sheereen-am*, you, *Savta* and *Saba* are going to a magical place where mountains touch the sky. Are you ready?"

She nodded bravely, her trembling body betraying her fear.

Cyrus carried her on board and buckled her into her seat. He kissed her head and said a silent prayer God would keep her safe. The engines of the jet warmed up as the crew prepared for take-off. "Remember your promise Cerise to listen to *Savta* and *Saba* and be a good girl. I'll see you soon, okay?"

Tears filled her eyes, and her small arms wrapped him in a hug. With a final squeeze, he stood, blinking back his tears. He shook hands with Morris. "Take care of her."

"God's speed. She's safe with us."

He leaned down to give Dina a peck on the cheek. She grabbed his hand with a strength that belied her petite size. She pulled his ear to her lips, whispering. "*Y'va-re-khe-kha, Adonai v' yish-mere-kha.* May the Lord bless you and protect you. Bring my granddaughter home, Cyrus."

He met her eyes and nodded. Forcing himself to smile, he waved to his family and exited the plane. He stood on the tarmac and watched the jet taxi down the runway and take-off into the cloudless blue sky. Mossad security would meet the plane in Zurich and see them to the chalet safe house in the Alps where they would be protected. He blew out a breath. Relieved that his family was safe and protected, he was free to do whatever was necessary to rescue Layla.

Cyrus read the previous night's intel coming out of Iran when the phone on his desk rang. It was Rafi, the director of the North America desk. The Ramsad had requested he join a meeting in the white room—a secured conference room swept each day electronically. The room was equipped with the latest jamming technology. He was the last man in, and a quick glance at the grim faces in the room told him he was about to learn something he would not consider good news.

The Ramsad, as the head of Mossad was referred to, wasted no time getting down to the issue at hand.

"Gentlemen, Rafi just heard from Director James Carter at FBI." He picked up a remote. "This just broke across multiple social media channels. The NSA and FBI are doing their best to remove it, but I'm afraid the damage has already been done." The agents turned toward the high-definition screen mounted on the wall. They watched a woman wearing a burqa speak in English on a YouTube video. Beneath the video was a translation of what she said in Arabic and Farsi.

She recounted the standard tales of the West's war on Islam, and the superpowers' America and Israel, being the enemies of the Muslim world. She called on the Islamic nations to cease fighting among themselves, to unite and wage jihad on the real enemies of a new caliphate. Her final threat included a shadowy reference to 9-11, and a warning of another attack of a "large-scale target" was planned if their demands were not met. When her diatribe completed, the video went black for a moment before, once again resuming. The venue had changed.

Cyrus's heart leaped from his chest when Layla appeared on the monitor screen. Anger boiled up in him. On either side of her stood two men, their faces covered by hoods. Each held an AR-15 assault rifle pointed at her head. He knew whoever held Layla had coerced her to read a prepared statement. Thank God, he'd gotten Cerise, Dina, and Morris safely out of Tel Aviv. He glanced at his watch. They'd be landing in Zurich within the hour.

He scrutinized his wife, looking for telltale signs of drugging, or torture. She appeared to be fine, fearful to be sure, but unharmed. Whatever their affiliation, the terrorists that had taken Layla and made this video had taken a page from the Israelis. Their point being there was no place on earth safe from retaliation—not the US and not Israel. Of course, that's where the comparison ended. Israel would never threaten mass murder, nor would they use a woman with a rifle to her head to get their message across. Life, all life was precious to Jews. It was a commandment from God, and one every Jew was taught from birth.

Just before the video concluded, the sound was cut, but Layla still managed to mouth something to the camera. Cyrus wasn't sure what she said, but he sure as hell planned on reviewing it again. He needed to figure out what she wanted to tell him.

The Ramsad interrupted his thoughts. "Cyrus, I presume your daughter and wife's grandparents have left Tel Aviv?"

"Yes, sir, they should land in Switzerland within the hour."

"Good. Then we'll proceed without fear for your family's safety. Cyrus, you'll accompany a diplomatic team to New York. You'll be investigating side-by-side with the FBI. You leave tonight. Of course, you'll be briefed and given a suitable legend giving you diplomatic immunity. The collection department is working on your passport and an assumed identity as we speak." The Ramsad's eyes were forged in steel.

Cyrus nodded.

"We've received intel from our sources in Iraq. The group who kidnapped Layla and murdered Avi and the bystanders is a Hezbollah-Iranian collaboration. We think it's likely they've planned a much bigger attack than the restaurant. Ma Maison was simply the teaser. Our intel suggests a long-range plan and logistics were required to mount an operation of this magnitude. These people are well funded and trained. It's possible they may have been in place for years, and their covers are well established. They are most certain to have the best technology available. We've already had a taste of their bomb-making skills.

"It's unfortunate, but the Americans ignored our warnings not to grant Major General Qasem Solatani JCPOA sanctions relief and now the chicken has come home to roost. Hajj Qasem's imprint is all over this. He failed in Washington to blow up the Saudi Foreign Minister but succeeded with Avi in New York. Now there are dozens of Americans' blood on his hands. Obviously not enough based on this video."

Cyrus recalled the Iranian plot General Solatani had hatched. He'd recruited his cousin, an Iranian-born businessman living in Texas, to blow up a crowded restaurant in Washington, D.C., where the Saudi Ambassador was known to be dining. Fortunately, the DEA and FBI, through an under-cover informant, had been tipped off, and they were able to arrest the Iranian, who'd hired a Mexican drug cartel to help him carry out the plan. In that case, the disaster had been avoided.

"It is of the utmost importance to Israel that we be of service to the FBI in stopping this attack. I'm putting everyone on notice, this must end in one way, and one way only. This is an *ein efes*, a 'no miss' operation."

The Ramsad stood to conclude the meeting. "Gentlemen, I leave you to your preparations for Operation *Amud Ha'esh*—Pillars of Fire. Once the FBI has determined who and where these people are located, we must help them prevent another disaster. If everything goes according to plan," his eyes rested on Cyrus, "we will save Layla and return her to her family and adopted homeland. You have your mission."

Cyrus's preparations for his midnight flight to New York had culminated in a long day. He left Mossad headquarters with one last task to address. He felt the absence of Cerise, Dina, and Morris acutely, but it was Aleck Wallace, Layla's father, he needed to speak with before he left.

Plagued by his guilt, their contact had been minimal. Except for a brief call the morning after the kidnapping, he hadn't spoken with Aleck. Now that a plan of action was ready, he needed Aleck to be made aware of what was planned. In the video, the terrorists had said they intended to prevent Aleck from continuing to aid the Israelis in their nuclear program. Layla was the bait, Aleck and he were the intended catch.

After living for a year in the Ramat HaSharon safe house provided to him by the government when he first arrived in Israel, Aleck had moved to a chic apartment in Tel Aviv with views of the sea. Cyrus pressed the button, ringing Aleck's apartment. He looked up at the security camera.

Aleck spoke over the intercom. "I've wondered how long it would take you to show up here." His disapproving tone only strengthened Cyrus's resolve. The buzzer sounded, and the door's locking system released.

Cyrus got in the elevator and the doors closed. The elevator's electron-ically programmed access system rose to the twenty-eighth floor. Being one of only two apartments on the floor, the door to Aleck's apartment stood open.

Cyrus found Aleck on the terrace, a drink in his hand. On the table, next to him, was another glass filled with amber liquid and a bottle of twenty-five-year-old Macallan scotch. A warm balmy breeze blew in from the Mediterranean, where the twinkling lights of boats could be seen. In the foreground, sprawled Tel Aviv and Jaffa, where the ancient and the new competed with the stars for attention.

Without a word, Cyrus sat and picked up the glass of scotch from the table. He took a good long swig. The smooth taste gave way to a feeling of warmth and a false sense of well-being.

"I stopped to see Cerise tonight at Dina and Morris's house, and nobody was home. Where are they?" Aleck asked.

"They're somewhere far away. Somewhere where they'll be safe."

Aleck nodded. "I don't suppose you'll tell me where they are."

"I can't Aleck. It would endanger you, but more importantly, it would endanger them."

Aleck swished his glass, the tinkle of ice cubes broke the silence. His whispered voice was raw with emotion. "I know Layla's alive. Now what?"

"Now?" His brow furrowed, punctuating his response. "Now, I save her. I leave tonight."

"Do you know where she is?"

"Not yet, but I'll find her, you can count on it. But that's not why I'm here." He pulled his phone from his pocket, pulled up the terrorist's YouTube video, and hit play. Cyrus watched Aleck's expression change from joy at seeing his daughter unharmed to alarm as the real threat sank in. When it ended, Aleck turned to him. "Let me come with you? Maybe they'll be willing to swap her for me."

Cyrus had anticipated Aleck's response. "No, Aleck, the Israeli government will not risk your safety."

"I don't give a shit what they're willing to risk. She's my daughter goddammit! I'll halt my work just where it stands now. I won't lift another finger."

"I understand your frustration, but anger isn't going to free Layla. Even if we exchanged you and me for her, there's no guarantee they wouldn't kill her anyway. We're not dealing with rationality here. We're dealing with a suicide bomber mentality. Their goal is to take as many lives as possible."

Aleck's shoulders slumped in resignation. "Then how are you going to save her, Cyrus?"

"Trust me. I'll succeed. I have to." He paused. "Aleck, at some point, I may need you to play a part in this. I'm not sure yet in what way, but if I require your help, it will be something you must keep from everyone, including the Israeli government. I need to hear it from you that you're willing. I may have to go off Israel's radar and do this on my own. If it happens, you may be the only person I can trust."

"Whatever you need, I'll be there. I trust you completely. No one wants Layla rescued more than me, except you."

"Good. I knew I could count on you, go about your life, your usual routine as if nothing has changed. It's possible you're being watched, so Mossad has assigned a surveillance team to you. It's unlikely you'll see any sign of them, but it's their job to make sure you're not tailed and to protect you. Here..." He reached into his blazer pocket and handed Aleck a phone.

"This is a secure phone. I've programmed the name I'll be operating under, Zev Neshar, and my cell number if you need me. However, it's best if you don't contact me unless it's important because I'll be undercover. I'll keep you informed as best I can as events unfold. If the team needs you, Mossad will be in touch. If I need you, I'll be in touch with you on this." He pulled another phone from his pocket.

"This is a burner phone—it's untraceable." Aleck studied the two phones.

Cyrus took another sip of scotch and rolled the glass between his hands. "I'm sorry, Aleck, it's my fault Layla's in this situation," he whispered. "If she weren't married to me, she'd be safe. I've failed her."

Aleck laid the phones down on the table. He squeezed Cyrus's shoulder. "I appreciate your sentiment, but it's a foolhardy statement. Layla is as stubborn as her mother and grandmother. She comes from a long line of strong women who make their own choices. You, my dear Cyrus, were one of those choices. My daughter loves you, and I assure you, she wouldn't change any of the decisions she's made, and that includes you. Just focus on bringing her home."

Cyrus nodded. "I've things to prepare before my flight. You'll be hearing from me." He stood and shook hands with his father-in-law. "*L'hitraot.*"

"Go with God, Cyrus."

CHAPTER 11

Lancaster County, Pennsylvania
September 14th
9 a.m.

Layla woke with a pounding headache, uncomfortably tangled in the damp sheets of her bed. She felt unease when she realized not only was her hand not tethered to the bed frame by handcuffs, but she was completely nude. Her memory of the night before was a kaleidoscope of inscrutable images, which appeared and disappeared in vague flashbacks.

She had a fuzzy recollection of a storm raging outside, but what scared her was she didn't remember anything else. Just a sneaking suspicion that her dinner had been drugged and that something nefarious had occurred in her room. Her imaginings of what those possibilities were made her tremble in rage and fear. Her clothes lay in a pile, discarded as if they'd been torn from her in a hurry and cast aside. Vulnerable. She was completely and utterly vulnerable to the whims of her captors. She got up and hurriedly dressed.

Drawn to the window, she raised her face to the sunlight. Outside blue skies and trees adorned with fall colored leaves greeted her. There was no sign of the storm that had unleashed its fury on the countryside. Nor was there any evidence of what had happened during the night, which left her body feeling like she'd just gotten over the twenty-four-hour flu. She closed her eyes. She longed to fill her lungs with the clean scent of wet grass and damp earth that imbued the air with new beginnings in a storm's aftermath. She opened her eyes and noticed a ponderous, gnarled branch on the ground, smaller branches scattered around it, the physical evidence of a battle lost to powerful winds.

At the scrape of a key turning in the lock, she jumped back into bed, pulling the covers up to her neck. Ali entered carrying a tray of food. On the tray sat a vase with flowers in it. The romantic gesture made her even more suspicious and uncomfortable.

"I thought you might be hungry."

Something about the way he didn't look her in the eye and the sheepish smile playing upon his lips annoyed her. "You look like I feel."

"I didn't sleep much last night. The storm kept me up," he muttered, avoiding her gaze.

"Did it?" There were dark circles under his eyes. She wondered if her own bore the same signs of exhaustion. "How did my clothes come off, and why wasn't I handcuffed to the bed?"

"I came in during the night to check on you. I heard you crying. You were sick and running a fever. You'd removed all your clothes. You were thrashing on the bed, delirious. I didn't see the point in keeping you handcuffed. I'm sorry. If it makes you feel better, I didn't look at you."

Yeah, sure. You've been ogling me with my clothes on since I got here, walked into the bathroom while I showered—naturally, you wouldn't think of getting an eyeful with them off. The unsettling thought of being so defenseless made her want to grab his throat and wring his neck. *The good news is, I don't remember a thing. The bad news is, I don't remember a thing.* She had to be careful. Had to win him over while keeping herself safe from any more feverish nights.

"Do you want to take another shower? You were soaked in sweat last night."

She tried to keep her face as placid as she could, having learned a few spy tricks from Cyrus. "Yes, I would appreciate that." Her lips lifted in a smile. "Do you think we could take another walk?" The more time she spent outside, the more she could learn about her whereabouts and how to plot her escape.

He paused before he answered. "Maybe in the afternoon after the workers have left."

"What workers? Where do they come from?"

"This is a working farm. We employ Arab immigrants and Syrian refugees to do labor in the fields and orchards around the property. People we can trust. The local mosque sends us faithful brothers in need of employment."

"Are the workers aware of your terrorist activities?" She knew she was treading on dangerous ground, but she couldn't resist pushing the boundaries to see if she was having any impact on him besides the physical. She studied his face. "You've planned something bigger than Ma Maison, haven't you?"

"No, of course not. These workers are not involved with anything beyond maintaining the farm. We are a small group of devoted freedom-fighters who are well-trained and committed to our cause. Each has sworn to lay down their life for this mission. It would be best if you didn't ask any more questions. It puts your life in danger for you to know anything about what we've planned. I'm trying to save your life, not sign your death sentence." He ran his hands through his hair. "Do you want to shower or not?"

"Ali, what do you plan on doing to my husband and father?"

His body stiffened in response to her question, and he scowled. "The traitor will be eliminated, and your father, if he ever wants to see you alive again, will cease and desist his work for the Israelis. This has always been about taking vengeance on Cyrus, destroying him and everything he loves. Tehran will never forget the damage your traitorous husband inflicted on us. As long as Cyrus lives, you and your family will never be safe."

She clenched her jaw and dug her fingernails into her hands to keep from losing control and gouging his eyes out. "One more question, Ali, and then I'd like to shower. Have you received any more videos or photos of my daughter and grandparents? I miss them. It would mean so much to me to see they're safe."

He hesitated. "Yes, Layla, I have." But before I show them to you, you need to understand how serious this is and what's at stake." He reached into his pocket and retrieved his cell phone.

She got out of bed and went to his side, close enough to see the photos but wary of his hands.

"These were taken yesterday." He thumbed through pictures of Cerise, Dina, and Morris arriving at what looked to be a secluded chalet. In the background, she recognized the iconic snow-capped Matterhorn. "I don't understand—this isn't Israel. Where are they?"

"It seems your husband arranged for them to leave Israel. I'm sure he and Mossad believe a Mossad safe house, a chalet in the Swiss Alps is beyond our intelligence capabilities."

The breath froze in her chest. If Cyrus thought their daughter and her grandparents were safe and removed from any threats, he would be intent on Layla's rescue and putting a stop to the terrorists. He'd have no clue as to the danger their family was in. Blood-red rage exploded inside her. She grabbed his hand and dug her nails into his skin. "You bastard, you can't do this! I swear if you hurt Cerise, I'm going to kill you. I don't care if I die as long as you die with me." So consuming was her hatred that her strength was tenfold, and she clawed him drawing blood.

He wrenched his hand away and shoved her onto the bed, his physical strength overpowering her. Dropping his gun, he flipped her over and pinned her to the mattress, twisting her arm behind her back, nearly wrenching her arm out of her shoulder socket. The pain was excruciating, and she screamed.

He seethed through gritted teeth. "A cornered animal will fight to the death. I understand you're a lioness protecting her cub, fighting the only way you know how. But remember who you're dealing with." Like a snake, he hissed in her ear. "Cerise is such a beautiful child, just like her mother. I'd hate to see her become a victim of her mother's foolishness."

She wasn't sure whether it was her heart or his heart that she heard pounding in her eardrums. The pain was so intense the room spun. She was dizzy and close to fainting. Just as consciousness was about to slip from her, he released her arm but continued to press her into the mattress.

Panic jolted her awake. Had her attack inadvertently aroused him? She squeezed her eyes shut, expecting the worst. But then a moment later, his breath settled, and he rolled off her.

She couldn't contain the sigh of relief or the tears that spilled from her eyes. She bit her lip so hard she tasted blood.

He muttered under his breath in Farsi and got up from the bed.

"Your beloved husband is going to try to rescue his beautiful bride," he sneered. He's arrived on US soil."

His words dripped with resentment. *This is more than hatred of a traitor. This is personal. He's jealous of Cyrus.* "How do you know that?"

"The Russians know everything. They've alerted the general."

Cyrus is on his way. She could barely contain her joy. But then the full reality struck like a wrecking ball. And her hope collapsed, demolished in a pile of debris. If Cyrus came for her, Cerise and her grandparents would die. Her brain was branded with the image of her daughter and her grandparents at a mountain chalet. Branded with the image of an assassin watching and waiting with his eye on a riflescope ready to shoot when ordered. Her whole world was precariously balanced on the tip of a sword. She had to stop Ali. Stop the terrorists. Whatever the cost to herself. She needed to control her seething hatred and make him trust her, or those she loved would be destroyed.

Swallowing the bile in her throat, she raised her eyes to his. "Ali," she began in a soft voice. "I will do whatever it takes to keep my daughter and grandparents safe." She turned over and met his gaze. "Do you understand me?"

He returned to the bed and touched her cheek. She closed her eyes and tried not to flinch.

"I will keep your offer in mind, Layla." Standing, he swung the rifle around and pointed it at her. "I think you'd better take that shower while you can."

She took a deep breath and gathered her strength. He was right about her being a lioness. A lioness protecting her cub was formidable. He'd won the battle, but she'd win the war.

CHAPTER 12

Mossad Jet en route to New York
September 15th

Saving Layla is all that matters…

Cyrus stared out the passenger window into the black void of night and its endless array of stars. He had worked through the night on the red-eye from Tel Aviv to New York, absorbing the legend Mossad had created for his alias, Zev Neshar, until he knew it like his own skin. It helped that he had a photographic memory. So much of his work depended on learning pages of details and facts and then destroying the paper trail. Zev Neshar's bio read much like the truth, except where he'd been a deep-cover spy, Neshar was strictly an analyst who worked at a desk. Neshar meant eagle in Hebrew, a fitting name for what he was setting out to do.

I will swoop in like an eagle, a predator ready to kill. For years, I lived as a spy, an assassin, but nothing I ever did was as important as this, at least for me.

He repeated the mantra in his mind…*Saving Layla is all that matters…*

Every seat at the long oval table on the twenty-third floor of the FBI field office in Tribeca was filled with experts from multiple branches of law enforcement. Their haggard faces betrayed their frustration. The agents had worked through the night, around the clock. To a man, they were bleary-eyed. They guzzled coffee and vibrated from the caffeine. They bit the ends of their pens or drummed their fingers on the table.

As far as all the agents were concerned, Cyrus was Zev Neshar, a top Mossad expert on Iran. He and his team had been invited by the FBI to participate in all stages of the investigation. The threat of a deadly attack had opened the door for cooperation between Israel and the US that might otherwise be unthinkable. Cyrus listened and observed the players pigeon-holing them according to their usefulness to him.

The head of the threat-response squad of the Counterterrorism Division of the New York field office presented the evidence found at Ma Maison. When she'd completed her grim presentation of slides of the devastation and DNA results from the crime scene, she yielded the floor to a red-headed agent from FBI headquarters in Washington.

Cass Saladino displayed the aggressiveness of a woman whose chosen profession meant having to prove herself in a world where her measure was taken by, and in comparison to Alpha men.

In preparation for the mission, Cyrus had read Cass's dossier and realized that this was the agent Aryeh had described as his source. Through her investigation, Layla's DNA had been found, proving she was alive. At least for now.

Cass's meteoric rise in the FBI was impressive. She had a reputation for doggedly pursuing her cases and successfully resolving a high number of them. He watched the petite redhead take charge of the room. Physically she looked as if she'd be easily overpowered in hand-to-hand combat, but he'd read she was a master of martial arts. He preferred the practicality of Krav Maga, the Israeli martial arts discipline. Under different circumstances, he would have enjoyed testing her skills with a friendly spar. He wished he'd spent more time teaching Layla. He'd shown her a few moves in case she was ever attacked while shopping or walking down the street.

If I had taught her more advanced fighting skills. If I had shown her how to be more aware of potential dangers, would she have been able to spot the terrorists ahead of time and alerted Avi? He swore to himself that when she was safely home, he'd train her in martial arts until she became a killing machine. Never again would she be vulnerable.

He'd tortured himself over and over again for letting her go in the first place. He'd been so deliriously happy the past few years that he'd let his guard down. And, he was so proud of her when she was given a chance to curate this major exhibit at MOMA, he couldn't find it in his heart to stifle her dreams.

Never again would he make that mistake.

He knew how the Iranians worked. If Layla tried anything foolish, they wouldn't hesitate to rape or torture her. But she was no longer the naïve young student he'd met five years ago. She was courageous and strong and smart.

I believe in you, Layla. I'll find you soon. I promise.

David Weiss, the young recruit the Mossad had labeled the Yeshiva boy, had been hand-selected by the FBI director to be Cass's partner. He'd been a detective with the Santa Barbara police force before being recruited by the FBI. Cyrus found it somewhat amusing that Cass was not only David's partner but his superior. In Mossad, he knew of several female agents who were considered the most lethal and who had commanded significant operations. Women had an advantage undercover. A man in heat was putty in their hands. Through female wiles and pillow talk, it was easier for them to gain access and information. Men rarely, especially men from chauvinistic cultures, believed a woman who shared their bed could be a spy. It was contrary to their beliefs and an insult to their egos.

Cyrus had never worked closely with a woman. A deep cover mole primarily worked alone for safety reasons, but from what he'd read and seen of these two, he determined they would make great Mossad agents, which in this business was the highest compliment he could give them.

He studied the dynamic duo. Knowledge was power, and if he was going to save Layla, he would need these two in his corner. He was keenly aware his goals did not precisely align with theirs. They were focused on stopping any further terrorist attacks at any cost and bringing the perpetrators to justice. But Layla would not be sacrificed, not if he could help it. He knew he'd have to be cunning to achieve their separate but inextricably linked objectives.

Rather than focusing on Cass as she spoke, Cyrus watched David, his body language, his eyes. It was subtle, almost imperceptible, a slight twitch of his lips when her voice went down an octave, a nostril flare when she walked by him. Cyrus had spent years honing the art of reading people. His instincts told him the younger man's relationship with his partner went far beyond the FBI.

A man in love.

Cyrus tucked the knowledge away in case it might prove useful.

Cass brought up a map of the Mid-Atlantic States. "We're focusing on a two-hundred-mile radius surrounding New York," she said, aiming her laser pointer at the area in question. "I've assigned a slew of technicians to pull records of real estate transactions recorded in the last ten years by any foreign nationals, Iranians, or Arabs. Whoever is behind this has implemented a well-executed plan, over years of preparation, with every contingency accounted for.

"Thanks to Israeli intelligence," she nodded toward Cyrus and his team, "we believe this attack was a joint Hezbollah Iranian Quds force operation. The decibels are up significantly among suspected terrorists across the social media spectrum. We must assume there's a credible threat to our infrastructure, which we need to prevent. We have good reason to believe Ma Maison was just a teaser for what they have planned next. The video suggests a strategic threat. Something more devastating than 9-11."

"Cass?" One of the agents interrupted.

"Yes, John."

"Are we placing this area in question on terror alert? Washington and New York in particular."

"We are going to go on quiet alert. I don't want to telegraph our intentions or our progress until we know more. I don't want to set off a panic, and I don't want these terrorists alerted and forced into action. I'd prefer to keep this as close to the sleeve as possible until we can confirm who these people are. I'm warning you now, no leaks."

The agents around the room nodded in approval. The current trend of communicating a plan of action before an attack eviscerated the surprise paradox. It endangered the success of any response and needlessly risked lives. In Director Carter's FBI, leaks were punished with expulsion and prosecution.

"We've divided our focus area up into grids where agents are questioning leaders of local mosques," Cass continued. "They're looking for odd comings and goings. Out of the ordinary behavior, anything that might appear suspicious. We know the chemical ingredients necessary to build the type of bomb used at Ma Maison, and the handling of those materials would require a factory of some kind. We're looking for isolated outbuildings on a farm or estate. It seems unlikely they've built a sophisticated bomb-making operation right in the heart of Manhattan, but we can't discount any possibility. Our analysts tell me it's more likely to be a remote location, geographically accessible to strategic targets, so they don't have to transport a massive unstable bomb over a long distance. I expect a full list of possible locations, hideouts, and targets by this afternoon."

Another agent raised his hand. "Cass, are we thinking soft targets like the restaurant or something much bigger?"

"Our intel at this moment points to a much larger target. I'm thinking power grid, transportation, a military target, something capable of bringing the country to its knees. I'm expecting a full report from the NSA momentarily."

She switched from the map to a series of photos. "These were taken in the Lincoln Tunnel just minutes after the explosion at the restaurant. The Chevy Tahoe matches the description given by witnesses. The problem is that this Tahoe and two other identical vehicles all entered the tunnel at the same time. All of them had fake plates from different states, and each of them took a different route after leaving the tunnel, so we can't be sure which one is our target. They all disappeared shortly after that off the main roads and were lost to camera surveillance. Cleverly planned, I'd say." Cass's forehead furrowed. Cyrus could see her frustration at having to admit any admiration for the adversary.

"We don't believe they attempted this kind of an operation from a distance greater than the two hundred miles we've delineated on the map. It would be too risky. I want you to focus on the area I've described. I know we might as well be searching for a needle in a haystack, but that's what I expect from you. Find me that needle."

She set the laser pen on the table. "Whatever assistance you require will be made available to you. We've just secured the support of the National Reconnaissance Office. As you know, the NRO controls all US spy satellites. They've already begun monitoring our target area. As soon as we get a lead, those satellites will start observing twenty-four-seven and be directed on the area we suspect. The transmitted feed will be received live here and in Washington. They won't be able to take a shit without us knowing."

Laughter filled the room, releasing some of the tension etched into the faces of the investigators. No one in the room knew better than Cyrus how important it was to get it right. If they made a mistake, a lot of people would die.

Cass concluded. "Once we've established what we're up against, we'll plan our intervention to stop, disarm, and apprehend." Looking again at the Israeli team, she added. "I want to remind you again that we have Israeli experts in this room who will be helping us with every aspect of this operation. Take advantage of their expertise."

Cyrus and the Israeli team shut down their laptops and stood to leave for the hotel. Cyrus had been awake for more than twenty-four hours. He needed to snatch an hour's sleep before he resumed his work, or he wouldn't be able to function, let alone rescue Layla.

"Gentlemen, hold on a minute."

The Israelis stopped and turned to Cass.

"I want you to join the rest of my team and me for lunch."

Cyrus thought about bowing out but decided against it.

———◦◦◦———

Lunch was catered by the Reade Street Pub, a burger and beer restaurant a short walk from the field office, and a favorite hangout for FBI personnel. Cass had suggested eating in so the teams could get to know each other in a private setting. Cyrus wasn't interested in forming friendships. Instead, he focused on finishing his pastrami sandwich. He wanted to get lunch over with, so he could check into the hotel and catch some shut-eye.

"You know, Zev, I can't put my finger on it," Cass began, pouring dressing over her salad, "but your accent sounds different than Zvi and Shlomo's. Why is that?"

He smiled. "You're very perceptive. I was born in Iran."

"Iran? Now there's a story I'd like to hear."

"I'm afraid we haven't the time, nor have I the inclination to bore you with the prosaic tale of how my family immigrated to Israel. It's a routine story, not unlike why the Pilgrims left England. Religious persecution has a way of driving people from their homelands. Perhaps another time." He gave her a slight smile.

The agents at the table chuckled at his reference to the Pilgrims, but he could see in her eyes she wasn't in the least bit satisfied with his answer. Sooner or later, he'd have to level with her if he had any chance of gaining her cooperation. But not when too many eyes and ears were about. He took a sip of sparkling water as he considered just how much he'd have to reveal about himself.

"Layla Hassani, the woman who was kidnapped, her husband, Cyrus, was from Iran, wasn't he?" Cass prodded.

Cyrus set down his glass. "Yes, that's correct, he too was born in Iran."

"Then I assume you must know him. You both work in intelligence. There can't be too many Iranians that work in intel."

He chuckled. "Actually, there are quite a few, but in answer to your question, we've met."

"There's not a lot of information available about him. It's almost as if he didn't exist before five years ago—it's like he just suddenly materialized."

"I wouldn't know about that, but if you'd like, we can request a more detailed bio for you."

"No, that won't be necessary. I was just curious why Cyrus is mentioned as a traitor to the IRI in the YouTube video. It's kind of coincidental Layla's husband, and her father, a nuclear physicist, is a target of the group and was mentioned in the video."

Cyrus had known the video would come back to haunt him, but being under the scrutiny of this woman was like being under the lens of a microscope. He wasn't used to being the focus of an interrogation. He was far more comfortable being the interrogator. He decided to turn the tables and get back to his comfort zone. "So, Agent Saladino—"

"Call me, Cass."

"Cass, how long have you and Agent Weiss—"

"Call me, David. Like Cass says, let's drop the titles, at least in the office."

"I'm curious, how long have you been partners?"

"Two years. Like they say—if it ain't broke, why fix it?" David chuckled.

Cass's Blackberry began to buzz. The table fell silent when she answered. "What have you got?" She listened. "All right. Keep on it. Good work. She hung up. "We've caught a break."

A pulse throbbed in Cyrus's throat, and he leaned forward, waiting expectantly for Cass to let them know what they'd discovered.

"Four years ago, a corporation in the Cayman Islands purchased a large farm in Lancaster County, Pennsylvania," Cass began. "Our analysts have determined the corporate shell is linked to a board of directors who reside in Lebanon, Hezbollah's playground. The farm is situated not far from the Islamic Center of Lancaster, in a thriving Muslim community. The Islamic Center is a well thought of, trusted institution, certainly not supportive of terrorism, but a perfect cover for those who might have less charitable aims."

She paused and looked at Cyrus. "I like to think coincidence is just the truth shouting to be heard. I've apprised the NRO, and they're directing our satellites to the compound. We should begin receiving live feed momentarily."

Her words were barely out of her mouth when an agent entered the room and announced. "We're live, Cass." The agent grabbed the remote and hit play. All eyes flew to the screen.

The satellite's camera zoomed in on a large red barn with an attached silo, a house, and numerous outbuildings. It was rural, private, and unobtrusive. The perfect hideaway. Far removed from neighbors amid a landscape of identical Amish farms. Cyrus wondered if the FBI agents found it ironic that a non-resistant Anabaptist community had been infiltrated by Islamic terrorists.

The camera zoomed in on a woman with red hair running through a field, and an armed man running after her. Cyrus froze, his eyes riveted to the image. He couldn't believe what he was seeing. He knew Layla was alive, but to see her live, walking around in real-time was a punch to his gut. A chill ran up his spine at the thought that she might be trying to escape. *Baby, don't run, he's armed.* When she stopped at the edge of a grove of trees, he suppressed his relief. Seeing her alive and unharmed made his heart beat faster. Mesmerized, Cyrus watched the action play out like it was a scene from a movie.

Stay calm.

He needed to remain objective, to behave like the analyst he was and gain as much insight as possible. The man's rifle hung casually from his back. *He's not worried about what she might do…He trusts her.* The man brushed a strand of hair out of her eyes, and Cyrus nearly exploded. The intimate gesture knocked him for a loop and awakened all kinds of crazy thoughts. It was eating him alive to see Layla and not be able to do anything while a terrorist held her life in his hands. He tried to read her expression. *What the fuck is going on?* Was he seeing things? She wasn't resisting. In fact, she was smiling at him. *Why is she encouraging the animal?*

He could feel Cass's eyes on him. She already suspected him of deception, she may have caught a flicker in his demeanor, the tightening of jaw muscles, the narrowing of his eyes, the pounding of the blood vessel in his temple. Her practiced eyes would read these clues with interest. The only thing that would remain hidden from her scrutiny was the desire pulsing through his veins, the desire to place his hands around the throat of the man on the screen and squeeze until he was dead.

There is no question. I'm going to kill him.

He fought the fear that crept up his spine. Maybe it was too late already. Maybe irreparable harm had already been done. Could this murdering terrorist somehow have seduced his wife? The relationship between Layla and her captor was irrational. It went against his beliefs, contrary to who she was.

No, she's just trying to survive the only way she knows how.

Willfully he fought to calm his jealousy and the scalding hatred ready to erupt. Everything going forward would depend on years of training and his honed discipline. Reluctantly, he lowered his eyes from the screen, pretending to check his phone.

CHAPTER 13

Watching from her room, Layla saw a van filled with men drive away. Earlier in the morning, she'd also seen a semi-truck pulling a flatbed arrive with Energex printed on the side of the cab. Energex Corporation, she'd remembered, was a Fortune 500 company in the energy business. The truck hauled a giant blue container. It left the compound in the late afternoon with the container still strapped to the flatbed. *Why would an Energex company truck come to some farm in the middle of nowhere? And why was it here for hours?* She racked her brain for a plausible explanation, but she was incapable of thinking like a terrorist. *And what are those blue containers anyway?*

She knew there was a large outbuilding on the property behind the house that she couldn't see from her room. The one time she'd glimpsed it on her walk with Ali, she'd noted the barn sized windowless structure with a massive steel door and a loading dock.

What is going on in that building?

The arrival of the container made no sense. Layla couldn't imagine how this pool of field laborers was involved in any plot against the United States. As far as she could tell, the daily workers were used for farm work. But she didn't doubt even if they saw something suspicious these recent Middle Eastern immigrants would be afraid to alert the authorities or anyone else. Afraid to attract unwanted attention on themselves.

She felt helplessly inadequate to figure out what was going on. In the video, she'd been forced to read about a second terrorist attack, which would make the La Maison explosion pale in comparison. She shuddered to think of what that might be. What skills did she possess to do something to prevent an attack? Totally out of her element, she was a minnow swimming in a shark tank.

Ali's attraction to her and willingness to talk to her was the only leverage she had. If she could somehow turn him, convince him that killing innocent people on American soil would only bring death and retribution on his own people, she might be able to get him to sabotage the attack. It was a long shot, but it was worth a try. Could she entrap him? How far could she push him? Would she have to succumb to his sexual innuendoes to protect Cerise and her grandparents? If she could stop hundreds or thousands of deaths, or even one person from being murdered, wouldn't it be her moral obligation, her duty to do whatever it took?

She closed her eyes and pictured Cyrus's beautiful Nile green eyes. She touched her fingers to her lips and remembered his kiss. Could she survive and save lives by allowing a monster to take advantage of her? If Cyrus found out, there was the possibility he'd never forgive her. She loved him so much, the thought of losing him would be like being tossed into the sea without a lifejacket. Tears rolled down her cheeks as she realized she had to take action.

Ali may have been sweet to her, but he was a mass murderer, a sociopath. The man who had taken pleasure in pressing the button that activated the bomb at Ma Maison hadn't suddenly transformed into a good person, no matter how well he treated her. Even so, she would be a fool not to realize she held some power over him but was it enough to turn him? Time was running out; she could feel it. Whatever the terrorists were building in that silo was nearly operational.

She swiped her tears away, resolved to do what she must to try to stop whatever madness they had planned. The irony of her situation didn't escape her. Women had always been used as spoils of war, even traded by fathers and brothers to appease the enemy. Throughout history, kings had sold their daughters into loveless marriages to seal alliances. At least she would control her own destiny, make her own choice.

I must kill him or be killed.

The slide and click of a key turning in the lock turned her spine rigid.

"Layla, the workers left early, would you like to take a walk?" Ali strolled in and unlocked the chain that tethered her to the bed.

A small smile lifted her lips. "Yes, I was hoping you hadn't forgotten." Ignoring the AR-15 that hung behind his shoulder, she fearlessly invaded his space, placing her hands lightly on his chest and looked up into his eyes. "Thank you, Ali, for your kindness. It's so hard to spend so much time alone in this room with no one to talk to."

His eyes widened in surprise, and she felt him shiver beneath her hands. She swallowed her revulsion.

"I look forward to our walk Layla. The day is half gone. I must have you back before dark. We should go."

Outside Layla took a deep breath, filling her lungs with fresh fall air. She lifted her face to the sky, her hair cascading down her back. What she was about to do sickened her. Flirting with a monster was like dancing with the devil. She felt his eyes riveted on her and was determined to keep him off balance. Hot bile burned her esophagus when she locked eyes with him. She swallowed and tamped down her misery. Outstretching her arms, she tilted her face up to the sunshine.

"What are you doing?" Ali asked.

She stopped suddenly, locking eyes with him. "I'm living, Ali. I'm young and alive. I want to live, to feel the beauty of the world. You can coop me up in a dungeon, but you can't dampen my desire to live."

He shook his head and smiled. "You're an extraordinary woman."

"Am I?" She coyly tossed her hair.

"Come on, let's get away from the house." Ali's gaze swept surreptitiously around the landscape.

"Yes, let's." She turned and walked toward the field with Ali following close behind. She headed toward a grove of apple trees. They walked in silence, but Layla felt his eyes on her. When she glanced back and saw his gaze fixed on her, she took a chance and started to run toward the trees. Fingers of fear tore at her rib cage. She didn't have to look back to know he was running after her. She stopped when she reached the grove. He caught up with her.

His chest heaved as he caught his breath. "Don't do that, Layla. Don't run from me." He brushed a strand of hair from her face and leaned in closer. Before his lips met hers, she turned and ran into the grove.

"Layla, stop. Don't run away from me."

"Why?" She giggled. "Catch me if you can."

He ran after her, tailing her as she darted from tree to tree. A large old oak tree towered over the apple trees. She hid behind it, pressing her back against the thick trunk. She was flushed, her hair wild about her shoulders. Her chest heaved, her breasts straining against her shirt with each breath. When he reached her, he placed both of his hands on either side of the tree trunk, trapping her between his arms. He towered over her.

"What kind of foolishness is this?" he breathed, gulping air.

"What do you mean?" She forced herself to lift her face to his.

"Are you playing with me?"

"Why do you say that?"

"I don't know. You just seem different."

She dropped her gaze shyly. "I don't understand what I'm feeling, but…" *God, the lies. I know exactly what I'm feeling. I'm feeling fear—dread—hatred.*

"But what?" He leaned in closer.

When she looked up, shadows filled his face. Only the dark burning intensity in his eyes was readable. As if an actor in a play, she reached up and touched him, her fingertips caressed his jaw, drawing him closer until her lips brushed his. She whispered, "It's crazy, but I've wanted to kiss you." *I want to kill you, you bastard.*

With a groan, he crushed her to his chest, his mouth blazed over hers. She fingered his thick dark hair and pressed her pelvic firmly against his. His hardness swelled against her stomach. There would be no turning back now. His hands traveled the length of her, exploring her curves.

When they broke the kiss, gasping, his lips traced a path up and down her neck inhaling her scent. A deep groan of want escaped him. "What are you doing to me?"

"What are you doing to me?" She slipped by him and sat on the ground, drawing her knees up, hugging them. She pressed her face into her knees so he couldn't see her gag. He removed the rifle and leaned it against the tree trunk and sat down beside her. He took her hand, raised it to his lips, and kissed her palm.

"What is it *eshgham*, what is wrong?"

Eshgham? His words triggered a flashback, a vision of arms and legs entangled. She clapped her hand over her mouth, physically holding back a wave of revulsion. *Last night the bastard drugged me. I didn't have a fever—I was drugged. But there's no way we could have had sex. I would know, wouldn't I? Even if he did drug me, I'd know.*

She wanted to scream like a banshee and claw his eyes out. She lowered her hands. Her fingernails bit into the flesh of her palms. She drew in a breath, trying to calm the waves of hatred crashing over her. She knew she had no way of exacting revenge for the violation. With her child and grandparents in the crosshairs of killers—she could only play along.

Controlling her rage, she studied his face. The obsession written in his eyes was the key to her dilemma. Ali was in love with her, or at least thought himself to be. His reckless behavior was a breakdown—he was unable to control his desire for her. She took a deep breath and plunged ahead. "Ali, I'm confused. I'm not supposed to have feelings for you. But I can't help it. What's wrong with me?"

He took her hand and pressed his lips to her palm again. She trembled, wishing she could pull away.

"Layla, there's nothing wrong with you. Allah sees everything, and he's granted me a last wish. He's given me you."

She stared into his eyes and could see he believed this to be the truth. He believed they were destined for each other. "But it's wrong, Ali. I have a husband and a child." *I can't be too willing, or the bastard will suspect duplicity.*

"You will return to your child when this mission is done. I cannot help your husband, his fate is out of my hands, but I give you my word I will see to it you are freed and your child safe. Until then, you are mine."

He held her gaze, his lips only inches from hers. He pushed her gently into a pile of leaves, on the ground. He rolled on top of her and kissed her, his hardness pressed against her pelvis. She wanted to push him away. Wanted to fight and kick and run as fast as she could. But she couldn't. She had to do whatever it took to stop this madness. She closed her eyes and kissed him back.

"I don't understand this need burning inside of me, but I want you so much it makes me ache," she whispered, her lips leaving breathless kisses down his neck and shoulders. She could see the desire burning in his eyes, hear his heart pounding in his chest. She needed to break down his defenses as quickly as possible. A man in heat was incapable of resistance. She had a small window of opportunity to get what she needed from him. She needed to find out what they were plotting—what the next target was.

"Layla, you're not playing with me, are you?"

She cupped her hands on either side of his face, praying he couldn't read the truth in her eyes. The fear and rage and loathing simmering inside her. *Forgive me, Cyrus, love of my life. I have no choice.* The lie passed her lips without hesitation. "Ali, I can't explain what I'm feeling. The passion I have for you is all-consuming." She pulled Ali's head down to hers and kissed him, hoping he believed her. Hoping she wouldn't throw up.

His tongue twisted against hers, and she fought against biting it and kicking him in the balls.

"You're a very good kisser Ali. Are you a good lover as well?" she asked, nipping at his lip.

His reply was a moan of pleasure as he pressed harder against her. He punctuated his kisses with fevered words of desire. "Layla, I've never wanted any woman the way I want you. My heart is yours to do with as you please. You won't be sorry for loving me, I promise. I will please you, *eshgham*. You are my destiny, the one who will bring me peace."

She could feel his manhood pulsing against her, throbbing with desire. She watched him struggle to control his need for satisfaction. He rolled off her and stood, grabbing the AR-15. "Come, we must return to the house before we're missed. Tonight, I will come to you. Tonight I will make you mine."

She groaned out her frustration. At this moment, he'd found the will to resist her. He was stronger than she thought, and it worried her. She was playing with fire. Regardless of his professed affection for her, she knew he would not be made a fool. He was a methodical man, hardened and trained by the military. Capable of controlling the urges and passions that raged within him. She would have to be convincing, or he would see right through her. She knew what he was capable of. If he suspected her deception, he'd have no compunction about killing her or ordering the death of Cerise and her grandparents.

Oh, God, please give me the strength to get through this.

CHAPTER 14

"Is that Layla Hassani?" Cass asked, turning to Cyrus.

Cyrus remained silent as Shlomo took the lead. "It's her. I know this looks suspicious." His expression was grave as he watched Cyrus. "But Layla is operating under duress. We are aware of nothing about what's happening to her, what she's struggling with—what she knows."

Cyrus barely registered Shlomo's words. His focus was on the monitor. Cyrus was shaken when Layla and the man disappeared beneath a canopy of trees, and the satellite lost sight of them. He squinted, hoping they would immediately reemerge. *Where is she? What the fuck are they doing under those trees?* His instincts were telling him Layla was in danger, but his ego was suffering from what seemed to be a betrayal. His blood coursed through his veins with the fire of vengeance.

Cass interrupted his thoughts. "For now, we have no reason to suspect Layla of any duplicity and have to assume she's the victim and is acting out of her own protection, or possibly someone else's. What we need to do now is formulate our action."

She looked around the room and addressed her team. "Go to your drawing boards. I want concrete plans as to how we take them down. Jim, put the Governor of Pennsylvania on notification that the FBI will be conducting a raid on this compound, and get our hostage rescue team and extraction team queuing up for action. This will be an all-out assault led by our counterterrorist tactical teams from the Critical Incident Response Group—CIRG. I want HRT and a CNU, local and national, on the ground in Lancaster County immediately. Find us a base for operations. We need a command post."

Cyrus, who'd listened impassively to Cass's directives, suddenly interrupted with a commanding, "No!" Anger flowed from him like hot tar pouring onto the pavement. Thick and oozing, it filled the cracks of silence. Everyone in the room froze. "We need to talk, now," he said in a low growl.

Cass's eyes narrowed. "Okay. Everyone clear the room and get to work. Proceed as I ordered. Nothing has changed." She locked eyes with David. "David, I want you here." She called after the departing agents, "Somebody bring coffee, please."

Cyrus knew he had to level with Cass and David. But before he could utter a word, Cass went on the attack. "Okay, Zev, I want the truth. What the hell is going on with you? I warn you if you don't level with us, I'll have you shipped back to Israel faster than you can say Mazel Tov. I will not stand for any insubordination on my team or any questioning of my authority."

Cyrus smiled, hoping to dissipate some of the anger he'd provoked. "I apologize for not confiding in you from the beginning, but Layla Hassani is my wife." He bowed. "Cyrus Hassani at your service."

Cass glared at Cyrus. "Oh, for the love of—"

David smoothly intervened. "We understand your stress and frustration, Zev—I mean Cyrus—but Layla's isn't the only life at stake here. We have a significant threat to our homeland, which could result in the loss of thousands of lives. We may be facing another 9-11 or worse."

"I think you need to listen to what I have to say before you take any actions." Cyrus sat, waiting for Cass and David to follow suit. David took the cue and sat, Cass, threw a scowl at Cyrus and began to pace.

"First, let me give you a brief synopsis of who I really am," Cyrus began. "I am Iranian born. I was recruited by Mossad, groomed to be a deep-cover mole in Iran. I provided Mossad with intel, which slowed the IRI's nuclearization. For years, I was a valuable asset, spying on Iran's nuclear program, helping Israel in many capacities I'm sure you've heard rumor of. I rose to a very high position in the IRGC as an aide to the second in command of *Oghab2*. I believe you call it Eagle2. My position gave me complete access to Iran's nuclear facilities."

Both Cass and David's eyebrows shot up at the mention of the most elite and secretive division of the Iranian Revolutionary Guard. Everyone in the intelligence field knew Eagle2 oversaw Iran's nuclear security and facilities, however little was known of their operations.

Cyrus could see they were impressed. "Check your files, and you'll find Layla was kidnapped in Dubai five years ago. Her father turned to Israel to rescue her. I was assigned to get her out of Iran, which, of course, blew my cover. We were hunted by the IRGC and barely escaped with our lives. You've watched the video by the terrorists— it's Layla's father and me they want. My death for treason, possibly Layla's father's death for his work on miniaturized nuclear systems. Their goal is to show the US and Israel they can inflict devastation on us at will.

"I believe Layla is merely the bait being used to draw me out. If you go into that compound with a SWAT team and start shooting, not only will I lose my wife, but it is highly likely they'll blow the place to kingdom come.

"I know the Quds force and Hezbollah's tactics. I also know their leader Major General Qasem Solatani. I know how he thinks and how devoted he is to their regime. If he's behind this plot, you can be assured, every detail has been well thought out and programmed to succeed."

Cass had stopped her pacing. She was studying him again like a bug under a microscope. "Go on."

"This cell is operating, most likely, as a suicide mission, they have no intention of living beyond the detonation and fulfillment of their mass murder plot. I'm certain Applegate Farms is wired to explode if threatened, and I'm positive they have a contingency plan operating. My guess is they've already planted a bomb somewhere, and they have more than one delivery system. A backup just in case something goes wrong.

"If they even smell an attack, their timeline will be escalated, and a weapon of mass destruction will be delivered. One event will guarantee the next event. You have no idea what their intended target is or the delivery system they plan to use. Without precise knowledge of what they have planned, we have nothing."

"So, what do you propose, Cyrus?" David's voice was grim.

"Insert me. Let me go in solo to assess the situation. I speak Arabic and Farsi. I can pass the smell test. Mossad will help, they can arrange for my cover by using an agent infiltrated into Hezbollah in Lebanon." Cyrus's initial reaction had cooled. It had been torture seeing Layla flirt with that terrorist, but he knew she was doing it for a good reason. He felt it down to his bones. "I know my wife, and there is no question of her loyalty. There's a reason she's dancing with the devil, trust me."

"We don't suspect her of being a double agent or a traitor. It doesn't make sense. So why do you think she's, as you say, dancing with the devil?" Cass questioned.

"My wife is resilient and smart. She's trying to survive. My guess is she's gained the information we're seeking, or will soon. She may even have figured out the target. I need to get to her to find out."

"And then what?" Cyrus knew she was pushing him.

"Once we are aware of their plan, we can implement a simultaneous operation and take out not only the compound but the bomb and the delivery system. This isn't a Clint Eastwood movie; you can't go in with your guns blazing. It's what they expect—it's the unexpected we need to surprise them with."

"What if you're captured?" Cass jabbed at him.

"Don't worry about me. I'm expendable," Cyrus leaned forward to make his point. "If I'm taken hostage, you do what you have to do. I'm prepared to die to save my wife. But I'm telling you now that I won't fail."

Cass crossed her arms over her chest. "This is a risky proposition. Not to mention, we'd be delaying acting on a deadly threat."

David interrupted, "I have an idea."

Cass turned to David. "What's your plan, partner?"

"I need a few minutes to make a call to Homeland Security and our agent investigating the Islamic Learning Center in Lancaster. I'll be back." David's long-legged stride bore him from the room.

"Cyrus, I know you're a professional, but this is personal for you. Your objectivity and loyalties will be tested. Are you sure you're the right man for the job? Won't you be recognized by these people?"

"I understand your concern Cass, but I think I'm capable of separating the issues. Avi Zaken was a dear friend, but I will not be operating under a revenge factor. I spent much of my life as a mole, trained to function in a hostile environment without allowing my emotions to rule my decisions. Besides, I trust you and David will have my back. That's enough for me. As for my looks, I'm a master of disguise. I've been trained to alter my appearance with prosthetics, voice control, and make-up. Give me a beard, costume, and contacts, and you won't recognize me."

"How long has it been since you were undercover?"

"Five years."

"Five years is a lifetime in this business." Cass's raised eyebrows questioned his sanity.

"I lived ten years undercover in Tehran. It's in my DNA. Besides, no one has more to lose than me, Cass. I'm the man for the job, and you know it."

She stood. "All right, we'll do it your way, but I plan on having that compound surrounded by an army of law enforcement, and nothing and no one is getting out of there alive. Let's see what David comes up with. His judgment is always spot on."

Cyrus knew Cass was straddling two sides of the fence. She might empathize with his position, but her job was to stop a terrorist attack and keep her country safe. He knew public safety trumped Layla's life.

"I spoke to Homeland Security," David said, rushing back into the conference room a few minutes later.

"It seems Lancaster is ground zero for the administration's refugee resettlement program. There's been a massive influx to the community, many of whom are healthy young males. I also spoke to our agent, who conducted an interview with the head of the Islamic Learning Center, the largest mosque in the area. The center is instrumental in resettling and finding jobs for these people. They provide a service where the men are shuttled to local farms and businesses as day laborers. Layla's being held at Applegate Farms—a front for this terrorist cell. The mosque regularly sends day laborers to work at Applegate Farms. They're clearly taking advantage of the vulnerable backgrounds and refugee status of those farmworkers. Those laborers wouldn't speak up even if they saw something odd going on, whether or not they harbor any sympathy for these factions, or are just plain scared." David sharpened his gaze on Cyrus. "I'm thinking we infiltrate you into the labor pool. It will give you safe cover and easy access. We could insert you as early as tomorrow morning." David paused, glancing from Cyrus to Cass. "What do you think?"

Cyrus waited for Cass to respond. In his mind, it seemed a perfect way for him to gain access to Layla. If he had to, he would go rogue, and no one would be able to stop him. He was confident he'd save his wife. He was a trained assassin and had faced greater danger many times in his life. He lived by the sword and thrived on it. But he hoped he wouldn't have to go it alone. With Cass and the FBI on his side, he'd have more clout.

She locked eyes with him as if trying to read his mind. If Cass refused, it would mean he'd have to find another way. He had no intention of failing.

"All right. We'll go with it, but I warn you, Cyrus, I'm giving you one day. I want you to go in on that shuttle and leave on that shuttle. Stick with the plan. You got me?"

"Got it," he nodded and stood. "That should be all the time I need to find out what we need to know and get to Layla."

Hang on, my love, I'm going to get you out of this just like last time, I promise.

CHAPTER 15

Millennium Hilton, New York
September 15th
5 p.m.

She screamed in ecstasy, wrapping her legs tightly around his waist as he exploded inside of her.

Cass fell back onto the bed with a satisfied sigh while David's lips lingered on the pulsing vein in her neck. Their fast-and-furious sex wasn't what either would have preferred, but they were supposed to be packing and getting the hell out of Dodge. They only had a short window of time before they were scheduled to leave for the command center in Lancaster.

Cass's conversation with the director had granted her full control over the operation. His belief in her placed an additional weight upon her shoulders. The pressure made her edgy, but David was used to bearing the brunt of her nerves. He was her rock.

Her feelings for her partner mystified her. She still couldn't get over how well he understood her. Before David, she'd taken random lovers whose only purpose was to relieve her stress physically. With David, she didn't have to pretend. He was never threatened or insulted by her purely physical desire. He didn't question her motives—he merely satisfied her. With time, she'd stopped seeking one night stands, and David became her lover exclusively.

Her heart was still pounding in her chest when she asked, "David, did you pull a file on Cyrus?"

"I know you so well, Cass," he said, flashing her a knowing grin. "Yeah, I did."

"Do they have kids?" The question was relevant; however, she knew it struck close to home—it was personal. She and David had never talked about marriage or children. But damn, he'd make a great father. The truth, recently, she'd begun to think more and more about what it would be like to have a child with him. To have a life beyond the FBI. She almost yearned for it. He was the only man she'd ever had this thought with and it scared her. She'd always rolled her eyes at the "biological clock" notion. But lately, she couldn't stop thinking about it. *What the heck is wrong with me?*

"A daughter, her name's Cerise. She's four. Layla also has grandparents living in Tel Aviv."

Cass frowned. "That worries me. They're vulnerable." *Am I thinking of Cyrus and Layla, or myself? If David and I had a child, wouldn't that make us vulnerable too? How could we raise a child in a "normal" household knowing the risks we face?* "And these grandparents only enhance the problem," she added. "What if these terrorists get their hands on her or them? Both Cyrus and Layla could become blackmail targets. We need to find out where the kid and the grandparents are, and whether they're being protected. I don't want to think about a father or mother's loyalties being tested. Shit if the child were threatened, there's no telling what they'd do."

"That's an easy one. I'll get on it." David rolled out of bed. He picked up his clothes and began to dress.

Cass gazed at her partner, enjoying the view. His muscled body and bed-messed curls never failed to arouse her. It amazed her how oblivious he was to his movie-star good looks. The rare occasion when they actually had some downtime to get dressed up and go to dinner, David was always the main attraction. As soon as he stepped into a room, every woman became laser-focused on him and quite a few men too. And yet he considered himself just an average Joe. She wondered at the director's foresight in handpicking him to be her partner. It's like he'd had some sixth sense that David would provide a much-needed balance to her inner chaos? Where she was impulsive, he was exacting. She was the firebrand, and he was the calming hand of reason. Together they struck a perfect melody, or as her Sensei would have pointed out, *David is the yin to your yang.* "David?"

He turned to her, his eyebrows lifted in question. "Yeah, boss?"

As quick as lightning, she was out of the bed and in his arms, her lips locked on his in a searing kiss.

When they finally broke apart, she was rewarded with a crooked grin. "Are you trying to coax me back into bed? Because if you are, it's working."

Her fingers threaded through his dark curly hair as she pressed herself deeper into his embrace. His hazel eyes held a spark of tender amusement. "Unfortunately, we don't have time for another round, but…" She searched for the right words. "I…I need to tell you something before we leave."

"Okay, I'm game." His lips quirked up in a curious smile.

"I-I've never said this before…" She swallowed the sudden lump in her throat, struggling to give voice to her feelings. "I care a lot for you—" *I'm such a fucking coward. Say it, tell him the truth.* "I need you to know this, just in case something goes wrong." Her lips began to tremble, and her gaze skittered away from his. "I've been afraid to admit it, afraid if I did, it would mess up what we have. Afraid…saying it out loud would make you think I was trying to—trying to get you to make a commitment or something."

"Afraid to tell me what?" he pressed, tilting her chin up.

"Dammit! I love you. Okay?" She blew out a breath. "There, I said it. The cat's out of the bag." His eyes were locked on hers as he held her upturned face, caressing her jaw with his thumb. "Even if you didn't say it, baby, I never doubted it," he said softly.

A single tear threatened. Cass fought to hold the pesky thing in, but it stubbornly refused to listen and chose to sneak down her cheek. Tenderly David bent to kiss it, and that caused another and another. Soon she was blubbering like a baby.

"Guess what?" He gathered her into his arms.

"What?" she said into his neck.

"I love you too."

She sniffled and leaned back to look at him. "I kinda figured that," she whispered.

"And you know what else?" He flashed her that Hollywood grin. "It's okay, Cass, your secret is safe with me." He squeezed her and kissed her forehead. "I've got your back, baby. You're not going to lose me. Not now, not ever." He chuckled. "I'll pretend I didn't even hear you say the *L*-word or the *C*-word." He bent his lips to hers.

His kiss always had the same effect on her. When their lips parted, all she wanted to do was crawl back into bed with him and forget everything else.

As if reading her thoughts, he chuckled again. "You'd better get dressed, boss, or we're never going to leave this room." He turned her around and gave her a gentle pat on her butt.

"Give me ten minutes. Call for the car. I'll be ready." She grabbed her clothes and headed for the bathroom, throwing him a kiss as she closed the door.

CHAPTER 16

Lancaster County, Pennsylvania
September 15th
5 p.m.

Her wrist was once more chained to the bed. The last rays of sunlight streamed through the window battling with the shadows. Soon darkness would supplant the fading light. Layla's emotional exhaustion had taken a toll on her, and she'd fallen into a fitful nap. Worried about Cerise and her grandparents' safety. Worried, she'd never see Cyrus again. Worried, that if Cyrus discovered her kissing Ali or an even worse possibility her having sex with Ali, he'd hate her. Would Cyrus believe her…believe all she really wanted to do was make a run for it. *Yeah, like that's going to work.* She was in the middle of nowhere, and they'd catch her before she could even get to the tree line.

Men's voices floated to her door. Her eyes flew open as she strained to listen, recognizing the raised angry intonations of Ali and his brother Omar.

I hope it's not me they're arguing about. What if Ali changes his mind and doesn't come to me? I need to find out how he's going to protect Cerise and my grandparents?

The brothers went at it for several minutes more. After she heard a door slam, there was silence. Minutes later, footsteps approached the door and a key scratched in the lock. Her heart thundered in her chest as the doorknob turned. It was down to the wire. She'd have to go all the way with him to get the information she needed. To convince him to stop the bombing. To help her escape. The cost—her soul to save thousands. Do whatever it took to protect her family. *For you, Cyrus. For us…* She pasted a sunny smile on her face, but it froze as she saw Omar step into the room. He was dressed in military fatigues tucked into work boots.

He glared at Layla.

The metal clanked as she sat up against the headboard. She was thankful Ali had handcuffed her to the bedpost. If he hadn't, Omar would surely have blown his stack.

"What are you doing to my brother?" Omar hissed. "Are you a witch or something? I've never seen him like this."

"I don't know what you're talking about," Layla said as calmly as she could, hoping he couldn't read the fear in her eyes. "He's allowed me to wash and brought me food. Basic decencies, nothing more."

"You're lying. He's given you too much liberty, letting you walk around outside. My brother has changed since we brought you here."

She forced a chuckle. "Last time I checked, having a rifle pointed at your back or being handcuffed most of the day and night isn't exactly freedom." She closed her eyes for a moment. "Look, all he did was allow me a few minutes of fresh air, to feel the sun on my face. He showed me some kindness, that is all."

"It's a weakness, unworthy of a great warrior. It's unseemly for a man who has sworn his life to Allah, to a cause he's vowed to sacrifice his life, to behave with anything but contempt for the enemy."

"His so-called weakness didn't stop him from blowing up a restaurant with hundreds of people in it. I doubt it will stop him from doing whatever else you've planned."

Layla tried not to flinch under Omar's unwavering gaze. "He's told you?"

"No. He's said nothing. I'm not a fool, though. It's obvious you're planning another attack."

Through his teeth, Omar snarled. "If you weren't the bait infidel, I'd kill you now. But soon enough, you'll join your husband in Hell."

Layla thrust her chin out bravely. "I'm not afraid of you, and neither is Cyrus."

Omar slapped her, banging her head into the metal frame of the bed.

"You bastard!" she cried out, her hand cupping her cheek. "You're a coward hitting a woman who's chained to a bed."

Omar snarled as he stepped forward.

"Omar! Stop!" Ali rushed into the room, grabbing Omar's fisted hand before he could land another blow. "Don't hurt her. It's not her fault."

Layla watched the two brothers argue in rapid-fire Farsi. Both men's eyes were filled with deadly rage.

"Speak English," Ali ordered.

"Why do you want her to understand what we're saying?"

"Because I want her to know there's no reason for her to be fearful. I want her to know we're not animals. Cyrus is the target, not her."

"You just want to show off for her," Omar snorted. "You're thinking with your cock, Ali."

"Am I?" He stared icily at Omar. "I see no reason to abuse a woman who is chained."

"You grow weak, brother, she's controlling you."

"Enough, Omar!"

"Fuck her, if you must. But don't let it interfere with your duty."

"I don't believe I need your permission, Omar, one way or the other."

"I've seen the way you look at her. The strange hold she has over you."

"You need to pull yourself together, Omar. I know the stress is getting to you, but you're out-of-line. You know nothing of what I think or what I intend. You may be overseeing this operation, but it is my duty to see it through. The prisoner is of no concern to you. She poses no threat to you, to me, or to our plans. You are not to enter this room again. Do you hear me, Omar? I demand you do not enter this room again."

"I warn you, Ali. The woman is a witch, and she will be your downfall."

"And, I warn you, Omar, not another word. I'm not a boy. I'm a man. I've been as loyal to the cause as you have. I've sacrificed just as much as you."

The two men stared hard at each other. The intensity in their gazes unwavering. Layla didn't know if they were going to kill each other or burst into tears and embrace.

Finally, Omar nodded and stepped back. "As you wish, brother. Forgive my outburst. I should not have questioned your faith. I know you would never fail to do your duty."

"Thank you, Omar." Ali clapped his brother on the shoulder. "We still have much to do before tomorrow night. I suggest you get ready, Buraq will be here soon to pick you up."

Omar returned the gesture, laying his hand on Ali's shoulder. "Forgive me for forgetting what a great warrior you are." He walked to the door but hesitated before leaving. "Your dedication to our cause was never in question."

Ali nodded and closed the door. He leaned his forehead against the wood for a moment and then turned back to Layla. "Are you hurt, Layla?" he whispered. His dark eyes reflected concern.

She tentatively touched the swollen welt on her cheek. "I'll be fine, thank you. I think he would have done a lot more damage if you hadn't intervened."

"I'll be right back with an icepack,"

Returning, he sat on the edge of the bed and gently pressed the icepack against her face.

She winced. "Why does he hate me so much?"

"He's a product of our upbringing. He hates because he was taught to hate. Do not judge him, please? He-he used to be different. I can assure you—he won't bother you again."

Ali stood and walked to the window. Looking out for a few minutes, his face reflected some sort of inner battle he was fighting. It appeared to Layla that his demeanor in the last couple of days had changed from determination to regret. But what kind of regret? Regret for killing all those people or regret knowing his life was going to soon end. Watching him, Layla tried to understand. How could a person be driven to kill thousands of innocent people and still retain their humanity? Was it even possible? After so many years of indoctrination, of giving up everything for the cause, what was left of a person's true self?

Ali was, without a doubt, a Doctor Jekyll and Mr. Hyde, a reminder to her that nothing was ever black and white. Good and evil and love and hate could reside side-by-side in a man or a woman. *Given the right set of circumstances, we are all capable of murder.* He had killed without a thought. Could she do the same? If it meant saving those she loved? If it meant saving innocent people? She couldn't answer those questions right now, but if the time came, she hoped she'd have the strength to do so.

He turned back to her, and their eyes met. Her cheeks heated at being caught studying him, and she dropped her gaze in embarrassment.

"Already the sun has set on another day," he said. "I must perform my evening prayers. When I'm done, I will bring you dinner, and then you can shower and prepare for bed." He fixed his eyes on her. "Does that suit you, Layla?"

She knew the question bore more than one meaning. This time she met Ali's gaze. "I look forward to your company."

After Ali left, she leaned her head back against the headboard. *Oh, how I wish you were here, my love. You would know what to do.* Cyrus would make everything all right. He would keep her safe. He would tease her until she forgot about being afraid.

Ali and Omar's conversation had revealed the attack might come tomorrow night. She shuddered. That would explain his inner turmoil. He might be having second thoughts. Time was running out. A tear slipped down her face, and she brushed it away. She needed to stay strong. She needed a miracle.

CHAPTER 17

Millennium Hilton, New York
September 15th
5 p.m.

Cyrus paced his hotel room like a caged animal.

On the bed, his bag was packed and ready. Any minute the call would come from Shlomo telling him that he and Zvi were to report downstairs to a special operational vehicle that would transport them to their command headquarters in Lancaster, Pennsylvania. The FBI had fitted it with laptops, surveillance gear, a satellite feed, and all the bells and whistles necessary for them to work in complete comfort on the road.

He'd spent an hour researching the area known as Amish Country, its history, topography, and geography. Two hours driving time from Washington, and less than four hours from New York City, Lancaster lay centrally located, dangerously within striking distance of strategic targets. In Pennsylvania alone, he'd discovered five nuclear power plants, several of which ranked in the bottom third for safety and security standards. There were also plenty of military bases located nearby, but those weren't the kinds of targets guaranteed to devastate the morale of the country. It was the densely populated urban areas like New York and Washington that would arrest the heartbeat of the nation and cause complete chaos should they be attacked. 9-11 had nearly brought a mighty nation to its knees. A repeat would be catastrophic.

He retrieved a burner phone from his bag and dialed. It was midnight in Tel Aviv.

"Hello? Cyrus?"

"I'm sorry to call you so late, Aleck, but I may not get another chance."

"It's okay, Cyrus," he said. Rustling and a grunt followed as Aleck was obviously sitting up in bed. "Call me at any time. I've been going crazy with worry. Have you found Layla?"

Cyrus closed his eyes as he tried to block out the image of Layla and her captor, strolling beneath the canopy of trees. "Yes, we've found her. She's being held at a farm…as far as I can tell, she looks fine, unharmed."

Aleck sighed. "Thank God. You saw her? How?"

Cyrus couldn't help but smile at hearing his atheist father-in-law, giving thanks to God. "From a satellite feed. We got lucky. She was outside." He didn't mention the man who accompanied her, and how he seemed far too familiar with her. He didn't say what the optics appeared to be—the intimacy. He didn't want to pile more worry onto Aleck's plate.

"So, what happens now? What are you going to do?"

"I'm afraid I can't discuss the details with you, but rest assured action is being taken." Another cell phone began to vibrate in his pocket. "Hold on. I have to take another call."

"Go ahead. I'm not moving."

"*Ken?*" Cyrus listened and then answered in Hebrew. "I'll be down in five minutes." He switched to the burner phone. "Aleck?"

"I'm here Cyrus, go ahead."

"I need you to do something for me."

"Whatever you need, I'll do."

"Aleck, I'm going to text you a message in code. You won't be able to read it, and neither will anyone else should it fall into the wrong hands."

"I understand."

"I need you to copy and seal it in an envelope and take it to a restaurant called Edna in Ramat HaSharon. Arrange a lunch date. Meet a student or a colleague. Go early before your guest arrives. Ask to see the chef. His name is Eran. Big burly guy. Bald. He cooks Persian food like no other. Come up with a ploy. Get him to the table and drop a glass, something to get you both on the ground. Whisper to him, you need him to deliver a message to Aryeh, from a friend."

"All right."

"I'll tell you now, Aleck, he's going to give you a lot of bullshit. He'll say that he has no idea who you're talking about, and he'll deny he's ever heard of this Aryeh guy. Tell him it's from the man who met Aryeh a few days ago, outside at the table with the umbrella—behind the restaurant. Tell him he made us a special meal. Aryeh's favorites. Get a pen, Aleck."

"I'm writing."

"*Khorest fesenjan,*" he spelled it out. "It's a pomegranate and walnut stew. Tell Eran I said it was delicious. At this point, Aleck, I'm certain he'll believe you and take the envelope. You can do this, Aleck. It's important. Crucial."

"I'll arrange it for today as soon as I get your text."

"Good. Thank you, Aleck. I don't want you to worry, but you won't be hearing from me again for some time. Just know that I'll do whatever it takes to rescue Layla."

"I know, son. I know you will."

Cyrus swallowed the sudden lump in his throat. Hearing his father-in-law call him son was something he'd never heard before. "Thank you for believing in me," he said, his voice thick with emotion. "It means a lot. It's not likely we'll have a chance to speak again until this is over. Take care of yourself and get the envelope to Eran."

"Don't worry, I will see to it. Cyrus, I want you to know I couldn't have asked for a better son-in-law or a better husband for my daughter."

"Thank you, Aleck. Pray, I don't let you or Layla down."

"I trust you, son. I know you won't."

Cyrus hung up, grabbed his bag, took a last look around the room, and headed for the door. The time for talk was over.

It was time for the eagle to hunt.

CHAPTER 18

Ramat HaSharon, Israel
Edna Restaurant
September 16th
12 p.m.

The restaurant was bustling when Aleck was shown to a table at Edna. He'd requested one in a corner as far from the windows as possible. He didn't know for sure if he was being tailed by a security team, but Cyrus had indicated he was probably being watched for his own safety. He was nervous enough, and he didn't want to raise any suspicion. Covert activity wasn't something Aleck felt comfortable with. He glanced around the room, everything looked unremarkable. Just another busy lunch hour in a popular restaurant. He'd arrived a half-hour earlier than his colleague, exactly as Cyrus had suggested.

The waiter brought him a drink menu, which he browsed briefly, finding his favorite spirit, Macallan scotch whiskey. He usually didn't drink at lunch, but if ever there was a time or a reason for it, it was now. The server returned with his drink, and Aleck sipped it gingerly. He patted his pocket for the umpteenth time. The envelope containing the secret missive from Cyrus to Aryeh was where he'd put it. *I think I'm going crazy. To hell with it.* He downed the shot and motioned for the waiter.

"Bring me a menu, please. Oh, and another Macallan." He felt his nerves fray more and more with each second.

"Yes, sir."

When the waiter returned, he asked, "Can I get you anything before your guest arrives?"

Aleck quickly scanned the menu and shook his head. "I don't see what I want on the menu. I know this is an inconvenience, but would you mind asking Eran to join me for a minute?" He smiled. He hoped it conveyed that he and Eran knew each other.

"But sir, I'm sure I can help you. The kitchen will be delighted to fill any special request if they can."

"No, it's not about food. I just want to say hello."

"Oh, you're a friend. No problem. Let me get him. I'll just be a moment." The waiter disappeared through the crowded tables heading for the kitchen.

Aleck sighed with relief. *First hurdle. Check.*

A few minutes later, a large bald-headed man wearing chef's whites headed toward him. His brow was lined and shiny with perspiration. When he reached the table, he glared down at Aleck, no recognition written in his expression. "Excuse me, sir, do I know you?"

"No, not exactly."

"Is there anything I can help you with?" The man frowned down at him. His hands were on his waist while his fingers drummed impatiently against his hips.

Aleck picked up his glass, his hand shaking and took a sip. When he went to put the glass down, it slipped from his fingers, falling to the floor with a crash shattering. "Oh, I'm so sorry." Both Aleck and the big man dropped to the ground, careful to avoid the glass shards.

"Please, sir, let me take care of this. I'll have a busboy over here in a minute. I don't want you cutting yourself."

Aleck's voice replied in a strained whisper. "No. I have something for you, Eran, an envelope. I need you to get it to Aryeh."

Eran's eyebrows shot up. "I don't know what you're talking about. Who's this Aryeh fellow? I don't know him or anyone with that name. You must be mistaken."

Aleck trembled. The mere thought of failing Cyrus, and in so doing failing Layla, made him ill. He tried to sound convincing instead of desperate. "Eran, please listen to me. A week ago, my son-in-law Cyrus met Aryeh at this restaurant. The restaurant was closed. They sat outside under an umbrella. You made them a feast." He furrowed his forehead, trying to remember the name of the dish he'd made sure to memorize. "It's not on the menu for some reason today. It's called…ah…*koresht fensen*…? Shit, what's the damn thing called?" *Damn it. I'm a nuclear physicist, not a chef de cuisine.* "I'm so damned nervous. I can't remember the name. Please help me. You must remember my son-in-law Cyrus?"

They were still under the table together. Eran studied his face. "*Koresht fesenjan.* I remember. I remember your son-in-law. He was quite agitated. Didn't eat much."

"Thank God. The truth is, Eran—I'm not very good at this subterfuge stuff."

"What do you have for him? Give it to me, and I'll see what I can do."

Relieved, Aleck handed him the envelope, happy to be rid of it. "My son-in-law says it's critical, Eran. Life and death." The knot in his throat brought a hoarse whisper. "My daughter's life."

Eran placed his hand on Aleck's shoulder. "Leave it to me, my friend. Now get up off this floor and let me get back to my kitchen. I'll have this cleaned up in a wink and a new drink brought to you."

"Sorry about the mess."

"Next time, order a cheaper scotch."

The two men stood and shook hands. "Sorry that I can't do. I only drink Macallan. I'm of Scot descent. It's in my blood."

"Okay, Scotsman, I just happen to have some *khoresht fesenjan* on the stove. Any other special requests?"

Aleck looked at the menu, his eyebrows raised. "I really don't know a thing about Persian cuisine."

Eran chuckled. "Is anyone dining with you, or are you solo?"

"I have a colleague meeting me. I had to insist this restaurant was the best in the area, and…" he laughed, "that I was an expert in Persian cuisine."

Eran laughed heartily. "Let me prepare you a tasting feast. I promise you won't be disappointed."

"Thank you. I'll be able to save face."

"And, enjoy the best Persian food in Israel."

They shook hands again, and Eran strode back to the kitchen. A minute later, Aleck was sipping on another glass of Macallan, happy he'd done his part but worried it might not be enough. *Now, just let Cyrus do his part,* he prayed.

CHAPTER 19

Philadelphia International Airport
September 17th
6 a.m.

A disguised Aryeh arrived at PHL a bit disheveled, but none the worse for wear. He'd traveled with the passport of one of his many aliases, Dov Klein. His black suit was rumpled from his nap on the plane, but other than his wrinkled clothes, he looked like any other Orthodox Jew. He rarely drew attention from US customs officials, and he didn't expect to today.

When he exited the airport, he got into the blue Mercedes parked at the curb.

"Shalom, Yitzhak." He tossed his briefcase in the back seat. "We need to stop at the bank so I can get these diamonds into the safety deposit box."

Yitzhak raised his eyebrows. "Aye-aye, boss. Is that our payday?"

Chuckling, Aryeh pulled on the *tzitzit*, the knotted fringes religious Jews wear on the four corners of their body, which had somehow tangled in the seatbelt. "Bankroll for the operation, plus extra as needed for whatever comes up." He said, teasing good-naturedly, "You, Yitz, are overpaid already."

Yitzhak laughed. "How was the flight?"

"You know me, a couple of whiskeys, and I can sleep anywhere. God bless the IDF and its training. Is everything ready?"

"Yes, just as planned, the team, Ziva, Daniel, and Ben are coming in from Newark." He gestured to the clock on the Mercedes dashboard. "They should be meeting us within the hour."

"*Tov.*" Aryeh quickly calculated the time difference. "Ash should have arrived in Zurich hours ago. He knows what's at risk. Ash will never let the killer harm the child. He'll find and kill the sniper. There isn't a better assassin I know of. Have you heard from Zvi?"

"Zvi's at the FBI command post outside of Lancaster. He should be checking in soon."

"Perfect." He threw the felt hat he wore in the backseat. "Good Lord, I can't wait to get out of these clothes, and dump this beard." He scratched the thick black mass of hair that shadowed his jaw. "Man, the Orthodox attire is definitely not my thing."

Yitzhak laughed. "I get it, boss, me, either."

"I heard from Cyrus through his father-in-law. I hate keeping the guy out of the loop, but it's best if the bait doesn't know what's about to happen to him. He's going to get to Layla. He's convinced the FBI to let him case the farm before the shit hits the fan. I want to give him every opportunity to save Layla without risking the outcome of the operation. From this moment forward, the team must function precisely and accurately as the movement of a Chopard Swiss watch. I expect perfection."

"The team is ready, boss."

Aryeh sat back, relaxed. "That's why they pay us the big bucks, my friend."

Overnight the advanced operations team of the FBI set up a tactical command center at a dairy farm just a few miles from Applegate Farms near Lancaster. Under the cover of darkness, unmarked semi-trucks rolled in with equipment necessary to the operation. By dawn, TV monitors, smart boards, satellite systems, secured phones, and tactical gear were on site, along with the FBI's bomb squad, HRT, SWAT, JTTF, and various other law enforcement teams were housed in portable housing in the pastures.

A large barn had been converted into a state of the art technology center, the cows having been relocated to an adjacent property until the terrorist operation was shut down. The farmer who'd been taken to a secure location would be well paid for his displacement and discomfort. Regardless of the price of milk, his bottom line would reflect a better than average profit this year courtesy of the US of A. When the operation successfully wrapped, everything would return to normal as if law enforcement had never been there. The cows would enjoy a holiday from the milking machines and return no worse for wear. The selection of a dairy farm was ideal and would raise no eyebrows with the comings or goings of commercial vehicles.

Cass wrinkled her nose as she walked back and forth across the temporary floor. Even with the air filtration system in place, the scent of livestock still lingered in the air. She brought her coffee cup to her lips and took a sip as she peered over the shoulders of the FBI tech geeks who monitored the satellite feed and screens. The live shots from Applegate farms showed no activity, a complete contrast to the beehive in the FBI's mobile command center.

As the queen of the hive, Cass was immediately alerted by the increased buzz behind her. She turned and cocked her brow at the stranger. Dressed in what looked to be work overalls, the man sported a dark beard, a bigger than average nose, and dark eyes that regarded her beneath thick black brows. Dark black curls with a smattering of gray framed his head. The man walked ponderously in work boots toward her, his gait indicated a pronounced limp. When he broke into a smile, her jaw hit the floor.

"I told you I was good at disguises," he chuckled.

"I'm stunned. Even Layla won't be able to recognize you."

Cyrus's brows furrowed. "Yeah, I'm worried about that. I don't want her frightened when I try to approach her."

"The transformation is uncanny." She glanced at her watch. "Are you ready to go tomorrow morning? Where's your transmitter and earpiece? Have my people prepped you as to our communication protocol, the use of roger and over?"

"Transmitter is sewn into my shirt collar, and my earpiece is in. Yeah, I've got the lingo. Same as Israel, except not in Hebrew."

She walked to the other side of the barn. She wasn't taking any chances. She whispered, "Are you reading me."

"Roger, Cass, reading you loud and clear. Over."

"Cyrus, remember what I told you. You're to be on that five o'clock shuttle when it leaves the farm. There can be no changes in the plan?"

"Roger, boss."

"Okay, you're ready to go." She walked back to where he waited. "Drake will drop you tomorrow at the mosque where the men gather for daily pickup. I'm putting a lot on the line for you, I expect you to deliver."

He smiled. "I always deliver Cass."

CHAPTER 20

Lancaster County, Pennsylvania
September 17th
8 p.m.

Somewhere outside the window of Layla's prison, the mournful hoot of an owl struck a chord. It reminded her of the precariousness of her situation. She'd been granted a reprieve. Yesterday, Ali had been bogged down and not been able to come to her. Omar had never let him out of his sight, and Ali had been forced to behave as if it didn't matter. However, at lunch, Ali had promised he'd come to her tonight.

Any minute he would come through the door. Layla forced herself to swallow the bitter pill of truth. She was about to break her marriage vows. A verse from the traditional marriage vow replayed in her mind. *"Let no man turn asunder."* She couldn't recall if the vows included the phrase *"Let no woman turn asunder,"* because what she was about to do was in violation of those vows. She was about to cross the line, turn asunder, cheat, call it what you will. The reason didn't matter, even if she was doing it to save the lives of Cerise and her family. The one good act could not negate the other.

She fought to stay the tears brimming in her eyes, and guilt threatening to consume her. She was petrified with fear, but she mustn't let Ali see any telltale signs of crying. If only she had a glass of wine, something to blur the lines of her reasoning, something to dull her guilt. Layla fidgeted on the bed, yanking at the handcuff with frustration. She wanted to get up and pace. To burn off this anxious energy bubbling inside her. She wanted to tear her hair out. For the first time in her life, she understood the reason people became cutters. She'd remembered reading about the late Princess Diana, who'd admitted to cutting and physically hurting herself. Self-flagellation was used by some traumatized people to relieve emotional stress.

How would she be able to pretend a desire for Ali? How would she be able to let him touch her, kiss her, invade her body? And then afterward, would she ever be able to return to who she once was?

Maybe if I close my eyes and picture Cyrus? If I convince myself that it's Cyrus making love to me, then I'll be able to get through it...

She began to tremble. It seemed insurmountable to do such a thing. Fear threatened to overwhelm her. *Would Cyrus forgive her? Would he be able to get past her betrayal?*

The dam burst within her, and a flood of tears drenched her cheeks. Her heart was broken, she was broken, and she had no way of knowing how she'd ever find herself again.

The pedestal she'd inhabited like a goddess would be kicked out from under her, and she would become a mere mortal woman, no different than any other woman in the eyes of her husband. She was trapped, imprisoned, in more ways than one. How had she come to a place where there seemed to be no way out? She prayed to God for an answer.

The click of the key turning in the door, for some reason, reminded her of the book titled, *"For Whom the Bell Tolls."* She quickly dried her tears as she tried to remember the meaning of that dour phrase. *Something about loss and death—its inevitability.* She pinched her cheeks and forced a smile of greeting on her face as she waited for the man who controlled the fate of her daughter and grandparents, the man who, in all likelihood, would destroy her marriage.

Cyrus, please forgive me for what I'm about to do...

Ali had prepared himself with care and thoughtfulness, not unlike what a bridegroom in Iran would do on the day of his wedding. He knew he was going to die. Layla would be the last woman Ali would ever lie with, the last woman he would ever love. He looked in the mirror, trying to see what she would see. He wore a white linen Nehru-collared shirt, and his long black hair was scented and oiled straight back from his forehead. Even though he was young and not out of his twenties, his face bore lines and scars etched from the years of living in military camps. An overwhelming sadness filled him as he thought about the children he would never have or the life he would never live. He couldn't bear the thought of becoming like his brother—an embittered man whose hatred had poisoned his blood.

Closing his eyes, he allowed the memories to rush in. The sound of Omar's laughter filled the silence. They had been inseparable. Together, brother with brother, barefoot, running through the orchard behind their farmhouse. When they died, it would be the end of their line. He and Omar had been poets then, believers that the world was a beautiful place with endless possibilities. Those beliefs had been lost in the ugliness of Hezbollah training camps, in the death and destruction of war. With time, everything of beauty had been driven out of them. Martyrdom had become their only desire. *Now, it's only hours away.*

Was this why he was so enamored of Layla? That somehow his soul could be cleansed when he went to meet his maker?

He stared into the mirror, and whispered a prayer to Allah, a prayer for his guidance and blessings, a prayer his seed would take life inside of Layla. He tried to imagine the beautiful son or daughter who would be created from a union of their bodies. Perhaps a child with hair the color of ginger and smoky topaz eyes, or a child with black hair and eyes as turquoise as the sea. It made him smile, this hope of leaving something of himself in the world. It was an irony, and he didn't know why, but it somehow pleased him that a child of his might be raised a Jew in Israel. It was something he could never have imagined. Something antithetical to his Muslim beliefs and culture. Yet it filled his heart with hope.

When he opened the door to Layla's room, he stood for a moment and allowed his eyes to adjust to the darkness. He could just make out the woman he considered his bride, sitting up in the bed. It pleased him she was awake and waiting for him. In three strides, he reached her and removed the handcuff that chained her to the bed frame. Taking her hands, he pulled her into his arms, "Layla?" He bent to kiss her forehead. "This room is not worthy of you or our union. You'll come to my bedroom where there is light. I need to see every inch of your beauty."

"But Ali, what about Omar? Isn't that dangerous?"

"Do not worry, *eshgham*. Omar is gone, he will not bother us tonight— no one will." Omar had left to meet with the suicide drivers to make sure they were ready for their final tasks. Saying this reminded him he'd most likely never see his brother again. The plan was for Omar to remain with Buraq, the driver of the truck carrying the bomb. Ali felt the stab of pain once more at the loss of his brother. He shook his head, driving the thought from his mind, and focused instead on Layla. In the darkness, Ali could just make out her delicate features. He needed to focus on her. He needed to see her smile. He needed to hear her cry out his name in ecstasy. "Come."

He took her hand and led her through the house to the other side. The house was as still as it was dark. He opened the door to his room, where the shimmering light of dozens of candles flickered on the bureau and the side tables, casting shadows on the walls. A large, wood-framed bed sat against the far wall.

Layla stood still, and a slight tremor passed from her hand into his. He understood that she must be nervous. Distracting her, Ali led her to two chairs near a small café table where he'd set a bottle of wine and two glasses. He let go of her hand and pulled out one of the chairs. "Sit, Layla." He poured them each a drink, giving one to her.

"I thought Muslims are forbidden to drink alcohol?"

"We are, but you're not Muslim, and I thought it would make you more comfortable." He took a sip and looked at the glass in his hand. "It's good, isn't it?"

She inhaled the bouquet and took a sip. "Yes, Ali, it's excellent, but why are you drinking?"

"I made a trip into town yesterday, to the state store." He shrugged one shoulder, and his lips turned up in a slight smile. "I've given myself to Allah. I'm sure he will forgive me for this one indiscretion. Tonight is very special. I want to feel what you're feeling." He drank deeply, enjoying the warmth that spread through his limbs.

"Tell me about your life Layla. I want to know everything about you. We're not in any hurry. We have all night. Let us share this wine and talk. I want to savor you and this moment."

"Okay." She took another sip and set the glass back down on the table. She proceeded to tell him about her life, the unbearable years of her mother's battle with cancer that finally claimed her life. The closeness she shared with her father. She told him about her time as an art history student at Harvard and the Saudi boyfriend she'd thought she was in love with.

"You and the Saudi were kidnapped in Dubai and taken to Tehran. That's where you met Cyrus?"

"Cyrus got me out of Evin Prison and rescued me from Iran. He risked and nearly lost his life, getting me to Israel." She dropped her eyes and then raised them.

Ali watched her intently when she spoke, absorbing her words, losing himself in her story.

"I'd rather not talk about Cyrus." She closed her eyes. "I thought he would come flying in like before and rescue me. I guess even Superman can fail."

"I would never fail you, Layla," Ali said fervently. For the length of time she spoke, Ali remained silent, watching the light dance across her features. He'd restrained himself from reaching out and touching her. He wanted to learn as much about her as he could in the short time granted to them. In this blink of an eye, he was able to court her.

He remembered that first night when he carried her into the house after the kidnapping. He'd sat by her bed and watched her sleep. She had been curled up like a child, and he'd felt the first stirrings of love. It was unaccountable and irrational, but it had swept through him like a storm surge. At first, he'd thought God had presented him with a temptation meant to undo him, a test of his loyalty. His attraction to Layla was so great his heart had thundered in his chest, and his longing to possess her had stolen his breath away. As he stood guard over her, the truth dawned on him, that Layla was not a temptation but a gift. He'd nurtured the thought until it grew into a love and passion that filled his mind and heart.

Layla finished her story and drained her glass of Burgundy. Setting the glass down, she took a deep breath and reached across the table, laying her hand on his. The heat of her touch shot to his groin. "Ali, I had no intention of falling in love with my captor. Why do you think this has happened?" Her eyes filled with tears crumbling whatever was left of his ability to resist her.

He was out of his seat and on his knees before her in an instant. His hands cupped her face as he gently pulled her toward his lips, whispering, "Oh, Layla, you can't know what your words mean to me. I've been struggling with the same questions since I first saw you. I believe Allah brought us together for a reason."

Her body shook uncontrollably. "And what reason is that, Ali?"

Right now, the thought of a philosophical discussion was impossible. Ali had no control over his heart, and his desire was aching between his legs. To believe it was he she desired was more than he could have ever imagined. When he'd drugged her, he'd felt her passion, but that had been for Cyrus, the man he'd been sent to kill. This time she was responding to him, and it overwhelmed him. He knew later when he'd satisfied her a thousand-fold, and she was lying in his arms spent, entirely his, he'd answer her questions. It was important to him that she understood what was in his heart.

"I will tell you my darling, but first—" He drew her against him, his tongue seeking the pulse point in her neck. His lips traced kisses from her chin to her collarbone as he inhaled her delicious vanilla scent. Her head fell back, and she moaned softly. Her acquiescence encouraged him to take more of her. Her body, which at first had felt rigid, with each kiss had softened as she leaned into him, her resistance falling away like the clothing he would remove from her.

Words of adoration poured from him. "Oh, Layla, you are the only woman I've ever loved. The only woman I swear I'd die for. You've bewitched me." Each time he gave voice to his love for her, the more deeply he truly felt it. Ali knew the human psyche was persuadable. He was aware that if one said something or thought something enough, it became the truth. But this was different. He hadn't felt this alive since he was a youth.

He was drowning in emotion, dizzy with need, lost in a flame that threatened to consume him. He ignored the voice in his head that condemned what he was doing. He squelched the nagging possibility that everything she said and did was a lie. He refused to believe that she didn't care for him.

When Ali first entered her room, Layla pushed her fears of losing Cyrus aside. She needed to focus on the stranger who'd promised to save her family. His face was in shadow, but she knew his eyes were locked on her, like an animal stalking its prey he was bent on assessing every nuance shadowing her face. He released the handcuff and took her hands, raising her to her feet. His kiss on her forehead was unexpected and oddly relaxed her nerves. She'd expected him to take her swiftly, but instead, he took her to his room.

Shimmering candlelight greeted her as she looked around, taking in his preparation. The satin sheets, wine, and candles, and their romantic symbolism made her want to throw up. *This is madness—the man is deranged. He's created a fantasy, like a play on a stage.* When she turned, she found him studying her face. His invitation to sit and talk disconcerted her. She hoped he perceived her shudder to be one of pleasure instead of the fear she felt. She would have to be more careful.

God help me, I must convince him I've fallen hopelessly in love with him.

Ali was courting her. She realized he actually believed he was in love with her, and that more importantly, he believed that she was in love with him. All his efforts, the wine, the candles were part of his romantic vision of a love born by the will of Allah.

Thank God for the wine. Something to dull my revulsion.

He pulled her into his arms. Her guilt was tearing her apart. All she wanted was for it to be over. She didn't know how long she could keep this deception up.

I don't want you. I could never want you. I'd rather die than want you.

She had to bite back her tongue. Stop herself from becoming a screaming madwoman.

She wanted to dig her nails into his eyes and gouge them out. She imagined scratching his face and kicking him in the groin. She wanted to run as far away as she could. Complete and utter despair threatened to overwhelm her. The fact that Ali was so delusional to believe she could want him when he'd annihilated hundreds of innocent lives with only one push of a button. Believed she would want him after he'd kidnapped and drugged her several times and kept her handcuffed to a bed. Believed she would want him when he and his brother were plotting some evil and nefarious bombing that would kill thousands of people. She would never forget being forced to read vile words on a video that was out there for all the world to see. How could he imagine she would feel anything other than hatred when they were holding the lives of her daughter and grandparents in the palm of their hands. Brandishing her precious child as a way to gain her cooperation. Oh, God, and now he was touching her all over and kissing her as though *he* were the love of her life and not Cyrus...

Oh God, please help me get through this.

She reclaimed her breath, pushing all those thoughts away. She needed to relax. She needed to let this happen. It was the only way...

His lips sought hers, and his tongue filled her. His tongue had become another form of communication, another way for him to express himself. He began to undress her as he pulled her toward the bed.

She closed her eyes and pretended she was far, far away...

CHAPTER 21

On the shuttle from the mosque, Cyrus struck up a conversation with the man seated next to him. He'd spent enough time in different parts of the Middle East to distinguish and emulate different Arabic accents. He recognized his Syrian accent.

"*Salam alaikum*."

"*Wa alaikum assalaam*. My name is Wajid." The two men shook hands.

"Zubayr, pleased to meet you."

"I've not seen you before?" Wajid observed.

"My wife and I just moved to the area. We were living in Philadelphia, but my wife is pregnant, and she doesn't want to raise our child in the city."

"A wise woman, your wife. The city is filled with temptation."

Cyrus smiled and touched his heart. "My wife is my jewel."

"You are a lucky man."

"Yes, Allah has blessed me. Have you worked at this Applegate farm before?"

"Yes, many times. It is owned by an Iranian couple. They hire mostly Arab immigrants to work in the apple orchard and the fields. It is apple picking time now, which is what we'll be doing."

"Sounds like pleasant enough work."

"Yes, but occasionally they have us loading or unloading trucks with heavy equipment. They have a large barn on the property no one is allowed into. Locked up tight, no windows. Sometimes, they allow a few of us who've worked there a long time inside to lift heavy crates. I do not like working like a camel. Hopefully, we will only be picking fruit today."

"What do you think is inside the building?" he asked casually.

"Don't know, don't care. They pay fairly, and they don't bother or demand too much. It certainly beats living in a war zone."

Cyrus nodded. He'd learned enough and didn't want to arouse the man's suspicions with too many questions.

The Syrian was correct. When they got to the farm, they were given bags to wear around their necks to fill with apples. A dozen ladders rested against trees amid a sizeable orchard. In the middle of the grove were wooden crates. Cyrus worked alongside the other men on the crew, filling his bag with red apples. The sweet, tangy scent of picked apples was intoxicating. As he worked, Cyrus kept an eye on the farmhouse, hoping to catch a glimpse of Layla.

Finally, the lunch break arrived. He wanted to slip away and prowl around, maybe get closer to the house, but he was wary of drawing attention to himself. When the other men each stuffed a few apples in their pockets, he did the same.

There were wooden picnic tables not too far from the orchard under a couple of large oak trees. The mosque had prepared them a light lunch of olives, figs, pita, and *baba ghanoush*. Cyrus ate with the other men, chatting amiably as he kept an ear to the ground. Around twelve-thirty p.m., just as they were about to get back to work, two flatbed trucks arrived carrying two large blue containers. Cyrus watched the trucks turn around and back up against the loading dock and the barn. The heavy doors of the barn slid open, and a group of men came out.

Cyrus asked one of the apple pickers where the bathroom was—he wanted to get a closer look. He followed the man's instructions to a couple of portable toilets not far from the locked barn, which the Syrian, Wajid, had described. He wanted to get a closer look at the canisters and the semis.

"You see what I'm seeing?" Cyrus whispered to his earpiece.

David, back at mobile command, answered back in his earpiece. "I sure do. We watched the trucks arrive. We can't get an angle on what the logo says, but we sure as hell know what those canisters are."

"Yeah, spent nuclear rod containers." Cyrus read the logo, "Energex. I'll bet my paycheck Energex owns and operates a nuclear facility close to here."

"As a matter of fact, they do." Cyrus could hear the tap of David's fingers on the computer keyboard. "Energex owns Limerick and Three Mile Island. TMI's about thirty miles from where you stand."

"Three Mile Island. I remember that place," Cyrus said.

"Yes, back in 1979, the TMI 2 reactor had a partial nuclear meltdown, and it's been closed down ever since. However, TMI 1 is still in operation until 2034, when it will be retired. The meltdown accident caused the decline of new facilities being built in this country."

"Damn, too bad they didn't retire it early."

"Yeah. It says here the Nuclear Control Institute warned Congress on several occasions that our greatest vulnerability to terrorist attacks is our nuclear power plants. TMI has been cited several times for poor security. Why do we only address these problems after a catastrophe occurs? Why the fuck don't we take a preventative approach?"

"Shit! What if a canister with a bomb was planted inside one of the nuclear facilities?" Cyrus felt his hands grow clammy at the thought.

"It's possible. I'm pulling up records now. Per what I'm reading, there've been many previous incidents and illegal actions from disgruntled employees in nuclear power plants all over the country." David groaned. "Jesus, the list is dozens of pages long...at one of the plants, three guys were killed when a worker intentionally caused a power excursion detonating a steam explosion that destroyed the reactor. One of the men working on the reactor was blown to kingdom come. He was found impaled to the roof with a control rod through his groin and shoulder. Some idiot taking revenge for his wife cheating with his co-worker. God help us. We not only have to worry about terrorists but crazy assholes homegrown in the US of A."

Cass interjected. "Okay, enough with the gruesome details. Of all possible scenarios, a nuclear attack would be the worst. I can't think of any other reason why there'd be Energex trucks loaded with spent fuel rod containers coming and going from a terrorist-occupied farm. I'm going to put TMI on lockdown and put the National Guard on alert. David, I want you along with the bomb squad at TMI ASAP. I want the place nailed down tight. It looks like TMI is the target. Just in case, I'm going to put every other nuclear facility within two-hundred miles on heightened alert as well."

"I'm on it, boss. Good luck, Cyrus."

Cass continued. "As for those trucks, Cyrus. I'll put out an APB and order a bomb squad to stop them en route."

Cyrus considered the repercussions of such an action. "Listen, Cass. I think we shouldn't stop them yet. Just keep them in our sights. They're not going to do a thing until they get to TMI. It's better not to tip them off, or make them aware we're onto them."

Cyrus waited while Cass considered. "Agreed. Makes sense. I'll put a dragnet around them. Cyrus, any sign of Layla?"

His gaze drifted back to the farmhouse. "No, no sign of Layla yet."

"I know you want to rescue her, but I need you to be on that van out of there at the end of the day. I'm planning on raiding the place tonight."

Cyrus sensed there was more to this than met the eye. It was coming together too easily. "I don't like the way this feels. Too easy. Too predictable. We're missing something, I feel it. I have to find Layla."

"You have until the end of the day."

"Roger."

Ali cradled Layla in his arms, watching her face and listening to her even breaths. Last night had been the happiest of his life, all he'd hoped for. He'd made love to her, giving everything he had and taking everything she gave. He bent to kiss her, not wanting to let go of what they'd shared. "*Eshgham*, the morning's arrived, my darling, and we need to talk."

Her words were muffled into the pillow as she slowly lifted her eyelids. Suddenly awake, she stared into his eyes. Placing her hands on either side of his face. "Ali, you have to stop this, whatever it is you've planned. You can't do this. It will destroy you. Please," she begged.

"Shh, let me talk. I need to let you know what I have planned for you. I'm sorry, but the wheels are already in motion—I can't stop it. Tomorrow night a truck carrying a powerful bomb will detonate close to the turbine building at Three Mile Island—"

"Three Mile Island?"

Her fear made him ache. "Please. Ali." She searched his eyes. "If you care about me at all, please tell me everything."

"I do care about you, Layla," he said, his voice cracking. "I l-love you."

"Then please tell me everything you know."

He closed his eyes, unable to bear the pain in hers. "It's a nuclear power generating plant not far from here. The bomb will explode close enough to set the plant on fire and cause a radiological release. The set back from the reactors isn't far enough away, and the exploding truck will likely spark a reaction, possibly a meltdown. Even if the suicide driver and truck fail, there is a backup plan. The explosion of the truck will coincide with a blast within the facility. Hidden in a tank used for holding and transporting spent radioactive rods is a bomb. One method is a guarantee against the other should the truck explosion fail to set off the reactors. The bomb planted inside guarantees a meltdown and a release of enough radioactive poison to contaminate and poison everything within fifty miles."

She gaped. "How many people are you talking about?"

Ali dropped his gaze, whispering. "Over three million."

"Oh, my God, you have to stop it! Ali, you said Three Mile Island is close, how close?"

"About thirty miles."

"You can't do this. You have to stop it." Her face was awash with tears. Her eyes were pleading. For a moment, he wished he could stop it for her, but the wheels were irreversibly in motion; he wasn't in control.

"I can't Layla. All communication stopped with the first light of dawn."

She turned her face to the window, her eyes frantic. Sunlight streamed through the window curtains. She rolled out of bed and ran to the window. "Tell me how to stop it?"

"I can't. Now listen to me. Cyrus is coming for you. The Russians confirmed his arrival in the US. He's probably trying to find your location now. I'm sure the Israelis are working with the FBI. When he comes for you, I'm supposed to execute you and Cyrus…"

She whirled around, her hands flying to her mouth.

"I'm not going to do it, Layla. I can't…" His vision blurred with tears. "I love you, Layla, I could never hurt you."

"But you plan on killing Cyrus?" she whispered.

There was only so much he could do for her. Cyrus was a traitor and had to be punished. "Cyrus isn't important. I'm talking about saving *you*."

"And my child Ali, what about my child? Is she important? When all Hell breaks loose, and we're nuked, she won't have a mother. But then maybe she won't need one since right now she's probably in the telescopic sight of a sniper and his rifle." She ran at him, her fists raised, ready to pummel him.

He caught her wrists in mid-air, holding her still. "Layla, I'm not going to let that happen. I swear to you, both you and Cerise will be safe. I have a plan."

She had a plan.

Cass thought about what she'd learned over the years working with the director of the FBI. She recalled him saying, "A good player doesn't show all of his cards, and a good commander of an operation doesn't lay all his strategy out to his troops." She'd taken his words to heart.

Following her instinct, she called her boss. Director Carter agreed with her. He put through a secured three-way call with the Commander in Chief. The wheels of government, when need be, can move quickly. Cass's request was fast-tracked. Protocols were already in motion when she called the commander of the 160th Special Operations Aviation Regiment —SOAR— at Fort Campbell, Kentucky.

The Night Stalkers were a special ops fighting unit of Little Bird and stealth helicopters. An elite tactical assault team, a special operations element of USSOCOM, the United States Special Operations Command. They'd flown missions in every hot spot in the world and specialized in the insertion/extraction of special operations forces, attack missions, and reconnaissance. This elite force was trained to parachute from a helicopter and commandeer a target or destroy it, exactly what she needed to stop the trucks carrying the bombs.

"General, I have authorization from the Director of the FBI and the Commander in Chief to request your service. Authorizing paperwork is on its way to you now."

"I got the memo. I'm fully apprised. What can I do for you, Agent Saladino?"

"Sir, I request the immediate deployment of the Night Stalkers for a mission in assistance to the FBI. We have a terrorist threat on the Three Mile Island nuclear generation plant. We believe three trucks carrying explosive materials will shortly be on the road to TMI. Those vehicles need to be either stopped or destroyed before reaching their target."

"Do we have a visual on these trucks?"

"Only two of them so far, sir. Our satellites are on a twenty-four-hour search and find so things should come together by the time the Night Stalkers arrive."

"Very well, Agent Saladino, consider the air cavalry on its way. We'll arrive within four hours."

"Thank you, sir. I'll be in touch with further details."

Cass hung up, feeling more in control of the situation. She was calling in the big guns. She had a feeling she was going to need them.

CHAPTER 22

Applegate Farm
Lancaster County, Pennsylvania
September 18th
12:00 p.m.

Layla lay with her forearm over her eyes. She felt nauseated, and her head ached. She'd slept very little, with Ali pressed against her all night. Guilt ate at her. She'd had sex with another man, betrayed her husband, and she had no guarantee it would save her child and grandparents. She hadn't seen Ali all day. She could only see the occasional worker emerge from the apple orchard.

The hours alone in the tiny room ticked away. So much time with nothing to do but contemplate one's fate. She tried to picture her life before the kidnapping. A tear slipped down her cheek. *It's only been six days since the bombing at Ma Maison. Why does it feel like a lifetime? How could so much have changed in less than a week?*

Stopping the images from the night before was impossible. She could still feel Ali violating her. It made her feel dirty, sullied. She wanted to stand under a hot shower and scrub away all traces of him. His professed love for her made her want to scream. Her guilt over what it would do to Cyrus was driving her to a nervous breakdown. Knowing that it was all for nothing made her despair almost unbearable.

The sound of shifting gears from trucks coming up the road diverted her attention. She sat up and watched as they drove past her window. The Energex logo on the two trucks was the same as before, and both were hauling blue canisters. *Ali said the attack was unstoppable.*

She was nearly frantic with worry by the late afternoon when Ali finally came to her carrying a tray of food. She bit her lip, suppressing her anger and the thousand questions she wanted to ask.

He laid the tray on the bed, sat, and gathered her into his arms, kissing her. "I'm sorry, *eshgham*. There was much to do." His body was heated, covered in a layer of perspiration.

She pulled from his embrace, the sickly sensation of bile rising in her throat, overwhelmed her. "You told me there's no way of stopping this. Why are you lying to me? What are those trucks doing here?"

"They're decoys. They will be driven by martyrs on suicide missions. When they blow, they will cause mayhem, distracting law enforcement from the real target, the nuclear facility. A truck carrying another bomb will be delivered by one of our brethren during the chaos that follows. I have no way of communicating with the driver. He is on a suicide mission. At this point, his only communication is with God. The other bomb inside the facility is already live. Last night a janitor activated it. The mechanism is set, and the countdown has begun."

She clenched her fists and bit her tongue until she tasted blood. *How dare you imagine God is communing with some murderous terrorist?* "How are you getting me out of here?"

"Tonight. I'll come to get you and give you the keys to the truck. You'll be free to go. Drive toward Philadelphia. Get as far from here as you can before the reactor blows."

She forced herself to make one last attempt to reach him. "Come with me, Ali. If you surrender to me and confess to the authorities—help them—maybe something good can come of this? Do you really want to be the cause of millions of people losing their lives?"

The saddest of smiles shadowed his face. "Thank you, *eshgham*, but I can't. My destiny is sealed."

You deserve to die a thousand deaths, you madman.

"How will you protect my daughter and my grandparents?"

"Once you're safely away, I will send the sniper an encrypted message to abort. I'll tell him Cyrus is dead, and your father has been neutralized."

"Oh, my God. My father. Please tell me you haven't harmed him."

"No, your father is safe. He's being protected by Mossad. I'm counting on you to warn him that none of you will ever be safe if he collaborates with Israel. I won't be here to protect you. After what happens here, I feel confident he'll see the truth of my warning."

"Why can't you send the message now?"

"I can't call the sniper off until the appointed hour of the timed explosion at the nuclear generation plant."

She fought to stop her hands from shaking. Her daughter, and grand-parents' lives would be in danger until the bomb exploded. Millions of people would have to die before the lives of her daughter and grandparents would be spared? And if her father kept working with Israel, they would still come after them? "What if the sniper doesn't listen?" She pressed her hands against her pounding chest. "How can you be sure he will?"

"He's relying on my communication of the mission's success. He will do as I order."

Cerise and her grandparents were hanging by the thinnest of threads. One misstep and their lives would be snuffed out. She wanted to slap Ali's face, to scratch his eyes out, but there was nothing she could do except see this madness through to the end. She'd been forced to choose between her own family and thousands of innocent people. Wave after wave of nausea hit her. "Ali, tell me you'll be able to save them. I don't want to live if you can't."

He took her hand and placed a gentle kiss on her palm. "Because of you, Layla, I have loved and felt love in return. I promise you I will save your family. I swear it to Allah."

She was dependent on the promise of a lunatic. How had it come to this?

Applegate Farm
Lancaster County, Pennsylvania
5:00 p.m.

The sun sat low on the horizon. Its rays reflected gold and pink on the clouds. The van carrying the workers with Cyrus on board left the com-pound. Within minutes of leaving the farm, Cyrus clutched his stomach and bent over moaning.

Wajid gripped his shoulder. "Are you all right, my friend?"

"No," Cyrus groaned. "I feel unwell. Please…please tell the driver to pull over to the side of the road. I need to get out…hurry."

After a considerable amount of fuss, the driver stopped the van. Cyrus gripped his stomach as he stumbled up the aisle toward the door. The Syrian followed him. Around them, the men complained loudly about the delay.

Wajid asked, "What do you want us to do, my friend?"

"Go, tell the driver just to leave me here. I'll call my wife, and she'll come to get me. My stomach is turning somersaults." He gulped air. "I can't get back in the van, or I'll throw up. Don't worry. I'll be fine. I have my phone."

"Are you sure? We can wait. Screw these guys."

"No. There's no point. It's a form of claustrophobia I suffer from—since the war."

"Ah…I understand completely. Okay, then we will see you tomorrow."

"Yes. With Allah's blessing, I'll be better by tomorrow."

"*Al-wadā*, my friend."

"*Ilá al-liqā.*"

The van pulled away. Cyrus sat in the dirt and watched until it disappeared. Brushing the dust from his pants when he got up, he jumped the fence at the side of the road and jogged across a cornfield back toward the farm and Layla.

CHAPTER 23

It was fifty degrees outside, but the gusty wind whistling across the mountain pass made it feel more like thirty. Ash, the *Kidon* team's sniper, lay bundled in his camouflage sleeping bag on an adjacent slope to the chalet where Cyrus's daughter and Layla's grandparents slept. He pulled the collar of his down jacket up around his ears, surveying the chalet through night vision binoculars. He could see one of the men from the family's security detail walking the perimeter of the chalet, smoking a cigarette as he made his hourly circuit. Everything appeared to be peaceful and ordinary. His gaze swept the slope leading to the chalet, searching for any sign of movement. So far, there was no sign of the assassin who'd been charged with killing Cyrus's family. *Where are you, motherfucker? Come to papa.*

It all began when Israeli airport security notified Mossad about the suspicious Iranian businessmen who'd slipped into the country. Mossad assigned a twenty-four-hour tag team to their movements. They needed to know who, what, and why they were there. The Iranians were found to be surveilling the movements of Cyrus's family. Arresting these spies would have been easy. However, they were only minnows, and what Mossad was after were the big fish.

Ash's satellite phone vibrated. It was Aryeh, the director of Ash's *Kidon* team.

"*Ken?*"

"Have you located the kill?"

"Not yet, boss."

"Everything quiet at the chalet?"

"Yes. The family is bedded down. No sign of them."

"Good. We've just received some intel on your target. He's Adnan Mahdavi, Quds Force, General Solatani's go-to assassin. He's been on our hit list for a long time. Putting him out of business will be quite a feather in your cap."

Ash took a bite of a power bar and chewed, grinning. "Solatani's boy, huh?"

"I know how you feel about the bastard. You should be paying us for the pleasure of taking this guy out."

Ash chuckled. "You're probably right, boss. Anytime I can stick it to that murderer is like fucking a supermodel. Purely orgasmic."

"Keep your dick in your pants, lover boy. He's not dead yet."

"*Yet* is the keyword, boss. So correct me if I'm wrong. Solatani is responsible for the bombing in New York and Avi's murder?"

"Exactly what I'm saying. Am I sweetening the pot?"

"Definitely. Though you'd think the bastard would have his hands full with fighting ISIS, not to mention financing and training all the other thug terrorists in the Middle East. Isn't Solatani directing operations in Iraq and working with the Americans? Why would he attack the hand that feeds him? Or am I asking a stupid question?"

Aryeh laughed. "You better stick to assassinating bad guys. Solatani has no moral compass. He has no compunction with being financed by the Americans while at the same time plotting death and destruction in the US."

"I'd like to get his head in my riflescope. The only thing he'd be plotting would be the ground." Ash held his hands as if holding his rifle, closed one eye, and squeezed an imaginary trigger. "Pow. Go find your seventy-two virgins, Solatani."

"Music to my ears, Ash. One day you'll get your chance. In the meantime, you make sure Adnan Mahdavi meets his maker. Better yet, send the bastard straight to Hell."

"You got it, boss. I'll message you when it's over. Happy hunting."

"You too, *achi*."

Brothers for sure. Aryeh and the rest of the team were his brothers. Ash would never let them down. He hadn't located his adversary yet, but somewhere out there was a predator, a killer, and Ash was determined to make tomorrow the last sunrise he ever saw.

He knew the family was safe so long as they were in the chalet. A couple of hours of sleep and he'd begin hunting his prey. He'd wired the area around him so he'd be alert and ready for any intrusion. If anyone tripped the wire, they'd be dead before they took another step. Satisfied that he and the family were well protected, he rested his head on his arm and closed his eyes. His other hand gripped his .22 LR pistol.

Tel Aviv, Israel
September 18th
12:01 a.m.

The knock on the door woke Aleck from a restless sleep. It was six days since Layla's kidnapping and two days since he'd heard from Cyrus. He had no idea where his granddaughter and his in-laws were. A lifelong agnostic, he'd lately taken to praying to a God he knew very little about. Oddly, during those moments of prayer, he felt a solace he'd found nowhere else. The scientist and pragmatist was annoyed by that fact, but the devoted father and grandfather was grateful for the moments of peace that prayer brought to him. The knocking grew louder.

He shook his head and looked at the clock. *Midnight. Where the hell's my security?*

He padded to the door and looked out the peephole. He recognized two of the men. *Mossad security. Well, at least I know there's no problem with the security team.* He pushed the intercom. "What the hell is going on?"

"I'm sorry, Doctor Wallace, but we have orders to take you into custody and bring you to headquarters."

"Now? Why? Is there something going on? Is Layla all right?"

"Dr. Wallace, we're just following orders. I'm sure the prime minister will inform you when you arrive."

Aleck grumbled to himself, "Dammit, Dodi," it was impossible for Aleck not to think of the prime minister of Israel simply as Dodi, his former college roommate, "you certainly take advantage of our friendship when it suits your purpose." He slid the locking bolts open. "Come in. Just make yourselves at home while I get dressed and brush my teeth."

"Yes, sir. Take your time. We have security all around the building."

Aleck stopped dead in his tracks. "Why security all around the building? Has there been some kind of threat made against me?"

The agent looked as if he'd been caught between a rock and a hard place.

"Never mind," Aleck said, waving his hand in frustration. "I get it—you're just following orders, and you can't tell me anything. I wish someone would write you guys some new material. The 'I don't know' line has become a tad boring." He walked toward the kitchen, turning on lights as he went. "I'm not moving from here until I get some coffee. I'll make a pot for all of us."

Quds Force Encampment, near Mosul, Iraq
September 18th
12:01 a.m.

General Qasem Solatani opened the flap to his tent and stepped outside. He was greeted by his shadow, Achmed, an adjutant who followed his every step. The man merely nodded, acknowledging the general who he was sworn to guard. He rarely spoke unless spoken to.

It was midnight, and a rare silence filled the air. The temperature was a comfortable sixty degrees, and the general wore only a light camouflage jacket. The camp lay not too far from Mosul, where intense fighting with ISIS militants had been ongoing for weeks.

Solatani knew he was an enigma to his men. He'd heard their whispered accounts of his late-night sojourns through the camp. They called him the warrior ghost. Years of battle had turned his hair and beard silver, and in the moonlight, his dark, deep-set eyes glittered with an otherworldliness he knew enhanced his followers' reverence.

Some nights he walked through the camp wordlessly, guarding his precious moments of contemplation and strategizing. However, tonight he felt magnanimous and nodded his acknowledgment to the occasional Quds Force soldier he passed.

Fingering his beard, he smiled at his aide. The man had long ago become the keeper of Qasem's thoughts and secrets, his sounding board.

"My brother, *alhamdulillāh*, our plan is finally a go. Very soon, our brothers in America will bring down a living hell on the Americans."

His aide nodded. "*Alhamdulillāh*, Allah be praised."

"A nuclear meltdown will serve to deter them from any hostile intervention in the affairs of our beloved republic."

The general affectionately patted his aide's back. "It is Ali and Omar who will deliver us this victory. I have loved them like sons, and it breaks my heart to know I will lose them. But it's Ali, I will miss the most. He has a poet's soul. He should have lived to bear sons."

A chilling foreboding took hold of the general. He shivered. He felt as if he'd stepped on a grave.

"Are you all right, General?"

"Yes. The voice of Allah has whispered in my ear. I must speak to our leader Khamenei about erecting a fitting monument to immortalize Omar and Ali's heroic act."

The general picked up his pace. Soon he would get the call from Omar informing him of the elimination of Cyrus Hassani and his family. The sweet knowledge scented the very air he breathed. Cyrus and his family's deaths would serve as a warning to any Iranian who dared treason. It was one of the things he admired most about the Israelis. They understood vengeance must always be exacted. It didn't matter how long it took so long as it was delivered.

A thought came to him after circuiting the camp. He turned to his shadow. "Come, Achmed. I believe Allah will favor us if we honor our brethren with prayer. Today we bring glory to our people."

Achmed bowed his head. "As you wish, General. You do the work of Allah, and for that, we are blessed."

CHAPTER 24

Lancaster County, Pennsylvania
September 18th
7:00 p.m.

Long shadows grew in the fading light of the setting sun. Cyrus had remained hidden, waiting for darkness to fall over Applegate farm. He'd received several frantic messages from Cass through his earpiece ordering him to leave, but he ignored them. It was better for Cass to wonder where he was and what he was doing. The uncertainty of what was happening would buy him valuable time and might dissuade her from acting before she heard from him.

He knew the plan of action Cass intended to take. The FBI was positioning themselves for a raid. He hoped Cass wouldn't come bursting onto the farm with an army of law enforcement before he rescued Layla. He had to get a lay of the land and what the terrorists were planning. But he needed to find Layla before all Hell broke loose.

He changed into a black sweater and pants and strapped his *Glauca* combat knife into his leg harness. He dry-tested the Glock pistol the FBI had issued him, before loading and holstering it. Armed and ready, he felt more confident.

Searching his backpack, he found the apples he'd picked earlier in the day and took a bite. Eating something before combat calmed him. It was hours since lunch, and the sweet fruit would have to sustain him for hours more.

He thought about Layla and how happy she'd be when her Superman made his appearance. He remembered the promise he'd made to Cerise, to bring Mommy to her. He allowed himself a quick smile, thinking of the reunion they'd have as a family, and the reunion he'd share with Layla alone in the privacy of their bed.

He crept toward the barn where the loading dock was located, and the trucks full of spent fuel rod canisters had been parked. He covered the ground like a Ninja, silent and invisible. First, he checked for an alarm system and was surprised to find there was none. Then he decided to break into a side door not visually seen from the house. It was locked. He dropped his backpack and pulled out a flashlight and a lockpick. It took him less than a minute to gain entry. He took a last glance around and slipped through the door.

He shone the flashlight, illuminating the interiors. The terrorist cell was well organized. Along one wall was a bank of laptop computers, their screensavers displayed images of frozen landscapes, mountain tops with billowing steam clouds rising from the sun's heat, and waves crashing on monolithic rocks rising from the sea. Above the computers was a map. Shining his flashlight on it, he recognized the location of Applegate Farms, which was circled in red. He studied the map, looking for Three Mile Island. He traced the beam of light across the map, following Route 283 West until he reached an island, shaped like a fish, floating on the Susquehanna River. Three Mile Island was circled.

He dropped the flashlight beam to the table and spied a black leather folder in a basket of papers. Opening it, he turned the pages. There were additional maps, aerial photographs, tide charts, and alternate route maps, all highlighted in yellow. From what he could see, each one led to the TMI nuclear generation plant. Photos of the outside gates and the security checks were taken with a telephoto lens. The time stamps indicated they were made over the course of several months. The last photograph, just a few days ago. One of the images showed a truck with the now-familiar logo of Energex painted on its side doors, carrying a blue canister, arriving at the gate, and gaining entrance. He took out his phone and took a picture of the license plate on the truck. Then he flashed the beam around the room, checking to see what other intel he could find.

In the back of the room was an area blocked off from the rest of the workstation. He walked over and pulled a canvas sheet aside, he knew immediately he'd found a bomb makers' paradise. Displayed on a shelf were labeled containers of nitric acid, pentaerythritol, lye, sodium bicarbonate, timing mechanisms, C-4, and other plastic putty materials. *How the fuck did they amass all this?* Unfortunately, he knew the answer to his question. If a person was intent on gathering chemicals, much of what he saw could be acquired through industry catalogs and the "dark web," a secret part of the Internet where criminals and terrorists plied their trade in a shadow world undetected. The darknet provided virtual safety, a black market for everything, and anything existed, including the slave trade, bomb-making materials, arms, drugs, the list went on and on. Whatever pestilence the criminally minded desired.

Initially, Cyrus had considered delaying communication with the FBI, but he realized now what he'd discovered had to be relayed to Cass and the team immediately.

"Agent Saladino," he whispered.

"Goddammit, Cyrus! What the fuck is going on with you? You agreed to be in the van when it left. You are intentionally disobeying my direct order. I have a good mind to—"

"Whoa, Cass. Circumstances forced me to remain, and I'm glad I did."

"This better be good, Cyrus."

"I'm confirming that Three Mile Island is the intended target."

"And how do you know that?" Her angry tone modulated into curiosity.

"I'm inside the bomb-making facility, and the evidence is definitive. TMI is their target. I'm talking about photos, maps, chemicals, the works. From what I'm looking at, I can infer the delivery system is in those blue spent fuel rod containers. My guess is one of those armed containers is already inside TMI. You need to send a bomb squad and bomb-sniffing dogs there immediately. You also need to find those Energex trucks. I'm sending you photos now with one of the license plate numbers."

"Roger. Can I count on you to get the fuck out of there now?"

"Sorry, Cass, I can't do that. My wife's being held by these animals, and I'm not leaving without her. My vows to her trump my vows to you. My advice to you is to forget about this farm—there's nothing here. Focus on TMI and the trucks. I'll handle this place."

"Cyrus, this is too dangerous for one man."

Cyrus smiled. "Maybe, but this one man works best alone. See you on the other side of this nightmare. Over and out."

Cyrus pulled his earbud out and stashed it in his pocket, not waiting for Cass's reply. She couldn't accuse him of disobeying orders if he hadn't heard them. He couldn't afford any more distractions.

8:00 p.m.

Layla rubbed her eyes and wondered what time it was. It was nearly dark, and a sliver of moon rose in the sky. Out in the country, where there was no city pollution, the stars lit the sky earlier in the evening, carpeting the heavens in a blanket of twinkling ornaments. If the reality of an attack didn't exist, she might have taken comfort in the serenity of it all.

Where is Ali? She'd seen very little of him except for the obligatory meals. A few hours earlier, from her window, Layla had seen the Energex trucks carrying the blue canisters, then several hours later, they left. At the day's end, she'd seen the van that delivered the workers leave with all of the men on board. She'd been intrigued by one of the workers. The man had stood apart from the others. Tall with a dark beard, he seemed to be watching the house. He wore dark sunglasses and a fisherman's knit cap, so she couldn't get a good look at him. He limped when he walked to the van to get in. She couldn't help but wonder if it was Cyrus. She shook her head, wishing her heart would stop playing games with her emotions. She was so anxious to be rescued from her prison, her overactive imagination was seeing things that weren't there. After the van left, there'd been no activity, nothing to break the monotony of the endless hours. Drained from the ordeal, she'd fallen asleep.

The scrape of the key turning in the lock drove the sleep away. Layla sat up, a prickle of fear creeping up her spine. "Ali?" She fought her feelings of dread. She knew she needed him to help her.

"It's okay, Layla. It's just me."

"What's happening?" She tugged on the handcuff. "When are you going to let me go?"

"Are you ready?" He unlocked the cuff and pulled her to her feet. He embraced her, burying his face in her hair, inhaling her. "The time has come *eshgham*. I need to get you away from here."

Cringing inside, she reluctantly returned his embrace. "But how, Ali?"

He pulled apart from her, enough to see her eyes. "I told you, you'll take the truck. It's got a navigation system in it. We'll plug in Philadelphia, and all you have to do is follow the guidance."

"But what about Cerise and my grandparents? How do I know you'll call off the sniper?"

He bent and brushed his lips over hers. "Just drive and don't stop for any reason. Make no contact with anyone until you reach Philadelphia. By then, it should be over. By then, I promise you they'll be safe."

She could feel his heart pounding in his chest. He kissed her deeply, and she forced herself to respond. Before he broke from the kiss, she felt the wetness of his tears on her cheek.

Tears? He dared to cry tears when he was behind a plot that would kill or injure millions of people?

He let her go. "Come on, there's no time to waste. The bomb is set to go off in two hours."

She felt the color drain from her face and her stomach turn. Ali took her hand and led her from the room. The empty house was as silent as a tomb, and she shivered. Ali must have felt her shudder because, in the kitchen, he grabbed a coat. Fear had numbed her, and her movements were slow and clumsy. Saying nothing, he helped her on with the coat and zipped her in. He grabbed a few bottles of juice from the refrigerator and a set of keys off the counter.

Outside, a cold blast of air stole her breath. Ali grabbed her hand and pulled her forward to a black Escalade truck near the barn. He helped her into the driver's seat and strapped her in.

Her voice trembled as she turned to him. "I don't know how to get to Philadelphia. I don't know where I am?"

He smiled. "I'm going to program the navigation system. Like I told you before, just follow the instructions." He closed her door and walked around to the passenger side and got in. "Turn the ignition, *eshgham*."

"Oh…of course." She searched the steering wheel, locating the key in the ignition. The engine gave a smooth roar as it came to life.

Ali pulled up an address in the Navi system. "I'm sending you directly to the FBI offices in Philadelphia. They'll take care of you." He turned to her, his face etched with pain. "Layla, what you've given me I can never repay, but I promise nothing is going to happen to your daughter or your grandparents. Now you must promise me you'll drive straight to Philadelphia and not stop no matter what is reported on the radio."

She nodded numbly. Ali reached across the center console, his hand caressing her cheek. It was all she could do not to cringe. Had her acting like a love-struck fool worked? She had placed her faith in the hands of a madman. A terrorist. She prayed he was telling her the truth. Prayed, he would spare her daughter and grandparents. Prayed that Cyrus was safe. Prayed that her father was protected. Prayed that she wouldn't fall apart.

Ali leaned in and kissed her, his breath warm on her lips.

Oh, God, no more kissing…

When his lips left hers, he hesitated as if unsure what to say next. "Layla, if by some chance, you become pregnant…you would never hurt the child— our child—I mean, you wouldn't kill it before it was born?" His face was shrouded in misery.

She paled, nearly mute at the possibility. A tear rolled down her cheek when she thought about what Cyrus's reaction would be. "No, Ali, I could never destroy a baby—even your baby—not any baby. I would keep it, raise it, and love it. It would be God's will that the child is born." She regurgitated words meant to reassure him. She prayed she wasn't pregnant. How would she ever be able to bring his child into the world?

He smiled, his eyes filling with tears. "Yes, God's will. Thank you, Layla."

Middletown, Pennsylvania
Three Mile Island
8:30 p.m.

An FBI mobile command center RV, tech trucks, and personnel vans arrived at the gates of Three Mile Island and roared up to the main entrance. The crew swung into action, setting up their base of operation.

David ordered snipers to the gatehouses and stationed others along all of the approaches to the complex, just in case, the bomb-carrying trucks happened to get through Cass's dragnet. He, like every member of the team, was dressed in body armor and helmet. He jumped out of the command center vehicle and was met by a supervisor of the facility. They briefly shook hands and introduced themselves. "Thanks for getting here so quickly, Jim. What I need is a layout of the facility."

"I've got that right here for you." The man handed David a roll of architectural blueprints. "I know Three Mile Island like the back of my hand."

"Good, because your assistance is going to make this a lot easier. We suspect TMI has been compromised. We've received intel on two Energex employees, a truck driver and a janitor, probably homegrown terrorists who were enlisted into a terrorist plot. With no prior record, they cleared your background security checks and delivered and activated a bomb. We believe the bomb is set to blow in the next hour or so. I hate asking you to risk your life, but we need your help."

"I've got family and friends less than fifty miles from here. If a bomb explodes anywhere near those reactors, it will cause a meltdown. I'd lose my family, everything I care about in this world. I'm not leaving until the reactors are safe. I've brought in my most trusted crew of engineers and support staff. Whatever you need, we're at your service. All of us feel the same. We know what's at stake."

David walked to where different members of the Joint Terrorism Task Force and FBI support staff were setting up tables, chairs, and equipment. He rolled out the plan pinning it flat. "Where do you store the spent fuel rods containers. We're particularly interested in the blue ones."

Jim pointed. "Here. We keep the empties here." He looked confused. "They're all blue."

David eyed the blueprint. "Naturally, they're all blue." He continued to study the plan. "That's a relatively large space. How many of those babies do you house here?"

"Maybe twenty. The canisters are stacked to the ceiling. Over here," Jim pointed, "we have a storage pool where the rods must be kept for ten years in special water containers until their radioactivity has significantly subsided. Then we transfer them into dry storage containers and keep them in a secured area outside. The storage tanks are special plastic, steel, and concrete. They're impenetrable, and they're monitored. Of course, the whole place has a sophisticated CCTV system, cameras everywhere."

David motioned his hand at an agent. "Mike, get a couple of your men and start going over the video footage of the CCTV cameras. I want you to pay close attention to the delivery of blue canisters. See if there is a match to the license plate photo Cyrus took. You should be able to get the date of delivery and then match it up to footage in the canister storage area. Maybe get a pinpoint on which canister was delivered from that particular truck. Who knows, maybe you'll find a video of the bomb being activated."

He turned back to the supervisor and asked, "Why the hell is this waste kept on-site within proximity of the reactors? Isn't that just asking for trouble?"

"The states have been dragging their feet. Nobody wants a hazardous waste site in their backyard. It's all supposed to change in 2022. The NRC has ordered all hazardous waste to be stored at special facilities. Unfortunately, they haven't been able to get any states to agree to be a guinea pig." He scratched his head. "Until we have a place to store this shit, most nuclear-generating plants store the waste on-site."

David stared at the man, speechless. "Are you fucking kidding me? It's an accident waiting to happen. We have a ticking bomb and no time to search twenty or more canisters, not to mention the radioactive pool and dry storage containers. Do you keep them in any order? Like last ones in. Tell me you know the latest ones delivered."

"Sure, I do."

"Okay, let's go." He turned to his assistant. "Bring the secret service bomb-sniffing dogs. They're our best chance of finding this baby before it blows. Where's the EOD guy?"

One of his agents answered. "He's being loaded into the bomb-tech suit. They're almost ready."

David couldn't imagine wearing one of those hundred-pound space-suits the Explosive Ordinance Disposal bomb experts wore to defuse a bomb. Those guys were the craziest mothers on the planet, but he praised the Lord, such men existed.

Usually, they'd use robots or a water cannon to disarm a bomb, but in this case, there could be no controlled removal or detonation. The bomb-meister was going to have to get in the canister, disarm it, and pray the mother didn't implode. Not that it would make any difference because if it exploded, they'd all be joining him in the next world, and so would the millions of people within fifty miles of here.

A minute later, he saw what he hoped would be the hero of the day, lumbering toward him accompanied by three other assistant bomb experts from EOD. These guys had to work as a team—this was not a one-man job.

"Okay, let's go." He yelled back to his second in command, "We're going inside to find that bomb. Remember, nothing gets near this facility. Any vehicles unless authorized by the FBI are to be stopped or destroyed."

Helicopter above PA Route 283

Cass, attired in full body armor and radio helmet, sat behind Captain Hughes and his co-pilot in the AH-6M Little Bird helicopter. She'd commandeered Captain Hughes, a decorated Night Stalker who'd flown several tours of duty in Afghanistan and Iraq. Cass would make the calls as she saw fit, and Captain Hughes would carry them out with his team of Special Forces Rangers.

"I'm curious, what kinds of ammo do these birds carry?"

"Folding fin rocket pods, hell-fire laser-guided anti-tank missiles, and 3-barrel Gatling guns. We brought our top rappellers, as you requested. They're ready to go."

"Right. If we can safely commandeer the truck, it would be better than allowing, what we think must be a four-thousand-pound bomb to go off in a populated area."

Captain Hughes whistled. "That's one big baby. Lots of fireworks if she blows."

"It is Captain. A damn big baby. I'd like to miss that show if you don't mind."

He chuckled. "I plan on handing you a sparkler, which is more than enough excitement as far as I'm concerned."

"Amen, Captain."

Both Cass and the pilots wore night-vision goggles compatible with the digital glass cockpit, which also served as a computer screen where information scrolled continuously.

They flew low over PA 283, monitoring the vehicles cruising below them. In the sky, the satellites were searching all possible routes into TMI.

"Cass?"

David's voice broke in her ear. "Roger, David, I read you. Over."

"Good. I just wanted you to know we're inside the canister storage facility, and the bomb-sniffing dogs are beginning to search the canisters. We brought in a hydraulic lift and platform because the canisters are stacked high. We're lifting the dogs and handlers so they can get close to each container. I'll keep you posted. Any sign of the truck? Over."

"We're tailing two of them, but what we think is the big megillah we haven't found yet. But we've got you covered. The satellites are at work, and we should have something soon. I'm not going to let that truck get anywhere near you."

David chuckled. "Well, just in case, I've got snipers covering the roads and snipers covering the gates."

"You won't need them."

"I hope you're right, boss. Wait a second, Cass."

Cass drummed her nails against the transmitter impatiently."

"We've got something, Cass, one of the dogs has found something. They're opening the canister now, and the bomb tech is getting in to see what kind of a monster we've got."

Cass furrowed her brow. She felt a prickly sweat break out on her skin. "David be careful."

"Roger, Cass. Over."

CHAPTER 25

"Get out of the car! Put your hands up." Both Layla and Ali nearly jumped out of their skins. They stared into the muzzle of a Glock pistol pointing at Ali. Ali's hands immediately rose in the air as did Layla's. The man with the gun was shrouded in darkness.

She squinted and tried to make out the face behind the voice. Her heart banged like a drum in her chest. *Oh my God, please let it be him!*

"Take it easy, friend." Ali's voice was barely above a whisper.

"Slowly lower one hand and open the truck door and get out."

Cyrus was here! Her Superman was here. It seemed like a miracle. She sobbed her relief. But the elation swiftly ebbed when the truth hit her. Cyrus might have moved heaven and earth to save her, but there was nothing he could do to save Cerise and her grandparents. Only Ali could call off the assassin.

"Layla, get behind me," Cyrus said.

Layla jumped out of the car and got behind Cyrus. Ali slowly did as he was told. "The devoted husband and traitor has finally arrived," he said quietly.

"Husband, yes. Traitor depends on your perspective."

"Hassani, what happens between you and me is one thing," Ali said, "but you need to get Layla out of here. She needs to leave now."

"And why should I listen to you?"

Ali walked slowly around the truck, his hands on his head, and faced Cyrus. "Because if she doesn't, in two hours, she'll be dead or dying."

"What's he talking about, Layla?"

As if she'd been sleepwalking and suddenly woke up, words poured from her. "It's true, Cyrus. They've somehow managed to place a bomb in a nuclear facility, and there's another one they rigged in a blue canister that's going to be delivered and detonated right in front of the gates. He told me it's a backup. Just to confuse the authorities, they have two additional trucks with smaller bombs that are going to be detonated to cause chaos and distract from the blowing up of Three Mile Island." Panic made her voice sound high and out of breath. She grabbed his arm. "We've got to get out of here now. He told me we're twenty-seven miles from the reactors. When they blow, everything within fifty miles will be contaminated with radiation from the meltdown. Leave him—he doesn't matter. Please, we need to get out of here."

Cyrus turned his head slightly to look at her. "What the hell? Are you crazy? I'm not leaving this motherfucker alive."

She was frantic. "You have to, do you hear me. You can't hurt him!"

"What is going on with you and this monster? What's happened to you? Why are you protecting this bastard?"

"I'm not. You have to believe me. I will explain later, but you need to let Ali go."

"Never! I'm going to kill the bastard right now." Cyrus held the pistol to Ali's temple.

Layla screamed, "No!"

Before Cyrus could pull the trigger, the muzzle of another pistol pressed against Layla's temple, and she screamed again. Cyrus turned and froze.

Layla stifled her cries with her hands over her mouth. Ali lowered his hands and moved away from the pistol Cyrus had pointed at his head.

"Omar, I didn't expect you back here." Ali smiled at his brother. "Although I can't say I'm not happy to see you."

Layla forgot her fear and whirled. "You bastard! You lied to me. You had this planned all along!" Tears gushed from her eyes as she ran at him, her fists raised.

Ali glared at her and rebuffed her with ease, pushing her away. "Keep silent. Don't speak." He turned to his brother. "I thought you were planning on accompanying the transport right to the gates of Hell."

Omar hissed. "You're a traitor, Ali. Buraq will deliver the payload. I came back here because I didn't trust you. You were going to let the witch go free. You were going to disobey orders. The General was clear. They both must die."

"Don't be ridiculous. I had no intention of letting her go. She was the bait, remember? How else could we have lured Cyrus to reveal himself? This is exactly what we planned, and now we have him."

"No, brother, it's not. I begged you, have all the sex with the bitch you want, but don't fall under her spell."

Omar's revelation made her knees grow weak. When she turned, she saw the look of devastation on Cyrus's face. The anguish in his eyes.

"Omar, I swore an oath I would never break," Ali insisted.

"Your promise is meaningless. You allowed this infidel and your unholy desire for her to rule your logic. But I will give you one chance to redeem yourself." He pushed the muzzle of the pistol firmly against Cyrus's temple. "On your knees, Cyrus, and put your hands on your head. Now!"

Cyrus's face revealed nothing as he knelt.

"Remove his weapons, Ali, and throw them under the truck."

"Wouldn't it be wiser for me to hold on to them?"

"Just do as I say, Ali." Ali removed Cyrus's weapons and tossed them beneath the Escalade.

Cyrus watched both men with a cool-eyed stare. Omar swung the muzzle away from him and pointed the gun at Layla, both he and Ali flinched.

Omar chuckled. "All for a bit of ginger pussy. You both deserve your fate, and I plan on delivering it to you by making you both watch as I execute her. Then I'm going to send you off to join her, Hassani. Finally, your debt to Iran will be paid, and a clear message will have been sent to our enemies. They will think twice before threatening us. Israel will know that just like them, we never forget or forgive those who betray us."

Cyrus felt powerless to move with Layla in the crosshairs of a fanatic. "Kill me, Omar," Cyrus said in a calm voice, "but let her live. She's a mother, and she's innocent of any crime." He could never explain to a brute like Omar what it meant to love, or why he had no desire to live in a world without Layla. He would welcome death rather than see her die.

"She must die for leading my foolish brother, astray. Once he sees her lying in a pool of blood, he will be cured."

Omar's words froze his heart. The thought of Layla lying with another man was like a knife being thrust into his gut. He couldn't imagine she'd willingly betray him, but even the possibility filled him with despair. Right now, the answers eluded him. The only thing that mattered was saving her. Cyrus's gaze locked on Omar as he prepared to launch himself at his legs.

Omar moved just out of range of Cyrus's reach. He racked the slide on the Glock and slowly released the trigger preparing the gun to shoot. Cyrus heard the click of the reset and watched Omar's finger squeeze the trigger. He roared and lunged at Omar, but not before a shot rang out. His attempt to tackle Omar fell short, and he lay sprawled in the dirt. Omar trained the gun on Cyrus.

Behind him, Layla screamed. "No! You can't die!"

He turned and saw Ali lying on the ground, blood gushing from a wound in his chest. Layla crawled to him, lifting his head in her lap, pleading with him to live.

Cyrus couldn't process what he was seeing.

Omar was shouting and waving his gun like a madman. "Ali, why? Why? Why would you sacrifice yourself for her? For an infidel? She dies now." He aimed the Glock at Layla. "*Allahu Akbar.*"

Cyrus yelled, "No!" and again launched himself at Omar. He made contact with Omar's legs and felt him falling. Simultaneously, he heard the unmistakable sound of a gun with a silencer. He'd always thought of the telltale puff of air from a silencer as the quiet wind of death. Before Omar hit the ground, he was dead, a bullet to his head.

Cyrus, still on his knees, twisted around. He watched as a man dressed all in black materialized from the shadows. The barrel of his gun with silencer pointed at the ground. The man pulled the three-hole balaclava off his head and revealed a face Cyrus in a million years didn't expect to see. "Aryeh?"

The man's sardonic smile revealed a set of gleaming white teeth. "None, other. I told you we'd rescue Layla. But it looks like you needed a bit of rescuing too," Aryeh chuckled.

Taking a breath of relief, Cyrus turned to see the prostrate figure of Layla holding the terrorist in her arms. It made him sick to see her weep and plead for him to live. She sobbed, begging him to keep his promise.

What kind of promise had he given her, and what had she given in return? The dying man whispered to her, and she bent her head to listen.

Watching Layla beg Ali to live felt like someone pulling the pin from a grenade and it detonating in his gut. Bile rose in his throat as he watched his wife bid her lover farewell.

Tears poured down her face. "Ali, please, don't die. You have to help me. God damn it, you promised." She held his head in her lap. She needed him to save Cerise, but he was dying, and there was nothing she could do about it. She didn't care if Cyrus watched, she'd seen the devastation on his face when he realized she'd been intimate with Ali. At that moment, she knew she'd lost him. It was something she'd have to face later. None of it would matter if she didn't stop the sniper who threatened her daughter and grandparents' lives.

"Ali, please make the c-call!" she screamed. "I'll hold the cell phone. You can save her. I'll do anything. Tell me how to save her."

"*Eshgham,*" his voice was barely discernible. "It will be all right, but you need to get out of here. You need to get yourself and our child away from here before the bomb explodes. Go..."

Oh God, he's delusional. My baby, Cerise, is going to die. She shook him. "Ali, Ali?" A sound like air escaping from a balloon rose from his chest. He shuddered with his last breath.

Layla covered her face and sobbed.

Cyrus couldn't draw his eyes away from the drama unfolding between his wife and the terrorist. When the man took his last breath, she seemed to collapse in sorrow.

Aryeh insisted. "Walk away, Cyrus. Give her a minute. Let me talk to her. Maybe I can get to the bottom of this."

Cyrus tried to get past the pain that was eating him alive. The betrayal nearly brought him to his knees. Layla was everything he'd ever wanted, needed, and loved. He couldn't believe she was weeping over the dead body of a terrorist. Was this some version of Stockholm Syndrome? Had the terrorist somehow gotten into her psyche? "Do what you can, Aryeh," he rasped. "This whole thing is making me sick."

Aryeh ignored Cyrus and bent to his knees beside Layla. "Layla, I'm Mossad, a friend. Let me help you." He pried her hands from Ali's body and lifted her to her feet. "Talk to me, Layla. Tell me what you know. Lives depend on you."

Cyrus watched from a few feet away as Layla tried to catch her breath from her sobbing. "T-there's a s-sniper in Switzerland. H-he's going to kill Cerise and my grandparents. There's a bomb inside Three Mile Island and another one on its way."

"We know all about the sniper. I have an operative watching the chalet, protecting your family. Nothing is going to happen to your daughter or your grandparents. The assassin will be eliminated."

Cyrus went ballistic. "What sniper?" he roared. What the hell are you talking about?"

Aryeh's gaze never left Layla's face when he answered. "Calm down, Cyrus. Layla knows there's a sniper in Switzerland. The Iranians have been following you and your family for months. They've monitored every move you've made, including tailing Cerise and Layla's grandparents to Switzerland. There's a Quds force assassin targeting them."

"Oh, my God. Are you sure you can stop him?"

"Our man will not fail."

Cyrus paced, his fingers spiked through his hair. "Those fucking bastards. I want them to die all over again."

"Through gathered intel, we put the pieces of the puzzle together, this was planned by the commander of the Quds Force, General Solatani. I'm afraid you've made a serious enemy," Aryeh added.

Cyrus glared at Aryeh. "How long have you known this?"

"Calm down Cyrus. It didn't all come together until after you'd left for the US. We've responded accordingly."

Aryeh turned back to Layla and spoke to her in a calm voice. "Layla, what happened between you and Ali was based on you trying to save Cerise and your grandparents. Am I correct?"

Tears washed down Layla's cheeks, and she spoke in a broken whisper. "Y-yes…I didn't want to. I never wanted to. I had no choice. I had to s-save them…"

Aryeh took Layla in his arms and rocked her as she sobbed against his chest.

Cyrus's knees buckled, and he staggered. Shame washed over him for thinking Layla had betrayed him. Watching Layla break down, shredded his insides. He took great gulps of air as he calmed his pounding heart. He and Layla needed to talk. But right now, they had a terrorist plot to stop.

He pulled his transmitter from his pocket. "Cass? Are you there?"

Cass's voice crackled over the line. "Cyrus, what the hell is going on? I'm pretty sick and tired of you turning me off and on whenever it suits your purpose. What's the status at Applegate? Over."

"All suspects at the farm are disabled, and Layla is safe and unharmed." He didn't mention Aryeh. "Layla confirmed what I told you about the attack. You need to stop the truck before it reaches TMI, and you need to find and neutralize the bomb inside TMI. Given what I've learned, I'd say you have less than an hour."

"David's found the bomb in a blue spent rod container. The bomb squad is in the process of dismantling it right now. Cyrus, I'm glad Layla's safe."

"She's safe, but the bastards sent an assassin to Switzerland to kill our daughter and Layla's grandparents. Mossad's on top of it. This won't be over until I know they've removed the threat."

"I'm sorry you must be going crazy."

"I'm trying to stay calm. What are you doing about intercepting the truck transporting the bomb?"

"I brought in the Night Stalkers, a military assault helicopter squad. We're searching for the vehicle, and are on our way to a possible sighting. I'm getting minute-by-minute satellite feed updates. I've set up police road-blocks in all directions. That truck isn't getting through."

He took a breath; there was still a chance they could stop the attack. "We're counting on you, Cass. And thanks for trusting me. Keep me posted. Over."

The co-pilot pointed, and Cass nodded. She switched channels. "David?"

She could barely hear him whisper back. "Not a good time Cass, I don't want to breathe, let alone talk. We've got a monster bomb in a spent rod canister, and the bomb-tech is inside trying to neutralize it. Over."

Instinctively she whispered back. "Roger. I just want you to know we've got the truck in sight. There's a police roadblock set up at River Road, which is still a good mile from TMI. They should be able to stop the truck there, but a little precaution goes a long way. Put your sniper team on notice, just in case. Over."

"Gotcha. Don't worry, they have their orders and are well prepared, but I'll put them on red alert. Over."

"David…"

"I know Cass. I know. Over."

"Over," she whispered with all the love in her heart.

The helicopter tailed the truck. In the distance, she could make out the blinking lights on the four conical towers of TMI. Her heart banged her chest like a bass drum. The thought of David inside that complex with a live bomb made her want to scream. She refocused her attention on the enemy truck and the terrorist bent on destroying not only the man she loved but the world she lived in.

Ahead, obstructing the road, she could see the flashing lights of a dozen police vehicles. There was no way the terrorist and his truck was getting through the law enforcement blockade.

One mile from Three Mile Island

Buraq rolled his prayer beads between his fingers. It was a chilly night, but he was dripping with sweat. Ahead, he could see the flashing lights of what must be a roadblock. He knew he was only about a mile from the target. He slowed and considered his options. He'd trained for this moment in Libya. The caliphate depended on his fulfilling his duty. This was it. Either he pressed on to a glorious end, or he died in vain having never reached the gates, and never bringing down the fires of Hell.

He closed his eyes and gripped the wheel. With a burst of bravado and a rush of adrenaline, he shouted, "*Allahu Akbar.*" He pressed his foot to the floor, downshifted, and barreled toward the police vehicles.

Helicopter above Three Mile Island

"Shit!"

From the helicopter, Cass saw law enforcement fire pistols and rifles at the truck barreling toward them. Like a bull seeing red, the truck picked up speed, and lawmen began to dive and jump out of the way. Cass's breath stopped. It was happening so fast, yet it seemed like slow motion. She clutched the overhead strap on the helicopter prepared for when the impact came.

The truck barreled through as effortlessly as a train hitting a car stuck on railroad tracks. Police vehicles flew and rolled over one another, landing in a blaze of burning metal. From her vantage point, they looked like the Matchbox cars her younger brother played with as a child. Her mind flashed to a memory of him, smashing them together and shouting *kerpow!*

She squinted through the smoke and saw the truck rampaging toward TMI. It was impossible to hear anything in the helicopter. She shouted into her transmitter. "Captain Hughes, I'm handing command to you and ordering you to blow him to kingdom come."

"Roger. I'm going to put the other two birds on the ground. Eagle two and three, you assist law enforcement on the ground. Get ready for some fireworks. Enjoy the show and hold on. Over."Through the window, Cass saw the other two helicopters break away and head back to assist ground operations.

Cass clutched the overhead strap. The turbos kicked in, and the helicopter surged toward the truck. Through the night vision goggles, Cass could see the computerized cockpit light up with streaming coordinates as the rocket system locked on to the truck that careened at full speed toward the TMI gates.

"Permission to fire, Agent Saladino?"

"Granted!"

The whoosh of the rockets sounded quiet as death. *Five-four-three-two-one.* The explosion lit the night sky. The only thing left of the truck was raining debris. Pieces of flaming metal flew over the river, splashed down, and released a white cloud of smoke as the cold water doused the flames. The helicopter shook from the boomerang effect when reverberations hit it. Her stomach turned over, and nausea gripped her. The truck had carried a massive bomb. It exploded in a fiery display of flames and smoke. The hoots and hollers from the Rangers on the ground resounded over the radio and were echoed by the exuberant howls of the men in the helicopters.

Captain Hughes laughed. "Did you see that baby blow? Holy mother of God, what a sight to see. Where to now? You got any more target practice for us?"

"Not at the moment, Captain." Her fear receding, she grinned back. Then she remembered David.

"David? What's happening? Truck bombs destroyed. Update?"

"Yeah," David whispered, "We heard and felt it go off. Scared the crap out of us. According to the engineers, this place could have blown had they gotten closer. Good job taking it out. Over."

His forehead was damp as he watched the live feed coming from inside the canister. Two cameras were trained on the bomb technician inside the spent rod canister. One camera was focused on the device. The other on the technician's face. David could see the man inside the suit, his brow wrinkled in concentration. A thin layer of perspiration shimmered eerily on his fore-head. He knew the guy was probably boiling in the bomb suit. Even with his specialized training, the undercurrent of fear would be impossible to suppress. David kept his eyes on the monitor display showing the bomb tech's elevated pulse and heartbeat.

"What's happening there?" Cass asked.

"Technician's inside. I can't tell from the cameras what kind of progress he's making. I know we don't have much time before this baby blows. I've got my fingers crossed."

"He's the best, David."

"That's what his assistants say. But the suit makes it difficult. The heat can cause confusion. From what I can see, he's sweating like a pig. They keep talking to him to make sure he's thinking straight. We all know what's at stake if he fails."

"Is he familiar with this type of bomb?"

"Yeah, the assistants are confident." David peered closer at the screen. "Wait…something's happening." He heard Cass's sudden intake of breath and knew she was afraid for him.

The bomb technician smiled up at the camera and gave a thumbs-up. Everyone expelled a collective breath, and rowdy applause broke out.

David's heart resumed its normal rhythm. "We're good, Cass. Bomb's neutralized. Crisis over."

"Thank God. I've got to call the director and the general. I hope we didn't lose anyone on the ground. Waiting for a report now."

"I'm sorry, Cass." David knew how hard Cass took law enforcement casualties on her watch. He watched the technician being helped out of the bomb suit. Other assistants took his place inside the blue spent fuel rod canister to clean up and remove the disarmed bomb. "What about Cyrus?"

"I wanted to kill him. The guy marches to his own drum. Disobeyed my orders at every turn, but it seems he got the job done. Unfortunately, we won't be able to interview the terrorists. They're all dead. He rescued Layla—she's safe."

"What a relief. That's good news."

"Roger. Okay, got to make those calls. See you back at base camp. We did it, David."

"Yes, we did, baby." David knew he'd broken protocol calling her baby, but he didn't care. The only thing he wanted was to hold the woman he loved in his arms, to feel a semblance of normalcy return to his life.

"David!"

"I know, Cass, I broke the rules. Don't lecture me, I don't care anymore. We need to talk. This mission has convinced me you're the most important thing in my life. Get used to it."

"We'll talk. I'll try to see it your way. The thought of losing you would have destroyed me."

"That's never happening, Cass."

"Roger that."

Zurich, Switzerland
6 a.m.

Ash swept the area back and forth with his binoculars. He didn't have to wait long for his prey to reveal himself. The sniper crawled on his belly toward the chalet.

Before joining Mossad, Ash had been an IDF sniper assigned to a regiment on the Golan Heights, where he had plenty of opportunities to become an ace sharpshooter. It was a job he enjoyed.

He had no intention of waiting for the child or anyone else in the house to show themselves. He was taking no chances with their safety. Ash pressed his eye to the Galatz rifle scope and calculated the distance and wind velocity. Adjusting his aim, he held his breath and slowly squeezed the trigger. The gun blast echoed around the mountains. The assassin sprawled dead, his blood gushed out of his head, turning the snow red.

From the chalet, Ash watched Mossad agents emerge with their guns drawn. He grinned. *Mission accomplished.* He swung the rifle to his back and strolled to where he'd stashed the rest of his gear. After he loaded up and removed any trace of his being there, he sent the signal from his satellite phone that his mission was successfully completed. He put on his snow-shoes and began the trek down the mountain to where he'd stashed his motorcycle. He looked forward to some Swiss hospitality. First, he'd make his report for Aryeh, then a hot bath, followed by coffee and breakfast. He looked at his watch and smiled. *Perfect. Plenty of time for a nap before my flight back to Tel Aviv.*

Quds force encampment Mosul, Iraq

General Solatani rubbed his prayer beads together, his head bowed in deep meditation. In a quiet voice, his adjutant gently interrupted. "General, forgive the intrusion, but I have received news. I'm afraid it isn't good."

General Solatani opened his eyes, frowning. "What is it?"

The man's eyes darted nervously around the tent.

The General controlled the anger bubbling up inside him. "It's okay, son, I have no intention of killing the messenger." He forced a smile.

"Yes, sir. Our sources tell us the bombs were neutralized. There was an explosion outside of Three Mile Island, several infidels were killed, but the facility was undamaged. There's been no word from Ali or Omar. We must assume they're dead, sir. May Allah bless their souls."

"And the child? The grandparents?"

"Our intel out of Israel says they've left for Tel Aviv. No word from Adnan, we have to assume he's dead too. Cyrus and his wife have left the US and are on their way back to Israel. I'm sorry, sir."

The General looked down at his prayer beads. Hatred surged in his veins. *Defeat.* He flung the prayer beads across the tent. "Thank you. Continue to monitor the situation. Get our men out of Tel Aviv as soon as possible. Do not disturb me again. I need some time to reflect." The man saluted and backed out of the tent.

The General stared at the spot where the man had stood. Years of planning down the drain. His most trusted aides probably dead. Repercussions were sure to follow. The hated enemy and traitor, Cyrus Hassani, still walked the earth. It would take him days, perhaps months, to regroup and formulate his response. The war on ISIS, the war in Syria, and Iraq was never-ending. The dream to bring Iranian hegemony over the Middle East still elusive. He picked up his prayer beads and rubbed them.

"Forgive me, Allah, I have failed you." He took a deep breath, allowing the energy of Allah to invigorate him. He dreaded reporting the setback to the Ayatollah.

Yes, I've lost this round, but there will be another one. Allah will see to it. I must stay focused on the goal. I must remain faithful to the one God.

You and your family will never be safe, Cyrus Hassani. Never.

CHAPTER 26

FBI Command Center
Lancaster County, PA
September 19th
12:10 a.m.

The FBI temporary command center bustled with activity. Agents busily typed up reports, while crews began the arduous task of breaking down the facility and preparing it to return to its former glory as a dairy farm.

Layla sat, huddled in a blanket drinking coffee. From the corner of her eye, she watched Cyrus conversing with a group of men, who she pegged as Israelis.

At the farm, Cyrus had called in his report to a woman named Cass, who'd overseen the FBI's operation. Then came organized chaos. Hundreds of law enforcement personnel inundated Applegate farm. They quickly took control of the situation and began to process the crime scene.

She'd been relieved when they finished photographing Ali and Omar's bodies, and the coroner cleared them for removal. She couldn't bear to look at them but found it difficult not to. It had felt as if any minute, Ali would get up and come for her to take her back to the room and handcuff her once more. The mere thought chilled her to the bone.

Cyrus had assured her the terrorist plot had been prevented. The bomb-carrying Energex truck was destroyed a half-mile from TMI. The other two vehicles had been commandeered by rappelling Special Forces Night Stalkers before the bombs they carried could be triggered. Before being taken into custody, the two drivers, wearing suicide vests, had blown themselves up. Fortunately, there were no other deaths, but several officers were injured in the TMI blast.

She'd fainted when Aryeh informed them that Cerise and her grandparents were safe and on their way back to Tel Aviv, and the sniper had been eliminated. When she came to, she found herself in Cyrus's arms as he carried her to a chair. She'd wanted to wrap her arms around his neck and sob her relief, but the wary look in his eyes made her turn inward.

Aryeh, who officially wasn't there, disappeared like smoke from a chimney, dissolving into the cold night air as if he'd never been there. When she'd asked Cyrus who Aryeh was, he'd stated he was part of some super-secret Mossad group he'd worked for when he was a covert operative in Iran. Aryeh had comforted her, she'd instantly liked him. He'd eased the tension between her and Cyrus. However, once he was gone, the strain returned.

As she sat and nursed her coffee, she occasionally noticed Cyrus studying her, but when their eyes met, he'd look away. His face wavered between disappointment, animosity, and contrition. She could see the battle being waged within him.

She slumped and hunched, burying herself in the blanket. *Maybe it's just as well.*

When he initially hugged her, she'd been unable to conceal her reticence. She withdrew from his touch, and when he called her on it, she cowered, answering him in anger. "I need time, Cyrus. Please. I need time." How could she tell him that even though she was free, her psyche wasn't? She still felt like a prisoner. Still felt overwhelming shame. Still felt Ali's touch on her skin. She felt it down to her bones. She almost wept when a wave of nausea overwhelmed her at Cyrus's touch. It was as if Ali had cast some evil spell around them, where even her husband's touch reminded her of Ali.

She wanted to tell him it wasn't him, it was a reaction to Ali and his brother Omar, and the horrors they'd put her through. She should have said something then, but she didn't. He hadn't touched her since. She couldn't help but wonder if he'd ever touch her again.

Her eyes were wet, watery, threatening a downpour. If she allowed even one tear to fall, she feared a torrential storm would be unleashed. She did her best to suck it up. The thought of breaking down in front of strangers who were ebullient at having stopped the terrorist plot was something she didn't want to do.

She distracted herself by watching the beehive of activity. A petite red-head with spiked hair approached Cyrus. She was accompanied by a tall, handsome man who grinned from ear-to-ear. The man pounded Cyrus on the back, and the woman shook his hand. Cyrus nodded toward her, and the man and woman turned to scrutinize her. The petite woman barreled toward her reminding her of a tornado carving a path through a field. *Tiny but mighty*, she thought.

She thrust her hand forward. "Cass Saladino. Nice to meet you, Layla."

Layla shook the hand of the woman who appeared a force of nature. "Nice to meet you, Cass. Thank you for what you did to help me."

"Oh, I didn't do much. Cyrus was determined to rescue you, and convinced me to try his plan. He's quite persistent. I thought about kicking his ass back to Tel Aviv, but I'm glad it all worked out."

Layla smiled. "Yes. I'm sure he made your life a misery."

Cyrus, accompanied by the guy who'd come in with Cass, walked over to them. Cyrus scowled when he looked at her, while the other man grinned.

"Layla, meet Agent Weiss. He's Cass's sidekick."

"Nice to meet you Layla, my named is David." The guy was like a big affectionate puppy, hugging her. He was definitely different than anyone she'd ever met in the intelligence business. "Nice to meet you too. I'm so glad it worked out."

It was impossible to feel an aversion to this man. She hugged him back. From the corner of her eye, she saw Cyrus studying her. His scowl deepened.

"Thank you, David." Layla avoided making eye contact with Cyrus.

"I guess you can't wait to get back to Tel Aviv?"

"Yes, I want to get home as soon as possible. I need to see my daughter. I'm afraid what started out as an incredible trip turned into a nightmare. All I want is to hold my child in my arms again."

Cass and David kept glancing at Cyrus, who stood in stone-faced silence.

"We'll have you out of here in no time," David said in warm encouragement.

What followed became a blur. Layla was tired. Worn down by all she'd been through, and depressed by the widening distance between Cyrus and her. Their communication whittled down to as few words as possible. Her stomach was in knots, and she could only imagine what he was feeling. She was too tired to think, too tired to do anything. She was grateful when they were released. She dozed in the van on the drive to Philadelphia International Airport. The Israeli team, she, and Cyrus were directed to a private jet. The aircraft took off immediately and had barely reached altitude when Layla fell into a deep sleep. She slept the entire flight back to Tel Aviv.

CHAPTER 27

Washington D.C.
September 19th

Cass barely made it through the door of her townhouse. She was wiped from the intensity of the operation, and the drudgery of paperwork she'd felt compelled to complete before she allowed herself to go home. She dropped her bag and briefcase at the door. *I need to wash every last speck of farm dirt off my skin.*

She leaned against the door, determined to muster enough strength to shower and check her messages in precisely that order. Then she'd joyfully answer the swan song of her bed that called to her. She needed twelve hours of sleep, and then she'd be good as gold.

She was throwing her clothes in the hamper when she heard the doorbell ring. *Who the fuck is that?* She grabbed her robe and stumbled to the door. Opening it, she saw a smiling David, overnight bag in one hand, and an unwieldy case in the other. Two bags of groceries sat on the ground at his feet.

"Where's your key? I was just about to get in the shower. And what the heck is that case for?" She nodded toward the black case.

"Can't find my key. It must have fallen off my keychain. Sorry."

Her gaze returned to the mystery case. "The case, David. What's in the case?"

"The case is a surprise," he flashed a devilish smile.

"I'm too tired for surprises, David."

"Not this one, you're not." He moved past her, leaning the case against the wall, then went back and picked up the grocery bags. She closed the door behind him.

"Go take your shower." He bent and gave her a peck on the lips. "Have you eaten anything? I picked up some stuff at the market."

She eyed the shopping bags, realizing she hadn't eaten all day, and there was probably nothing in the house. "I'm so tired I didn't think about food. Okay, I'll let you do your thing, my shower calls." She headed toward the bathroom. "When I get out, you can explain the hitman case. What do you have in there, a machine gun?"

David laughed. "No guns, and no clues. Shower, baby."

The shower invigorated her. *At least long enough for us to eat.* She smiled. *And maybe a round or two of sex.* She vigorously towel dried her hair, and spiked it up with her fingers. It was why she kept her hair short, easily managed, it kept her beauty regimen to a minimum.

When she pushed through the kitchen's swinging butler's door, her eyes grew wide. On the table was an ice bucket. Submerged in it, was a bottle sporting the telltale foil wrapper indicative of champagne. Two flutes stood ready to be filled. David was cooking at the stove, his back to her, and an apron tied around his waist. She giggled. *If he isn't the most fucking gorgeous short-order cook on the planet.* Enjoying the view, she watched as he expertly flipped an omelet in the air and landed it back in the pan.

"What's so funny, baby? Don't you like seeing your man wearing an apron?" He turned his head. "I made your favorite, just the way you like it, underdone and creamy."

She sat at the table, loving the pleasure of being served. So many years of the single life certainly made her appreciate having David in her life. David slid a plate in front of her, and the aroma filled her with warmth. Paper-thin slices of avocado blanketed the omelet. "Hmm, it looks yummy."

"Filled with sautéed onions and goat cheese. Hold on, bagels are warming in the oven, and I got gravlax and cream cheese. We're celebrating."

He brought the food to the table, popped the cork with a flourish, and poured them each a glass of bubbly. "To us, baby, we stopped the bad guys."

"*Cin cin.*"

"*L'chaim.*"

They gently clinked glasses and sipped.

She dug into the omelet that steamed enticingly before her. Between bites, she asked, "So are you going to tell me what's in the secret case?"

"You didn't notice it in the living room, all ready to go?"

She frowned. It wasn't like her not to observe the details of her surroundings. "I must be exhausted. I walked right through without seeing a thing."

"Good. It'll make the surprise even more exciting."

She shook her head and smiled. "Always the mystery man." She slathered a thick coat of cream cheese on a bagel half and topped it with a generous slab of gravlax. Taking a bite, she purred. "Oh, my god David, I think I died and went to Heaven. I'm having a food orgasm."

His eyes twinkled. "Hold that thought—there's more to come."

God, I love this man. For so many years, she'd avoided loving anyone. Avoided allowing her heart to be vulnerable. Her life was her career in the FBI. She'd dedicated herself to the continuous struggle of rising up the ladder of power. When David came into her life, all of her carefully crafted barriers crumbled. When he'd kissed her in the limo after the party at the Russian Embassy, her heart, an ice cube had begun to melt. The only problem she couldn't get past was the danger of being in love with your crime-solving partner. Suddenly the perils of the job were made real.

"Eat up, baby. I can't wait much longer. The suspense is killing me. I want to see your reaction to my surprise."

"If you think I'm going to leave one morsel on this plate, you are sadly mistaken. I'm thinking of licking it clean."

"Save your licks for more important things like me." The hunger in his eyes sent a current pulsing through her.

While she sat, satiated, and contemplating her happiness, David whirled like a dervish cleaning up the kitchen. When he'd finished, he removed his apron, folded it, and hung it on the hook on the wall. His neatness sometimes got her goat. It forced her to act in kind, something the rebel in her fought to resist. Before she could protest, he scooped her up and carried her to the living room. She didn't protest, didn't move, all she was capable of was resting her head against his broad chest. He placed her gently on the ground and commanded. "Get undressed." He crossed his arms over his chest and grinned, watching her.

"What about you? I don't see you removing any clothes."

He laughed. "Later. If you don't get started, I'm going to have to do it for you. I want you to lie on the table face down." He motioned toward the fireplace.

"Table?" When she followed his gaze, realization dawned on her. The gas logs were lit, and in front of them was a white-sheeted table. On the coffee table was an assortment of bottles filled with lotions and oils. "You were lugging a massage table? You planned a massage?"

"Exactly, smart girl, I'm going to give you a massage you'll never forget. In fact, I'm certain it will be the best massage you've ever had. I'm a pro, you know."

She eyed him quizzically as she removed her sweats. "How was I to know, you never mentioned it?"

"Then you didn't study my resume too well. It's just a footnote, but I worked my way through college and police academy supplementing my income with a thriving massage practice."

"Boy, you've really been holding out on me. Damn. How come you never offered before?"

He moved closer, his hands on her waist and pulled her against him as he bent and gave her a kiss. "I dunno…don't want to spoil you, I guess. Now get on the table." His eyes gleamed devilishly.

She saluted. "Yes, sir. All-hands-on-deck."

"Finally, I get to play boss, and I know just what to do with these hands."

A few hours later, they lay snuggled in Cass's bed after their sensuous love-making. Cass stretched, feeling completely relaxed, satisfied. Happy. "You're a quick study Agent Weiss. I think you're a keeper."

"I was just thinking the same thing, baby." He pulled her snug against him. He hovered above her smiling face and dove in with a passionate kiss, which she answered back, fingers entwined in his hair until gasping they broke apart.

Dark lashed, hazel eyes held hers. "Cass, I want to ask you something, and I don't want you to answer right away. I want you to let what I say sink in. Okay?"

Her stomach constricted. She felt herself at the top of a rollercoaster, suddenly plunging toward the ground. She couldn't imagine what he was going to say, but she knew whatever it was scared her, made her vulnerable. She breathed, forcing oxygen into her lungs, willing her heart to resume an even rhythm. "Okay."

He took her hand in his and drew circles with his thumb, easing the trepidation that stole her breath. "Cass, I know all of the reasons why we shouldn't, but I don't care. I-I-I…" He was stuttering. He flashed an *I'm-a-fool* grin. "What I'm trying to say, to make you understand, is I love you, and I want to marry you. There. I've said it." He searched her face, a look of hopeful anticipation on his.

A puff of wind could have bowled her over. She was so taken aback. "You want to get married, as in husband and wife?"

He grinned. "That's exactly what I want. I'm looking for forever with you. I'm pretty confident that's what two people who are in love with each other do."

"But David. Our work? We're partners. A great team."

"And we'll make an even better team married."

"It's against regulations. They'll never allow it."

"Then we won't tell them. If enough time passes and enough cases are solved, eventually we'll break it to them, and they'll see nothing has changed in our efficiency or our ability to handle the situation. I know it means sacrificing the big wedding and keeping two separate residences, but hell, we can have a wedding later. For all intents and purposes, I basically live here anyway. Right now, we'll just tell our closest friends and family."

She was speechless. "I don't know why, but this makes me think of Cyrus."

"Cyrus? Why?"

"I don't think I've ever met a man who seemed more in love with a woman than him. He was ready to lay down his life for her."

"Yeah, what's wrong with that? I'd do the same for you."

"I know. But you saw the way they behaved at the command center. You could have driven five Mac trucks between them. They seemed so distant, so far apart from each other. They avoided looking at each other or touching each other. Not exactly a great impassioned reunion."

"Baby, she's been to hell and back. They'll work it out. A little time at home, maybe some therapy, and they'll find their way back to one another. The marriage didn't cause them to distance from each other. It was the kidnapping, incarceration, being terrorized, and having her loved ones threatened that drove a wedge between them. They'll get past it."

"Maybe you're right." She looked at her hand in his. "I can't lose you."

"Then don't. Make the right choice, Cass. Marry me."

Tears of joy traced a path down her cheek. He bent and kissed them away. His arms wrapped around her, pulling her deeper into his embrace as he continued to kiss her, repeating, "Marry me."

Her head fell back, exposing her neck to his eager lips. "Yes…yes…I'll marry you." She felt him grow hard against her. Giggling, she moaned, "I said I'll marry you." He grew harder.

"Hmmm, baby, our sex is like two stars colliding, explosive. I want to love you from head to toe, real slow. I want to celebrate and remember those words forever. I love you, Cass." His kiss made her dizzy.

Somehow it will all work out. We'll make it work.

CHAPTER 28

Tel Aviv, Israel
September 20th

Nothing worked out the way they'd planned.

Layla wanted to go home. All she could think about was holding Cerise in her arms, and yet here they were pulling into an underground parking lot beneath an office building. Annoyed, she looked around in confusion. That's all she needed to add to her list of overwhelming feelings. The plane landing in Israel hadn't calmed her nerves. Nor had the drive back to Tel Aviv. The conversation between her and Cyrus had remained cold and clipped in the car. He'd texted the entire time while she had stared out the window, wondering how she was going to reclaim her life.

"Layla, I know you're anxious to see Cerise, but it's the official procedure for you to be debriefed and psychologically evaluated immediately following an incident of such consequential proportions. It needs to be done now before details slip away from you. It shouldn't take long."

"I don't want to do this now."

"I'm sorry, but you have to."

They took an elevator to the lobby, where they accessed an authorized only lift requiring security clearance to reach the upper floors. When Layla and Cyrus arrived on the top floor, a security guard waited for them. He escorted them down a long, nondescript hallway to a suite of offices with only numbers on their doors. They stopped at number 2022, and the door automatically opened. Inside, a receptionist greeted them. "Mr. and Mrs. Hassani, Orna Wiseman is waiting for you."

The receptionist buzzed them through another door where they were met by a tall woman with dark hair swept back in a severe bun. Kind brown eyes peered out through glasses resting on her hawkish nose. She clasped

Layla's hand firmly in her own. "Orna Wiseman. Layla, I'm so glad to meet you. I know you're anxious to get home. I promise you this won't take long. Cyrus, we should be done in about an hour."

"Don't worry about me. I know my way around here. I'll get some coffee and find a quiet spot to catch up on my email."

"Good. Come with me, Layla. I'm not as familiar with this place as your husband. They've assigned us a room for me to conduct our interview."

The room was surprisingly homey. A brown leather sofa rested against a wall with a photograph above it Layla recognized as the old port of Jaffa. On the opposite wall was a large mirror. Potted plants adorned two corners of the room. Layla sat on the sofa while Orna sat across from her in a wing back chair. On the coffee table was a tray with an urn and a plate of cookies.

"Coffee?"

"Yes, thank you."

Orna poured them each a cup, filled two plates with cookies, and sat back. "Layla, I'm a psychologist with expertise in PTSD. My job is to help you adjust and, of course, to document anything that might be relevant to intelligence."

"I was interrogated by the FBI, and I told them the full story of what happened."

"Yes, I know, but the FBI wasn't concerned with your state of mind. However we are."

Layla nodded in understanding, but inside she was wary of opening up to a complete stranger and pouring her heart out, especially so soon after it happened.

"Layla, I know how traumatic this experience was for you. Can you tell me a little about your captors?"

"Most of my contact was with the two Iranian brothers, Omar and Ali. Both talked about General Solatani, who they owed their allegiance to. Omar didn't speak to me except as a hated infidel, but Ali spoke a lot about his life. He'd spent years in Hezbollah training camps.

"Omar was a dyed-in-the-wool ideologue, a monster. He hated me, wanted me dead. I was terribly afraid of him. He hit me and would gladly have killed me." Her voice broke as fear and helplessness returned to her.

She took a moment to breathe and regain control of her riotous emotions. "Ali stopped him from hitting me. What they really wanted was

Cyrus. I was just the bait—the dangling carrot used to tempt the fox out of his hole."

"But Ali was different…"

Layla had taken a few psych courses in university when she'd contemplated doing a master's in art therapy. She knew Orna was "mirroring". On the other hand, Orna seemed genuine. *Maybe she can help me.* "Ali was different. Without a doubt, a monster, but not as gung-ho as Omar. I think Ali had lost his desire to fight, to kill, even though he was the one who pushed the button setting off the explosion at Ma Maison." She shuddered, digging her nails into her palm. "I saw him do it. Set off the explosion that killed Avi. It was the most horrible feeling in the world—not being able to do anything—knowing people were being murdered. I keep racking my brain if there was anything I could have done to prevent it."

Orna reached across the sofa and took Layla's hand. "Layla, you are not to blame for what happened. You were the victim."

Layla took a gulp of air. The pressure in her chest subsided just enough for her to continue. "After what I heard Omar say, I knew Ali had changed. He blamed it on me, but I don't know. I don't know what changed him, but I think Ali didn't want to die. I think Ali created this whole fantasy about me, made himself fall in love with me, believed he was in love with me. He was convinced God meant us to be together. I hated him so much." She whispered, "All I wanted to do was escape and run away. Instead, I pretended…" She looked at her hands and frowned. "He didn't hide his attraction to me or his jealousy of Cyrus. He made me nervous. I was afraid he would rape me."

"Did he?"

"No, he didn't—I-I don't know…"

Orna's eyebrows shot up. "What do you mean you don't know?"

Layla whispered. "He-he-he didn't beat me or tie me down or anything, he didn't force himself on me."

"I see." Orna studied her for a minute. "Layla, I have to ask you this. Did you have sex with Ali?"

Her eyes filled with tears. "Yes…yes, I did."

"And you believe it was consensual?"

"Yes," she sobbed, covering her face with her hands.

"Why?"

Sucking in a gulp of air, she wiped the tears from her eyes. "I-I knew he wanted me, so I-I used him t-to get him to save Cerise and my grandparents.

He-he promised to stop the sniper in Switzerland. I h-had to save them, and I would do it again. It cost me everything, but I'd still do it again." She looked at the mirror trying to regain control of her emotions. "I feel dead inside."

"You have nothing to be ashamed of, Layla. You had no choice. You had to save those you love. By any definition of the term, Ali raped you. He coerced you, manipulated you, kept you a prisoner, he didn't have to use force to get what he wanted, he dangled the lives of your daughter and grandparents in front of you."

"Oh God, Orna, do you think Cyrus will understand? He-he saw me with Ali—he knows what happened. You don't know my husband. You don't know what we've been through. I think he hates me now. I think he's disgusted with me."

"No, I only know the facts, the events. I've read the official transcript of the first time you were kidnapped in Dubai and taken to Tehran. I know about Cyrus and your escape from Iran. Why don't you think he can get past this and forgive you?"

"Cyrus was the only man I've ever had sex with, the only man I've ever been with. He reveled in it, cherished it, loved me more than anything in the world because of it. It was one of the strongholds of our marriage. A tie that bound us together. I was his and his alone."

"Let's be clear, Layla. What you did was done under horrific circumstances. Do you want me to talk to him? I'm sure I can make him understand."

"No. Please. You can't. Right after…when he tried to touch me—I pulled away. I couldn't bear his touch—I couldn't bear the touch of the love of my life."

"Layla, you need a therapist to get through this. An objective listener to mediate the emotions simmering inside of you. Emotions bound to boil to the surface. This is an explosive situation. You need help coming to terms with this."

"I know…" She held her hands together, so tight, her knuckles turned white. She dug her nails deeper into her skin, leaving dark red imprints. "I need to try and explain this to him. To convince him, we can get past this. If I can't, then I'll seek help. I promise."

"Don't wait too long, Layla. Without help, these issues are only going to deepen, and Cyrus is more likely to erect impenetrable walls, which might become impossible to bring down. He's not an ordinary man, no spy ever is. They possess an ability to disconnect from emotion."

"I just need some time. Some distance from what happened at the farm."

"Layla, are you afraid of sex? Are you afraid that your desire to make love and be loved might be lost?"

"Yes…the thought of anyone touching me fills me with terror."

"I suggest you begin therapy immediately. I'd be happy to work with you. I know I can help you. You can trust me, Layla."

Layla trembled with relief. Could she find a way out of this terrible darkness inside of her? "Please…yes…I can't believe this is happening to me. I love him so much, and now I can't bear the thought of seeing my betrayal in his eyes. I can't believe I pulled away from him. I know he thinks I fell for Ali, but nothing could be further from the truth."

"Okay, take a few minutes and gather yourself. It's best if we get through this and get you home and reunited with your child. We need to focus on getting you and Cyrus back to living your lives."

"You can't imagine how much I want to return to the way it was before. To forget the bombing, the fear…Ali."

"I have to warn you, Layla, it's not going to be easy. You have to face your demons head-on, acknowledge them before you can banish them forever. Kind of like an emotional exorcism."

"But you think I can? You think Cyrus can forgive me?"

"First, you'll have to forgive yourself, and then we'll deal with Cyrus."

Layla nodded. A tiny seed of hope took root in her heart.

"Good, let's start at the beginning. The evening of the bombing at Ma Maison."

Cyrus watched his wife's confession, the pain in his chest, immutable. He was spying through the one-way mirror on Layla and Orna's conversation. He knew it was wrong, but he couldn't help it. Listening to her describe what happened between her and the terrorist tore his heart in half. The love that had been his redemption lay in tatters, ripped to pieces. The thought of Ali, a monster, touching Layla was unbearable. He wanted to empathize, to forgive her, but his compassion was eviscerated by the anger and hatred boiling within his veins. Deep inside, he knew it was his fault. She would never have been kidnapped, never been raped, if she wasn't married to him. How, he wondered, could he ever get past the image of Layla and Ali kissing? Worse was the thought of Ali and Layla in bed together, their bodies joined. It made him want to kill Ali over and over again.

He remembered in Iran when he'd quoted to her Thomas Wolfe's famous passage in *You Can't Go Home Again*, "You can't go back home to your family, back home to your childhood…back home to a young man's dreams of glory and fame…"

Her confession shook his world, eviscerated it. He was confused, unsure if their marriage was fixable. He thought they'd had a strong marriage, an invincible marriage, and yet now it seemed like a beautiful vase that had toppled over and shattered into a thousand pieces. He thought of Cerise and couldn't bear the guilt of knowing what this would do to her. Could he live a lie with Layla for the sake of his child? The thought of living apart from Layla and Cerise was unbearable. That would be torture he couldn't endure. It would kill him.

All he could think about was Layla saying those words—saying she couldn't bear the thought of him touching her. He didn't try to understand what she'd endured. He couldn't deal with the guilt that everything that happened was his fault. He was hurting, broken inside, and he couldn't get past the reality of that.

The pull of gravity and despair buckled his knees. He bent, bracing his hands on his thighs, fighting his desire to collapse to the floor.

"What the hell is wrong with you?" A man's hand gripped his shoulder.

"Don't touch me," he roared, shaking free. Then he saw who it was. "Aryeh."

"What are you doing howling like a wolf at the moon?"

"She's in there. She's in there talking to the shrink. I-I listened in."

"You're a goddamn fool, Hassani."

"Leave me alone, Aryeh. It's my fucking wife in there. I don't give a shit about her privacy."

"Cyrus, you're treading into dangerous waters. Your wife believes this debriefing is confidential. You're going to regret this." He went to the one-way mirror and switched it off.

"I'll tell you what I regret," Cyrus growled. "You not minding your own fucking business." Cyrus had a distinct urge to grab Aryeh by the throat and beat the shit out of him.

Aryeh must have seen it in his eyes because he braced his legs apart and crossed his arms over his chest, eyeing him with a glare.

Cyrus knew Aryeh was right. What he was doing was wrong, but he couldn't stop. He was caught like a fish on a hook. Resentment welled up inside of him. *I'm in a nightmare. How could she not know I'd move*

Heaven and Earth to save her? Why didn't she wait? Fight? Believe? As suddenly as it had seized him, the anger dissipated, and in its place came guilt. It ballooned, sucking the air from his lungs, leaving him limp and impotent.

"I'm sorry. I've never had to do deal with—forgive me."

"Cyrus, in life, we go through many trials, but what gets us through is the people we love."

"Since when are you such a philosopher?"

Aryeh threw back his head and laughed. "Ah, my friend, a man in our line of work, has to have a philosophical view of life."

"Why didn't she wait? Why didn't she believe that I would get to her in time?"

"Tell me, what made you fall in love with her in the first place?"

"Her courage. She was thrown into a horrific situation and never lost her humanity."

"So, don't you think it was that same courage that fueled her actions back at that fucking farm with those maniacs? She's not a trained killer. The only weapons she had were her courage and humanity."

Oh, God, he was right. Dafna was right. And he was letting those bastards win by wallowing in his feelings of anger and betrayal. *I'm pathetic. An apathetic excuse for a man.*

"You need to talk to someone about this, man. And soon. If you don't, you're going to destroy the most beautiful gift that God ever gave you." He needed help. He needed to see Dafna. She was the only one who could help him through this crisis. When he and Layla were trying to escape from Iran, he'd been stabbed, and nearly died. During his recovery from multiple surgeries, the Mossad shrink had taken him through the darkest period of his life. The thought of it brought a twinge of pain to his abdomen.

The real pain was remembering what it felt like to live without Layla. Dafna had steered him right, made him face his fears. She had miraculously turned the tide of his life and made him face his demons. He'd dealt with his feelings of inadequacy, and the insecurities that prevented him from experiencing happiness. She'd be harsh, merciless, brutal. He'd have to deal with his deficiencies, to accept her assessment, her condemnation.

"I have to go. I have to talk to my shrink again. If I don't talk to her now, I think I'm going to implode."

"Go, man, I'll drive Layla home. Just go deal with this so you can get back to your wife and kid."

———— ❧❦❧ ————

Layla braced herself as she left the interview room. Her conversation with Orna had awakened her demons, her worst fear that her life was slipping away from her. Cyrus wasn't waiting in the reception area when she finished with Orna. She needed to talk to him and explain what was happening to her. She needed him to understand their marriage was fixable. He needed to join her in therapy, to work with her to get past this. She needed to see Cerise, her grandparents. *I need to know love is still possible.*

"Layla."

She whirled at the familiar voice. "Aryeh, what are you doing here?"

"I'm here to take you home." He handed her a note from Cyrus.

Layla, I left the car keys on the kitchen counter so you can drive to your grandparents' house and be with Cerise and bring her home. I promised her I'd bring Mommy to her. I've kept that promise.

I need to think. I need some time to figure things out.

Tell Cerise I was called away on business...tell her I love her. When you get home, I'll be gone. Not sure where, but it really doesn't matter.

I've already informed my boss. I'm taking a leave of absence. My salary will be directly deposited into the bank account for you. Financially you have nothing to worry about. I'll be in touch as soon as I can.

I'm sorry.
Cyrus

"It's begun," she whispered. "This is how a marriage ends."

Tears soaked the page as she read the note over and over again. Aryeh was oddly quiet, giving her solitude to express her grief.

He escorted her to the front door of the duplex and, taking the key, went in first, making sure the house was clear. Cyrus had mentioned that Mossad had checked their home earlier, but Aryeh chuckled and said he wanted to make sure they double-flushed the toilet. Before he left, he gave her his number if she needed him to find Cyrus.

"You can call me day or night," he said.

"Don't you ever sleep?" she gave him a crooked smile.

"I'll sleep when I'm dead," he replied with a wink.

CHAPTER 29

Tel Aviv, Israel
September 20th

"Ima!"

Cerise flung herself into Layla's arms, kissing her. Auburn curls pressed against her cheek, and the pure scent of her child enveloped her. She squeezed her eyes tight, trying to hold back the flood of tears that threatened to pour like rain. It was the first moment of joy she'd experienced since she was kidnapped. Even the cold-hearted note from Cyrus couldn't dampen the love surging inside of her.

From the corner of her eye, she saw Dina's beloved lined face, glowing with a beaming smile.

"Cerise, I've missed you so much, baby." She pressed her lips into the mass of curls.

The ever-observant child lifted her head and looked around. "Mommy, where's Daddy? He said we'd have a party when you came home. Did he tell you we flew on an airplane, just *Savta* and *Saba* and me? Oh, and the pilots gave me a hat and some nice men on the plane played games with me, and a pretty lady gave us food whenever we asked for it. Did he tell you, *Ima*?"

"Yes, baby. *Abba* told me."

"Did he tell you we flew to the mountains and there was snow? Mommy, I wanted you to be there. Mommy, have you ever played in the snow?"

"Yes, angel. Mommy grew up in the snow."

"Did you love it? *Savta* read me a book about snow angels. Did you ever make a snow angel?"

Layla kissed the pale freckles on Cerise's nose. "Yes, I made lots of snow angels when I was a little girl."

"Would you make them with me, *Ima*?"

"Well…" she teased. "It doesn't snow in Tel Aviv."

Cerise giggled. "No, Mommy. When we go to the mountains. Will you make snow angels with me? Please, *Ima*? We can make them together and look up into the sky. Daddy can take pictures of us, and we can keep those angels forever."

A wrenching pain seized her. She grabbed the child, hugging her close. "Yes, darling, your daddy will take lots of pictures. I promise you, baby."

"Daddy promised we'd go back there. All of us and go sliding down the snowy hills. Where is he?"

What could she say? Words escaped her. "He-he's away, baby. He had to go away for a few days for work. He told me he's sorry, that he'll miss you to the moon and back, and can't wait to get home and hold you in his arms."

The child's trusting smile wrenched her heart. All the while, she felt Dina's gaze penetrating her. The lie to Cerise more than apparent to those discerning eyes.

"Okay, Mommy." Her gentle daughter laid her chubby little hand against Layla's cheek. Layla wanted to weep. "When he gets home, I want to make a party." She turned toward her great-grandmother, whose face instantly blossomed into a smile. "*Savta*, you and *Saba* can come to the party."

"Thank you, *metukah*. You are the delight of my old age."

Cerise ran to her great-grandmother and wrapped her arms around her. Dina bent to kiss the top of Cerise's head. "You're not old. You're like the sun, *Savta*—you will shine forever."

"Yes, my love, I will shine on you forever, God willing. Now let's have some cake and tea. Mommy must be tired from her journey. Go *metukah*, tell your *saba* that Mommy is home."

Clapping her hands, the child was gone in a flash. Her joyous cries to her great-grandfather rang in the air. Dina put her arm through Layla's. "So, where is he?"

Layla burst into tears. "Oh, Bubbie, I've lost him. I've screwed everything up. I want to die."

"Shush, I will not listen to such ridiculous prattle. We will sit down, and you will explain it all to me. Then we will figure out how to bring that stubborn man back to his family where he belongs."

Layla cupped the steaming mug in her hands. The warmth permeated her being. After celebrating as a family and feasting on Dina's honey cake, Dina had sent Morris and Cerise to the living room for a game of dominoes. Knowing nothing less than the truth would do, she bared her soul to her grandmother. The whole story of her kidnapping, her imprisonment, and her betrayal with Ali.

"*Savta*, if you saw his face, the way he looked at me." She shook her head, and a fresh wave of tears flooded her eyes. "He hates me. He doesn't want me anymore."

"Foolishness. The man risked his life for you. If you could have seen him when he thought you might be dead, you would know that's impossible. He wanted to crawl into the grave with you. I was worried he'd kill himself. Never have I seen a man love a woman more."

Layla whispered, "But, maybe I destroyed his love for me."

"He's wallowing in self-pity. He doesn't know how to put the pieces of his heart back together. Under no circumstance are you to give him a divorce. Listen to a woman who knows from whence she speaks. Many years ago, I nearly lost my Morris over something, not unlike what's happening to you."

"You, Bubbie?"

Dina's eyes burned bright with the memory. "Although you wouldn't know it now. At one time, I was quite the beauty."

"Of course, you were. I've seen the photos. Mommy looked just like you."

"Yes, my girl was a beauty too." A wistfulness filled her eyes.

Layla reached for her grandmother's hand and gave it a gentle squeeze.

"You know your *saba* and I were in the Irgun," Dina said. "In the paramilitary army fighting for the birth of Israel. There wasn't much time for romance in war-torn Palestine at that point. We married soon after we met. We'd survived the Nazis, but none of us expected to survive the war for Independence. We took our happiness where we could.

"I was a wild child with a devil-may-care attitude. I didn't care who I hurt. All I wanted was to make up for the years I'd been deprived of by the war. The Nazis. The concentration camps. Watching my entire family shot and killed before my eyes. Living in those camps, being leered at, spit on, mauled, and brutalized by the Nazis. Watching poor souls around me sicken and die from the filthy conditions, or hang themselves before falling into the hands of the Nazis." The tears seeped from behind Dina's closed eyelids.

Layla's heart wept for her.

"How could I ever be a normal wife, let alone live a normal life? I didn't think anything could be normal again after that horror." Dina pulled out a handkerchief from her pocket and wiped her eyes. "Morris and I were stationed in different places, and I had a short-lived fling with a *samal rishon*, a brigade leader. It was wrong. It was hurtful what I did, but Morris and

I had spent so little time together, and I was lonely. I fell for the brigade leader's seduction, but I was as guilty as he was.

"I need not tell you how angry Morris was when he found out. He wanted out of the marriage. He called me every hateful name in the book and asked for a divorce. I was never good at containing my wrath when cornered. His insults got the better of me, and I agreed. I wanted to hurt him, to make him suffer for his hurtful words. I told him I didn't love him, that I didn't want to be married to him anymore. I told him the marriage was a mistake."

"Oh, Bubbie, that was so cruel. How did you work it out?"

"I signed the divorce papers."

"But I don't understand. You're still married."

"He carried those papers with him into battle. He slept with them in foxholes. They were always on his person, but he never signed them."

Layla studied her grandmother's face. "How did you get back together?"

A nostalgic smile embraced Dina's lips. "It was Chanukah 1947, six months before the state of Israel was officially born. I was on leave in Tel Aviv. My girlfriends and I were having a great time bar hopping. We were young and carefree, but we knew the war with the Arabs was coming." She shook her head. "I was sitting on a barstool, and this fool began pestering me. He grabbed me, forced a kiss on me. I certainly lived up to my red-haired temper. I slapped him in the face. The drunken sod lost control and was about to slap me back when out of nowhere came Morris, who grabbed the guy by his collar and threw him into the street."

"Wow, *Saba* did that?" Layla couldn't help grinning. "Just by chance, he was in the same bar?"

"Well, I wouldn't call it a by chance. He later confessed he'd seen us and followed us. He was trying to work up the nerve to say hello to me."

"That's so romantic." Layla was on the edge of her seat, her own troubles muted. "What happened next?"

"You know your grandfather is a man of few words. He took the tattered divorce papers out of his pocket and ripped them up. Very dramatically, he let the pieces fall to the floor. Then he took the wedding ring I'd returned to him and put it back on my finger. He kissed me very passionately until there wasn't an ounce of fight left in me. Then he dragged me out of that bar to a hotel room. We shared a passionate night of love. One I'll never forget. We've been together ever since."

"Oh, Bubbie, that's the best story ever."

"Yes, Morris is, and will always be, the love of my life. Just as Cyrus is yours. Now you take Cerise home and put her to bed. If I know Cyrus, you won't have to wait half as long as I did for Morris to come to his senses."

Layla enveloped her grandmother in a tight hug. "Thank you, only you could make me believe again."

I'm going to fight for us, Cyrus. Fight to save our marriage. This is one battle you're going to lose. I'll get past this. I refuse to live without love. I refuse to live without you.

Dina hugged her fiercely. "I love you, *liebchen*. You have brought so much joy to my twilight years. You are the gift your mother blessed me with."

CHAPTER 30

All of his pent-up anger and pain tumbled from him.

For the past five days, he'd had daily sessions in Dafna's office. He'd spent hours spilling his guts, pouring out his anger, laying bare his fears… His communication with Layla had been minimal, via text, and a few brief phone calls to set up when he'd pick up Cerise from school or from Dina's. He still hadn't gone back home. He needed time. A few more days. He needed to heal the fracture in his heart so that he could go back to Layla, whole.

Dafna listened without comment.

He wanted to hold back, to filter his words, but once the dam was opened, nothing could stop the flood. Love, passion, and devotion turned into anger, jealousy, and hatred, and then just as suddenly, he buried his face in his hands and wept. It was nearly unfathomable this loss of control, this breaking down in front of another human being, whether a doctor or not. After a few minutes, he gathered himself and wiped his eyes. "I'm s-sorry," he stammered.

"You needed to release, to let it all out. Now we can analyze the situation. I need you to step outside of your pain and try to deal with what has happened objectively."

He nodded, knowing the worst was yet to come.

"So far, this is about you. Your thoughts, your jealousy, your inability to see the situation from any other perspective but your own."

"What other perspective is there?"

"Layla's."

"How can I?"

"You have to. There's no other way to get beyond what you're feeling. To fix what's broken."

"Tell me how."

"Layla is suffering."

"She can't bear the thought of my touching her. I heard her say it."

"Spying on her was wrong."

"I know, I feel terrible. It was unfair."

"You love Layla deeply, but you must learn to respect her as well."

"I know. You're right."

"Why do you think she can't bear the thought of you touching her?"

"Guilt."

"Guilt is part of it. No matter what she says, though, there's something Layla's going to need to come to terms with, something you're going to have to come to terms with. She was raped. She didn't consent willingly to have sex with that terrorist."

"But she—"

"No, buts," Dafna cut in. "Have you forgotten your training, the many years you spent as an undercover mole in Iran? Have you forgotten how torture works? She did nothing that you nor I nor any normal human being wouldn't have done under the same circumstances. First, she suffered through being kidnapped and had to watch helplessly as a hundred or more people, including her friend, were murdered. Then she suffered through a week of captivity. You know the term Cyrus—survivor's guilt. She asked herself why she was spared when so many good people were not. She is dealing with her own guilt, and God willing her therapist will help her see the truth of it. And you must help her too."

Cyrus nodded. He knew Layla wasn't equipped for psychological warfare. He knew she would blame herself, He knew she would do anything to save Cerise and her grandparents.

"Cyrus, I want you to close your eyes and breathe deeply. Relax your mind. I want you to visualize that room in the farmhouse where your wife was held captive for six days. Imagine her feeling so lost, so far away from anyone who could help her and at the mercy of two terrorists…"

Cyrus closed his eyes and breathed deeply. He'd done this visual exercise with Dafna so many times before. It helped that he'd learned to meditate. He drew on that ability now as he calmed his breathing and allowed his mind to empty itself. He visualized himself, standing in the room. He looked around. He saw the closed window, locked, a few feet from the bed.

He saw a twin size bed with a metal headboard. He saw Layla's left wrist red and raw, cuffed to the metal frame… His vision traveled up her arm to her bruised face. Her eyes were full of tears. She was trembling with fear as the door opened and in walked Ali, carrying a food tray, his machine gun slung over his shoulder…

"Tell me what you see," Dafna said in a calm voice.

"I-I see her beaten down, assaulted both physically, mentally, and emotionally. They drugged her and chained her to a bed, day and night. She's so scared that at any minute someone could just walk in, drag her out, and shoot her in the head or behead her. They showed her photos and videos of Cerise and Dina and Morris. They told her they were in the crosshairs of a riflescope with an assassin's finger on the trigger. They told her if she didn't cooperate, the killer's finger would squeeze the trigger and murder them. They told her they were using her as bait for me. They knew I would show up. They told her they would kill me when I did…"

He saw her used as a pawn in a twisted chess match between two madmen brothers bent on destruction. One brother, a violent brute who threatened to kill her and called her horrible names—whore and bitch; the other brother, a manipulative narcissist with a martyr complex who wanted to wash away his guilty conscience through emotional manipulation. Ali's so-called kindness was doled out at the tip of his gun…

"Cyrus, I want you to come back," Dafna said. "Open your eyes on the count of three, two, one."

Cyrus pressed his fingers into his temples. "God…what she went through was hell."

"Do you feel how terrorized she must have been? Think about it. Layla alone, frightened out of her mind, helpless, completely at the mercy of fanatics. Then these fanatics begin to make headway into her psyche. One of them makes promises, a sliver of hope. Just enough to make her feel she might have some power after all. He allows her to believe he's fallen in love with her. He shows kindness to her. Whether he fell in love or not doesn't really matter. The fact is she sees a way to save those she loves. To protect them. It becomes an obsession, all she can think about. What else is there to reflect on during the endless hours of being chained to a bed? The seeds begin to grow inside of her, the roots burrowing deep into her until all that exists is the misguided notion that she and only she can save them."

"But why couldn't she have trusted that I would move Heaven and Earth to save her, to keep our child safe?"

"Cyrus, she may have believed that at first, but the minutes, hours, and days dragged by bringing her ever closer to what she believed was the end. The end of Cerise, of her grandparents. The end of you."

Cyrus scrubbed his face, wishing he could wipe away this terrible pain. Wishing he could have gotten to her sooner. Wishing he could have saved her from what she had gone through.

He took a deep, shaky breath and felt Layla's agony to the depths of his soul...

CHAPTER 31

Cyrus braced himself as he approached the front door of their home.

A dangerous combination of excitement and trepidation flowed through his veins. He hadn't seen Layla since the day they'd returned to Tel Aviv. Ten long days.

Considering the incertitude of their marriage, they'd both agreed it would be better to give each other some space while they worked through their issues with their therapists. Cerise was another matter. She needed to see her father, and he needed to see her. During the week, he'd picked Cerise up from school and spent a few hours with her before delivering her to her great-grandparents. But the weekend had been like being stranded alone on a deserted island, left with nothing but interminable hours of loneliness. It was like returning to who he was before Layla, the unfeeling, cold spy, incapable of love, or truly living. It was like a living death, and he knew if he didn't change the path he was on, he would die.

Unable to bear what seemed an unfair punishment, he'd called Layla and asked if he might pick Cerise up at the house today.

The door burst open, and a whirlwind of bouncing curls came rushing at him, screaming, "Daddy! You're home!" Cerise flew into his arms, nearly knocking him over.

His heart overflowed with love as he picked her up. He closed his eyes and buried his face in the sweet intoxicating scent of bubble gum bubble bath and four-year-old energy.

"*Abba*, *Ima* says we can go to the snow and make snow angels. And we never had our party. You promised, Daddy."

He rubbed his nose against hers. "You know Daddy always keeps his promises, baby."

She whispered in his ear. "I saw Mommy crying. She misses you." Her arms tightened around his neck. She leaned back and stretched upside down, her neck and face toward the door. "Don't you, Mommy? You miss Daddy?"

"I told you, baby, Daddy has been working," Layla answered.

Nice, Layla, you managed not to respond to the million-dollar question.

Layla stood at the door with her arms folded around her waist. Seeing her for the first time in more than a week, he felt blinded. *God, she's beautiful.* It was impossible for him to look away.

"Hello, Cyrus, how are you?" A smile tweaked the corners of her lips.

He fought to control the desire welling in him. "I'm good, Layla. How are you?" He wanted so badly to kiss her.

"I'm managing."

"You cut your hair."

She blushed and smoothed it back.

Just brushing her shoulders, the shorter cut made her hair even curlier. The gold-red curls framed her beautiful heart-shaped face. She looked like an angel.

"Yes. I needed…" Layla looked at Cerise, "…I've decided to make some changes in my life."

He dragged his eyes from her face, and he took in the rest of her. He wanted to ask what those changes might be but refrained knowing Cerise was listening.

"You look like you're going somewhere." He wished he hadn't asked, but he couldn't help himself. It was taking a supreme effort not to interrogate her. His stomach churned. *Damn, she's dressed up head to toe.*

"Daddy," Cerise interrupted, "when are you coming home?"

"Cerise, Daddy will let us know when he's coming back."

"But Mommy, *Abba* doesn't have to tell us he's coming home. He lives here."

Layla smiled. "Cerise, run in, and get your overnight bag."

Before dashing inside, she exclaimed, clapping her hands. "I'm having a sleepover at *Saba* and *Savta's.*"

Cyrus fought the questions burning like acid in his chest. "You look nice." She was dressed in heels, a tight black skirt, and a blue silk blouse. *She doesn't usually get dressed up for work. Is she going out?* Desolation filled him.

"Thank you. I have an engagement tonight. After work. I need you to drop Cerise at Dina and Morris's after your day with her."

His eyebrows raised. "Where…" He caught himself. "Look, I'm sorry this has been all on you. Cerise, I mean. I know you've had your hands full trying to keep things as normal as possible for her." Before he could stop himself, he added. "I'm sorry—for a lot of things."

She nodded. "I appreciate that, Cyrus. It's been hard. She doesn't understand why you're not here."

"I'm not sure I understand, either."

"Yes, well, we both know it's better this way for now. You probably shouldn't even be here now. I have so many mixed emotions."

"Mixed?"

"Yes. I don't know if I'm ready—" Layla's voice trembled. "To be alone with you."

He could feel his face heat with anger. "I'm not going to attack you, Layla. You have nothing to fear from me."

"I'm not afraid of you, Cyrus," she fired back. "I know it's irrational. It has nothing to do with you. It never did. I just need more time. I told you what I was feeling, but you refused to understand."

Back down, you fool. She said, 'was.' He clung to that thought. "I'm sorry. I didn't mean to push. I'm trying my best to understand."

Layla looked away, so he couldn't read her expression.

"Mommy," Cerise called, "I can't find *Arnav*."

"I'm coming, baby. Your rabbit is on the bed." She rushed down the hall to the bedrooms. He looked around; nothing had changed. Framed photos of their life together hung on the walls and filled the shelves. Cyrus's heart twisted in a knot when he picked up their wedding picture. It was a photo of them standing under the *chuppah*. The canopy was draped with roses. The way they looked at each other was unmistakable. Between them, they held an infant Cerise. That was how they expressed their vows, not only to each other but to their daughter. *The happiest day of my life. How did it come to this, Layla? What happened to us?*

His heart clamped in a vise being tightened by forces beyond his control. Dina's words replayed in his mind…*Layla's love for you is endless. It fills her whole being. You are the other half of her whole.*

He needed to hold on to those words.

Layla returned to the living room carrying Cerise's pink patent leather overnight bag. Cerise clutched her favorite stuffed animal to her breast.

He returned the wedding photo to its position of prominence. Determined, he knew he had to level with her. "Layla, I wasn't sincere before."

Her eyebrow shot up. "About what?"

"You don't look good. You look breathtakingly beautiful. So good that I've been disoriented since I got here. It's hard to be this close to you and not touch you."

Her blush made him want to go further, but he didn't dare with Cerise standing between them. Cerise's face tilted upward, watching.

"Mommy, can we make a party tomorrow?"

Cyrus chuckled, his fingers tousling Cerise's soft curls. His daughter was his best agent, incapable of being sidetracked from her desires.

Layla started to speak, but Cyrus interrupted. "Cerise, Daddy has to go away on business tomorrow. We'll have to save the party for when I get back. But I thought we'd go to the park and then get some ice-cream. Just you and me, a daddy and daughter day. We'll make a little pre-party just the two of us, *metukah*."

"But I want *Ima*, *Savta*, *Saba*, and Pop-pop at the party." Her lower lip protruded in the same adorable manner as her mother when she sulked.

Cyrus clutched his hands to his heart as if his feelings had been hurt. "Mademoiselle, you wound me. I thought I was the love of your life."

Giggling, she reached up, and he lifted her into his arms, raining kisses over her face. "Oh, Daddy, you are."

"Well then, let's get this party started." He looked at Layla. "I'll drop her at Morris and Dina's when we're done."

"I wish you were coming, Mommy?"

"Cerise, Mommy has something important to do. You and I will have a good time, and I'll be home for good before you know it." His gaze met Layla's. "Everything will be just the way it's always been. Right, Mommy?"

Layla fidgeted, she ran her fingers through her hair. Before she could protest, he leaned in and kissed her on the lips. He felt her shudder before she drew away. He couldn't read her reaction, whether it was pleasure or distaste she was feeling. He smiled down at her, hoping she felt the same way he did.

The child clapped her hands. "Kiss her again, Daddy. I like when you kiss Mommy."

This time Cyrus bent slowly, watching her eyes, and delivered a deeper kiss. Her lips were soft and yielding, gentle.

"Okay, enough kissing," Layla gasped, pulling away.

This time he knew he'd gotten to her. He could see the flush on her face. It was something for him to hold on to. For a second, he'd felt her response, and it wasn't revulsion.

She'd returned his kiss.

It's a start.

He was, without a doubt, the most exasperating man.

Her cheeks lit on fire with the memory of Cyrus's kiss. She sat at her desk, staring at her screen, re-reading the same sentence for the tenth time. She'd had a devil of a time getting any work done all day, and she had a work function to go to that evening. How in the world was she going to concentrate?

Layla stared at the computer screen without seeing it, the image of Cyrus holding Cerise played over and over in her mind. Then when he'd kissed her, she'd fought to maintain her equilibrium, to hide how it affected her. It had taken her by surprise, the flame of heat igniting inside her. She hadn't felt any revulsion. Or the fear she'd felt before…

You haven't destroyed me, Ali. I will find a way back to my life.

Orna had been indispensable, and her family was a safety net ready to catch her whenever she slipped backward. Slowly, but surely, her life was returning to her. The person she had been, maybe even a new, improved version, was emerging from the chaos and horrors she'd endured.

And now, in an unusual breach of standard behavioral treatment, she and Cyrus had insisted their therapists speak. Orna had told her she'd talked to Dafna, Cyrus's therapist. He was seeing her regularly, which was encouraging. It was proof he was committed to saving their marriage.

Letting him take Cerise was a step forward. Since coming home, she'd had difficulty letting her daughter out of her sight. Cerise was her link to sanity and love. But wasn't Cyrus that link as well? He used to be.

I don't want half of him—I want all of him. I want us to be whole.

The admission felt like a gentle breeze floating in from an open window.

When he kissed me, I didn't want him to stop. I wanted the kiss to go on forever.

His kiss had ignited her the way it used to, and she'd wanted to press herself against him. For the first time since coming home, she felt hopeful about reclaiming her marriage.

If only she didn't have the fancy dinner to attend with the wealthy patrons of the museum. She was tempted to leave early and stop by her grandmother's house, knowing that Dina would insist Cyrus join them for dinner. Layla was thankful that her grandparents and Aleck cared about Cyrus and accepted him, wanted him back in the fold. They were doing everything they could to make that happen.

I want you back too, Cyrus...

She pressed her fingers to her lips, remembering the heat of his kiss. She closed her eyes and imagined that kiss leading to greater intimacy. Passion sparked inside her. *I feel desire.* Tears welled in her eyes. *I didn't think I'd ever feel it again, but it's there inside of me for him.*

But she needed to know he believed in her again. With Orna's help, she'd realized just how much her marriage meant to her.

Now she needed to know it meant the same to Cyrus.

Cyrus was feeling more hopeful than he had since they got back from the US.

The kiss he'd shared with Layla took his breath away. Her lips had trembled as she kissed him back. He'd sensed her desire, the same rush of desire he'd always felt for her. He wished they'd had some private time to talk.

Maybe it's time you got off your ass and asked her out on a date. Cyrus chuckled. He'd done that four years ago after they'd reunited. They'd been through so much together in Iran. They'd fallen in love under such volatile, dangerous circumstances. After he was wounded and nearly died, he couldn't bear the thought of seeing her again. Convincing himself, she was better off without him. He'd been such an idiot.

You still are!

"Daddy, what's so funny?" Cerise asked as he unbuckled her from the car seat.

"I'm just thinking about how much fun we had today."

"We did have fun, Daddy? I love going to the park and feeding the ducks. Maybe Mommy can come with us next time." Cerise clapped her hands in glee.

He tapped her nose, loving her exuberance, knowing exactly where she got it from.

Layla.

Spending time with Cerise eased his loneliness. He lost himself in the constant chatter and affection his daughter poured over him. Like a gazelle leaping without direction, her active mind jumped from subject to subject. But his daughter also made him feel connected to Layla. He knew Layla was back at work at the museum and that she often didn't get home until late. He imagined between work and seeing her therapist, she didn't have too much free time.

He steeled himself as they walked to the porch and knocked. When Dina opened the door, she welcomed him inside.

"I really should go." He hoped she'd let him off the hook. He'd managed up until today to make his escape without Dina grilling him.

"Absolutely not, Cyrus. Come inside. I want to talk to you."

Out of habit, he searched the street. He wished someone or something would rescue him from the probing interrogation sure to come from the shrewd old woman. "It's dinner time. I don't want to intrude."

Laughing, she waved his ridiculous excuse away. "What a good idea, you can join us for dinner. I have a delicious lentil soup on the stove, and chicken and potatoes. I baked strudel, your favorite. There is plenty for everyone. Don't argue with an old woman. You'll lose."

"Yes, Daddy, stay *pleeeeeze…*?"

Shrugging his shoulders, he surrendered following Cerise into the house. He'd been living on falafels and hadn't had a home-cooked meal in weeks. He loved to cook and was usually the one who made dinner for Layla, Cerise, and himself…but being on his own…it wasn't the same. The aromas floating from the kitchen made his mouth water.

Morris was sitting in the living room watching TV. The old man's intelligent blue eyes lit with pleasure when Cyrus and Cerise entered. His thick silver hair brushed back off his high forehead gave him a distinguished appearance reminding Cyrus of an elder statesman. The two men shared a mutual understanding, a friendship far beyond their familial relationship. Cyrus trusted Morris, and he knew he could confide in him.

"*Saba!*" Cerise climbed into his lap and kissed his cheek.

"How's my baby girl?" he said in thick, Polish-accented Hebrew. "Did you have a good day with your *abba, metukah?*"

"Yes, *Saba. Abba's* staying for dinner."

"Is he? Are you sure we have enough food?" He winked at Cyrus, tickling Cerise.

"Oh, *Saba*, you know how much food *Savta* makes. You're always asking if she's expecting an army for dinner."

He scratched his head. "Ah, yes, I forgot. Your great-grandmother is always prepared for company." He motioned to the chair next to him. "Sit, Cyrus. Tell me how you've been."

Morris was much easier to deal with than Dina. Cyrus hoped he'd be able to avoid Dina's questions for a while longer.

"*Metukah*, go see if you can help your great-grandmother in the kitchen."

Cerise jumped from his lap and ran into the kitchen. Cyrus watched her. *How I've missed that bundle of energy.*

"I don't know what's going on between you and Layla. Dina and Layla keep me in the dark. But I'm telling you, whatever it is, the two of you need to fix it."

"I know Morris. I want to, but it's difficult."

Morris waved his hands. "Don't tell me. I only know one thing, Layla's been here every night, crying. It has to stop."

Cyrus's heart constricted. He looked down at his hands as if an answer lay within them. "I don't know what to do. I'm getting therapy, and Layla is too."

"Therapy, schmerapy, what the two of you need is a romantic getaway. That's my suggestion. Between Aleck, Dina, and me, we can handle Cerise for a few days. You take my granddaughter away, and I guarantee the two of you will work it out."

Cyrus gaped at Morris. *Maybe the old man's right? Maybe what Layla and I need is some time alone together?* "How do I convince her? Right now, she's not very open to any of my suggestions. She's angry. Said she needed more time and space. Accused me of not understanding what she's going through. I'm just frustrated. I don't mean to dump on you."

"Forget it, son. I know all about red-headed women and their tempers. I've been living with it for more than fifty years." He chuckled, slapping his knee. "Wouldn't trade it for anything, although there were times when I came close to hauling her over my shoulder and giving her a sound spanking."

Cyrus grinned. How well he knew the feeling. How many times had he wanted to do the same? Although knowing their shared passion, he was certain they would have ended up in bed."

"Let me talk to Dina," Morris said with a twinkle in his eye. "If anyone has any control over Layla, it's Dina. Two kindred souls, those two. It's hard to refuse my wife when she's determined."

"So, I've noticed. She hasn't said a word yet, but I feel like any minute she's going to blast me into outer space. Has she said anything to you?"

"If you're asking does Dina confide in me her conversations with Layla, the answer is no. Those two are as thick as thieves. God help anyone who tries to get between them."

"I failed Dina. She must be really angry with me. I promised I'd bring Layla home to her, but I don't think she was counting on our marriage falling apart."

"Let me handle Dina. I've been doing it longer than anyone on the planet. Beneath that gruff exterior lies a heart of gold. She loves you, Cyrus. I guarantee she's not going to send you into orbit. At least not yet." Morris smiled.

Cyrus couldn't help but grin. "You missed your calling, Morris. You should have been a comedian."

Morris threw his head back and laughed.

Cyrus's cell phone rang, and he pulled it out. Recognizing the number, he answered, his face froze. "My God! What happened?"

CHAPTER 32

Lis Maternity Hospital
Tel Aviv Sourasky Medical Center, Israel
September 30th

Cyrus burst from the elevator and ran across the polished white tiles to the nurse's station, ready to take down anyone who got in his way. Not even an act of God could have kept him from getting to Layla.

"Where is she, my wife, Layla Hassani?"

The nurse looked up wide-eyed with her best professional smile on her lips. "And you are?"

"I'm Cyrus Hassani—Layla Hassani's husband. Please, I need to know if she's all right."

The nurse typed in Layla Hassani and studied the screen. "I'll take you to her in just a minute. Doctor Steiner wants to speak with you first. Please have a seat, I'll notify him you're here."

Cyrus ran his fingers through his hair, trying to control his emotions. All he wanted was to get to Layla and find out what had happened to her. He considered running the nurse's blockade and checking every room on the floor. He'd give the doctor five minutes before turning the place upside down.

The elevator doors opened, and a man wearing blue surgical scrubs exited the elevator. Cyrus's heart nearly exploded from his chest. *Please don't let it be Layla he was operating on.*

He jumped up. "Dr. Steiner?"

The man in scrubs turned to him and held out his hand. "Mr. Hassani, pleased to meet you. I'm Max Steiner, Layla's doctor."

Cyrus shook his hand, ignoring all pleasantries. "What's wrong with my wife? What is she doing here?"

The doctor placed his hand on his shoulder, reassuringly. "Your wife's not in any danger—"

"Then what is she doing here?"

"My wife and I are on the board of the Israeli Museum of Art and were at tonight's charity dinner when Layla fainted."

Cyrus felt the color drain from his face. "Do you know why?"

"Yes, but I wanted to do a few tests to confirm what I suspected."

Cyrus was having a hard time following the conversation. He didn't understand why Layla had fainted, she'd seemed fine that morning when he picked up Cerise. "What is it, what do you suspect?"

The doctor looked at him as if he might be missing a screw. "She has a tendency to forget to eat and drink during pregnancy. This is exactly what happened last time with Cerise. Layla had no idea she was pregnant, and she neglected herself, and as a result, she became anemic and vitamin deficient. It's not intentional on her part, but it is dangerous."

"Wait…are you telling me Layla's pregnant?"

"Yes, in fact, when she fainted at the charity dinner, I suspected it. When I told her, she burst into tears. She was very distraught, so we called an ambulance and I admitted her. I'm not sure how far along she is yet. I'll know better when the tests come back. But, the pregnancy I'm sure of. You're going to be a father again."

Cyrus's knees buckled, and he stumbled. Dr. Steiner grabbed his arm to steady him. "Am I going to have to admit the husband?"

"No, I'm fine, it's just that—stress. Layla's been under an inordinate amount of stress as of late."

"Let's go into my office, and you can explain what this stress is, so we can decide how best to handle it?"

"Wait. I-I have to see her. This is all my fault." Cyrus was breathing heavily as though he'd run a marathon. Sweat had broken out on his forehead, and his chest was tight, but he couldn't afford to lose it. *Layla needs me!* "It's my fault," he repeated.

"Layla is resting, and a nurse is on duty watching over her." The doctor put his arm around Cyrus's shoulder and led him down the hall. "Mr. Hassani, I think you should sit down. I'll get you some water and something to calm your panic attack."

A few minutes later, Cyrus was seated in Dr. Steiner's office, his breathing had calmed down, and he was able to think more clearly. *She's okay. Layla is okay. Trust the doctor.*

"Tell me what happened so we can help," Dr. Steiner said.

"I'm sure you heard about the bombing in New York a few weeks ago," Cyrus began. He gave the doctor a brief summation of Layla's kidnapping in New York and her captivity in Lancaster. Cyrus also told him about the terrorists and their brutality and manipulation of Layla and Ali's rape of his wife. And then he admitted what he feared might be the truth. "Layla may be carrying the child of a terrorist."

"My God, what a horrible ordeal. Layla should have had a complete physical as soon as she returned from the US, but that's water under the bridge now." He paused for a minute, jotting down notes on his laptop before continuing. "I can also recommend an excellent therapist for Layla.

"She has one, Dr. Orna Wiseman—"

"Yes, yes, I know her, she's excellent," Dr. Steiner cut in. "I'll get in touch with her first thing tomorrow." He sat back and steepled his fingers on his chest. "Mr. Hassani, how you want to handle this is completely up to you and Layla. We can do a DNA test, and if she's not too far along, it would be possible to terminate the pregnancy if it's not yours—that is if you both desire it."

It was as if Cyrus were being hurled back in time to his childhood. He remembered his mother pregnant with his sister Ester. Ester was the result of his mother being raped in prison by Jalal Rahimi, a man who would become Cyrus's superior at Oghab2, Iran's secret counterintelligence service. In the end, Cyrus would destroy him, but not before telling Rahimi the truth about the daughter he never knew. He also informed Rahimi that the daughter he fathered would never know of his existence.

Now, as Cyrus contemplated the possibility of Layla being pregnant with the terrorist's child, he knew just as he couldn't imagine a world without Ester—who he loved beyond reason—this child too must be born into a loving home just like his. Cyrus's father had loved Ester as if she were his own. In fact, to this day, Ester had never known different, and she never would...How could he then be less than his own father?

But what about Layla? She's the victim here. If the child is Ali's, isn't that up to Layla to decide?

Cyrus's mind was spinning with questions, none of which he could answer on his own. "Can I see my wife now?"

"Yes, but I don't want you to upset or excite her. Do you understand?"

"You have my word."

Cyrus couldn't control the rush of emotion when he entered the hospital room. Layla was asleep, curled in on herself like a small child. It reminded him of Cerise. He felt a punch to his heart. He'd been so intent on saving her life in Lancaster, on being the hero, expecting her to rush into his arms with happiness, that he'd failed to see the signs of Layla's PTSD. Despite years of training and experience working in the field as an agent, he'd failed to see the signs of her trauma. Instead, he'd wallowed in his own feelings of jealousy. He'd allowed his ego to override all else. Running off, abandoning his wife when she needed him most.

I promise Layla, I'll make it up to you. I promise.

He didn't deserve her, but dear God, he would spend the rest of his life trying to.

Cyrus moved a chair next to the bed, careful not to wake Layla. She mumbled in her sleep, and he leaned in, trying to decipher her words.

"Oh God," she moaned, "don't let him touch me."

Tears flooded his eyes as he gathered her into his arms, holding her against his chest, wishing he could banish away her terror. What she cried out next sliced into him like a knife…"No, Ali! He'll hate me… please…I can't. Please, Cyrus, don't hate me…"

Layla trembled against Cyrus, sobbing into his shirt, as she opened her eyes. It took a moment for her gaze to clear and register his presence.

"Cyrus? W-what are you doing here?" She sniffed back her tears.

"The hospital called me on my cell," he said, gently combing back the damp strands of hair off her face.

"Oh…" and then like a cloudburst, the tears began to rain down once more. Layla's hands flew to her face as if she were hiding from his gaze. "I'm sorry, so sorry, I wish I could change everything."

"*Eshgham,*" he kissed her hair, her forehead, her cheeks, "I'm the one who is sorry. I was such an idiot. Please forgive me for abandoning you. Forgive me for not supporting you. I love you so much, Layla. Nothing can ever change that."

She looked up at him, confusion clouding her eyes. "But, I rejected you and made you feel unwanted."

"I'm an ass. I should have been supportive and understood the ordeal you'd been through—I should have been patient and given you time. Please, my darling, forgive me? I'll do anything to make you mine again."

"I'm yours, Cyrus, always yours, but I need to be able to tell you everything. I can't hold this inside, it's eating me alive."

"Why don't we meet together with Orna and Dafna? You can pour your heart out, yell at me, slap me, so long as in the end, you tell me you love me." He kissed the tears from her face.

Her girlish giggle made him smile. "Yes…oh, yes. But come home, Cyrus, please come home. I don't want to face another night in our bed without you."

"You won't have to, baby. Never again." With a shaky hand, he caressed her face. "As soon as the doctor says you're okay to leave, I'm taking you home." He needed to reassure her, he needed her to know where he stood. "Layla, Dr. Steiner told me about your pregnancy."

Pain shadowed her eyes. "I only just found out myself. Please believe me."

"Shh, *eshgham*, I believe you. You've been through so much." He kissed her forehead.

"How do you feel about it?" she whispered.

His vision blurred with tears as he gazed into her magnificent turquoise eyes as fathomless as the sea. "I love you, Layla, and no matter what happens, I will always love you from the depths of my soul. I will always desire you with every fiber of my being. I will always be your husband until the end of time, and I will always love our children and protect them and you with my very life…"

CHAPTER 33

The taxi pulled into a marina and wound its way through the slips arriving at a beautiful sleek yacht with the name Bathsheba lettered in black and gold across its bow.

Layla leaned forward. "What are we doing here?"

"This is where we're staying." Cyrus opened the car door and got out.

"But…how…" She followed him out of the car and stood gaping at the luxury yacht.

"Close your mouth, baby, before something flies in. I mentioned to my colleague Saul who works the North America desk, that I was taking you to Eilat. The guy was so impressed with what went down in America he insisted we stay on his in-law's boat. I had no idea it was anything like this, though. I can't wait to get aboard."

They stood at the bottom of the gangplank, and a man in nautical whites appeared waving to them. "Welcome aboard Bathsheba, Mr. and Mrs. Hassani. We're delighted to have you."

Layla and Cyrus shook hands with Captain Efron and his crew, and then the steward, Ariella, showed them to their suite. After their luggage was delivered and the door shut, Layla squealed with delight and flung herself on the bed.

"I can't believe this, Cyrus. It's like a dream come true. Did you hear the captain say cocktails and hors d'oeuvres would be served at five? I feel like a movie star."

Cyrus looked down at her, amusement gleamed in his eyes. "I heard." He looked around the suite. "You know I've never dreamed about living this kind of over the top life, but I must admit seeing you light up like an Israeli Independence Day fireworks display has me rethinking my priorities."

"What do you mean?

"I'll never be able to give you this lifestyle, baby, and you should have it."

In a flash, she was up from the bed, her arms around his neck. "I don't care about any of this, Cyrus. I didn't fall in love with a stockbroker or a businessman. I fell in love with a spy who happens to be a nuclear physicist. A man who lives his life in service to others. I don't regret marrying you for one moment. What we share is so much more than the accumulation of things."

He kissed her. The warmth became a burning desire. She pressed herself against him, and he trailed his lips along her jaw and whispered in her ear. "I want to do this right, *eshgham*. I love you and Cerise. I need you, Layla. I was lost without you. You saved me once, save me again."

His words reminded her that he was not just her lover, he was her best friend, the man who understood her better than anyone ever had. The man who brought her home from the hospital two weeks ago and barely left her side since.

Cerise had been ecstatic but anxious as well. She began to sneak into their bed at night and crawl in between them. They finally got to the truth, Cerise was worried either one or both would disappear. They had both choked back tears as they reassured Cerise that sometimes Mommy or Daddy would have to go away for work or family reasons, but they would always come back, and they would always make sure she was safe and happy.

Layla and Cyrus had also had several sessions with Dafna and Orna together, which had helped as well.

Despite their rocky start when they got back from the US, Layla was thankful for Cyrus's strength and support. "Thank you for reminding me our love isn't built on sand. What we share is special."

Bathsheba cruised out of Eilat Harbor into the Gulf of Aqaba. Cyrus and Layla relaxed on the top deck in the blue terry upholstered sunbathing pen. The rays of the afternoon sun-bronzed their bodies, burnishing them with coppery splendor.

Cyrus found it hard to keep his eyes off Layla in her tiny peach crochet bikini. She lay on her stomach on the smallest of baby-bumps watching the yacht sail out of the harbor, wearing large *Jackie O* sunglasses, looking every bit to the manor born. No longer able to resist, he grinned and ran his hand over her derriere. Warm skin and muscle quivered beneath his touch, firming his desire protruding from his swim trunks.

She laughed. "I thought you wanted to wait for the moment when we hear violins playing and a chorus of angels singing."

"I'm beginning to enjoy the torture of restraint. Touching you just intensifies it all. Once we hit the water, I'm sure I'll deflate."

She turned to her side and caressed him, running her fingers over his leg. "I doubt that. It's been quite a while since we made love. I figure that part of your anatomy has been denied long enough."

"Fifty days, to be exact."

She giggled. "What? Have you been counting them off? I'd better prepare myself for fireworks."

"You bet I've been counting them off, and yes, you'd better prepare yourself." He wriggled, trying to make his trunks a tad more comfortable.

The teasing repartee put him at ease. Of all the numerous blessings, humor was the one that kept him under Layla's spell. Not a day in their life together had he not found himself amused and delighted. Decidedly serious and oft times morbid, around her, he found himself with a perpetual smile on his face. They'd only been back together a short time since her release from the hospital. It was part of their joint therapy. She slept in his arms, but they hadn't made love. They both needed time to readjust. This vacation was the honeymoon they'd never had, and it would also be their first lovemaking reunion since she'd left for the exhibition in New York. Already he felt the weight of the world lift from his shoulders. *Appreciate what you have,* he told himself, *and never let your damn jealousy and insecurities threaten the only thing that makes life worth living. You have nothing without her.*

They swam together through majestic coral gardens. The boat had anchored a safe distance from the reef, and a tender had brought them in close. Captain Efron had briefed them on some of the attributes of the reefs, but nothing could describe the magical paradise they found themselves in.

He'd told them the coral reefs of Eilat extend more than three-quarters of a mile along the shore. Both he and Layla were excited. Captain Efron promised to take them to many of the premier diving sights over the next couple of days.

Sunlight pierced the shallow canyons, mazes, and bays of the reef where hundreds of different species of aquatic life lived amid the gardens of colorful coral.

As beautiful as the underwater landscape was, Cyrus found himself unable to look away from Layla. He watched as she swam among the tropical fish, gliding through the azure blue water, her auburn hair floating around her like a halo. She looked like a mermaid. Eilat was famous for its unique species of fish. Amusing himself, he wondered if he should announce to the scientific community he'd discovered a new species, the Laylafish.

Cyrus held his breath as a sea turtle swam close to Layla, drawn to the flame of hair floating around her mask. The turtle stuck his tongue out as if to taste the auburn tresses. A stream of bubbles rose like a string of pearls from her snorkel. Her laughter rang soundlessly, silenced by the sea. She kicked to the surface, and Cyrus followed her.

Her laughter filled his ears. "Did you see that turtle?" She gasped, delighted, lifting her mask. "He wanted to take a nibble of my hair."

"I can't blame him. I want to nibble on you too."

She laughed. "It was amazing, surreal. The turtle actually rubbed his nose on my mask. We need to buy an underwater camera tomorrow and take pictures. Cerise will go crazy when she sees. Maybe we can convince her being a mermaid is more fun than being a snow angel. She's driving me crazy with wanting to make snow angels."

"We'll get a camera, and we'll convince Cerise she's a mermaid like her mother. By the way, I think that turtle fell in love with you. Maybe you should have kissed him like the frog in the fairy tale."

"I see. You think if I kissed him, the turtle would have turned into a prince? My prince?"

Cyrus looked over her shoulder at the purple mountains of Eilat. His jest suddenly made him uncomfortable. He wondered if he'd ever get beyond his insecurity of not believing he was good enough for her. "I've never killed a turtle, but there's always a first time," he joked. He knew there was an ounce of truth to his words. Regardless of his insecurities, he'd never let anything or anyone take her from him.

"Ah, but you see, I kissed an Iranian frog once upon a time, and he turned into my prince, my personal Superman." She swam to him and wrapped her arms around his neck. They kicked their flippers, holding each other aloft.

She left him nowhere to look but into her turquoise blue eyes that matched the sea around them. She kissed him, and time seemed to stop. They were in a world of their own. A world where anything was possible.

It was what she wanted, what she'd prayed for. Healing, trusting, and a new beginning with the only man she'd ever loved. Her grandmother and Orna had said it would happen, and now she knew it was true. She and Cyrus had found their way back to each other. Nothing stood between them.

He was sucking her neck, and it was making her crazy. "We've been talking all day and night, baby. Hmmm," he nibbled her neck.

She couldn't control the shiver of desire that rippled through her. Cyrus's lips did things to her body that were beyond her control. Her chest rose, and her nipples pebbled, her body arched toward him. When his hands encircled her breasts, his fingers delicately manipulating her nipples, in soft pinches, she gasped. "Oh…".

"Mmm, baby, I love it when you show me how I make you feel." His hands dropped to the button and zipper on her pants, undoing them. He slipped his hands down, beneath the fabric, lightly kneading her stomach, caressing her thighs, teasing her without touching her sex. All the while, he eased her pants to the floor.

Breathlessly she murmured. Make love to me, Cyrus. No more words, just show me."

Their lips met in a searing kiss. Their tongues touched, twisted, and spun around each other in a dance. Cyrus carried her to the bed. He wanted to take his time, to drive her crazy with the power of his desire, to lick and taste every inch of her, but when her hand dropped to his hardness and enfolded his shaft, rubbing him against her wetness, he went mad. All his plans fell by the wayside. *I have to have her now.* He lifted her leg over his arm, opening her, and swift like an arrow quivering toward its target, he drove himself into her.

"Ah…" Bliss filled her face as he slipped slowly in and out of her with a controlled rhythm. She gripped the tensed muscles of his buttocks and pulled him deeper, absorbing his thrusts. It was impossible to have control when she stole it away. Each time he penetrated, she moaned with pleasure. It was heaven seeing her desire. Whatever doubts he'd held about her conquering her aversion to sex were dispelled by her sighs, by the rapturous glow of her face.

"Cyrus?"

He'd been lost in the sensual moment, and hearing his name pulled him back into the physical realm.

"Yes, baby?" He breathed, continuing to fill her. He sank deep within her, pelvis to pelvis, skin on skin. An endless cycle of penetrating thrusts, driving them toward fulfillment.

She pushed him onto his back, catching him off guard. She rose to her knees, straddled him, and guided him back inside of her. She rocked against him with a rhythm that made him harder. "Touch me. Please."

He fingered her sex, pressing and circling in equal measure, his eyes riveted to her beautiful face, the way her back arched when she took him deeper into her body. He wasn't sure who was inside of whom.

"Cyrus!" He felt her orgasm surround him, clenching him as he continued to fill her with every aching inch of his passion. She collapsed on his chest, her body trembling, her breathy gasps making him throb even more.

"I've dreamt of this so many times," he whispered. He ran his hands down her back, sliding his fingers over the moisture glistening on her skin. He was hard as a stake inside of her. Throbbing.

She kissed his chest, giggling. "More. I want more. Take me again."

He pulled from her and rolled her over.

Lifting her to her knees, he slipped his hardness between her folds. He began to thrust deep as his hands held tight to her hips. Each time she tried to breathe, it was stolen by his possession of her. "Oh…Layla…I love you." When they came simultaneously, it was long and powerful. A release that had eluded him for what seemed an eternity. Without this connection, he was empty, without purpose.

He pulled from her, turned her over, and held her close. Kissing his way to her ear, he whispered, "*Eshgham*, you are mine."

With a contented sigh, she whispered back. "Yes. Forever."

She gazed into his eyes, and the love shining from her eyes brought tears to his own.

"My darling, you are mine," she whispered.

"Yes. Forever."

Exhausted, they fell asleep.

EPILOGUE

"*Abba*, *Ima*!" Cerise hurled herself into their arms, embracing them. Green eyes wide with excitement, her words tumbled from her. "We're having a party! A welcome home party! Hurry, come inside. Savta says I can't have cake until you come inside."

"*Metukah*, slow down and give your daddy a kiss," Cyrus said.

Cerise lavished kisses all over his face and then did the same to Layla, her exuberance like that of an overly affectionate puppy made Layla giggle, and soon all three were laughing.

Aleck and Morris joined Dina on the porch.

"*Metukah*," Dina interrupted, "Let your abba and ima come inside. We have a cake to cut."

Cerise squealed and clapped her hands together. "Cake!" She ran into the house.

Dina shook with laughter. "Just like your mother, Layla, Cerise has an excessive fondness for cake."

Morris put his arm around Dina's shoulder. "And we all know where that gene came from."

Dina elbowed him in his paunch. "As if you could go a day without something sweet."

"You are my something sweet, Dinala."

Cyrus took Layla's hand and squeezed. When she gazed up at him, he stole a kiss making her sigh with pleasure.

After dinner, Layla loaded the dishwasher listening to the sounds of her family coming from the living room. The reunion of her small, close-knit family was like a dream come true. The kidnapping nightmare no longer had the power to harm her or those she loved. Dina wrapped her thin arms around her and hugged her.

"See, *liebchen*, everything is as it should be. You and Cyrus are where you belong. Together. And you will face whatever comes together."

"Cyrus and I will find out tomorrow about the baby."

Worried lines surrounded Dina's eyes as she held Layla's chin and forced her to meet her gaze. "How is he with this?"

"He says he wants the baby no matter what, but I know it has to be killing him. I told you that in Iran, his mother was raped in prison. *Ester*, his sister, was born nine months later. Oh, Bubbie…" The tears she'd been fighting won their battle. She pressed her fingers to her eyelids, but it was no more effective than sticking her fingers in a dike. "We both want this baby so much. I don't know what I'll do if it's not his."

Dina patted her back. "Shush, *metukah*. We will survive this. You will see my darling. It's too soon to decide on a course of action. You and Cyrus are strong. It's the only thing that matters."

Layla's sobs subsided. "I never dreamed he'd be so supportive. I was so wrong to think we wouldn't be able to get past what happened."

Dina nodded. "It's understandable. He loves his sister. Cyrus is a complicated man. It's best not to form a belief in what he might or might not do. He will surprise you every time, I think? You need to believe one thing and one thing alone."

"What's that?"

"You need to know he will never leave you or stop loving you. This, I am sure of."

The next day, Layla and Cyrus sat together in Dr. Steiner's office. They held hands. Layla felt as if she were waiting for the verdict to come down from a jury. She'd agreed not to discuss what they would do should the child not be his. He agreed it was best to wait as well, and she clung to the hope it was his.

Cyrus held fast to her hand. He whispered, "Relax, *aziz am*. Whatever happens, we're in this together. Nothing changes."

Dr. Steiner entered and sat across from them. His face was beaming. "The results were incontrovertible."

Cyrus squeezed her hand.

"Cyrus, you're the father. Layla, the pregnancy looks fine."

Cyrus jumped up and pulled Layla to her feet, wrapping his arms around her, he twirled her around in joy. "Yes! I knew it, *eshgham*."

Layla's hands flew to her mouth, suppressing a cry of joy. Tears etched a path down her cheeks. The nightmare was truly over. Cyrus gathered her into his arms. "*Eshgham, eshgham*, it's okay, my love. Don't cry heart of my heart."

"I'm just so happy." Instinctively her hand caressed her abdomen where the embodiment of their love grew.

"I'll leave you two alone with your good news. Congratulations."

Cyrus shook the doctor's hand. "Thank you, doctor."

Layla nodded and smiled through her tears as she leaned against Cyrus for support. "Thank you, doctor."

"You're both very welcome." He smiled and left the office.

Cyrus brushed her happy tears away with his kisses. "A baby, we're going to have a baby." He picked her up and spun them in circles.

He held her tight.. She snuggled closer, molding herself to him, soothed by the echoing of their two hearts, which seemed to beat as one. Resting in the safe haven of his embrace, she lifted her face to his. Their eyes met, and he kissed her. His kiss was as necessary as breathing, drinking, eating, or sleeping. His love was the nourishment her heart craved. When he dropped to his knees and kissed her belly, adoring her, she knew all was right with the world. Their love had triumphed, and whatever the future held, it always would.

RANSOM: TIP OF THE SPEAR SERIES BOOK 3

SNEAK PEEK

Tel Aviv, Israel
December 25
8:00 a.m.

"*Ima*, when is the baby going to get here? I want a sister. Can't you order one of those?" Cerise, declared from her perch in her pink booster seat at the kitchen table. She blew away the red curls that kept tumbling in front of her eyes as she twisted and turned the colored rows of the Rubik's cube in her pudgy hands.

Cyrus Hassani and his wife Layla exchanged amused grins at their precocious four-year-old daughter. She was so focused on proving to her father that she could solve the puzzle as fast as he had. It was a wonder she had time to pepper them with questions about the coming baby.

Cyrus stood at the counter, dicing Persian cucumber and tossed it into the bowl of red onion, tomato, mint, and lemon juice already marinating for the Persian Shirazi salad they would have for breakfast. "*Eshgham, my love.*" He winked at Layla. "Do you want to take this one?" He always reverted to his first language, Farsi, when using terms of endearment.

Layla laughed as she stirred scrambled eggs in a skillet on the stove. "Cerise, it's not like going to the ice cream shop. You can't pick your flavor. You have to accept what God gives you."

"I think we should give it back if it's a boy." Cerise wrinkled her nose.

"Whoa, what do you mean, give him back? What's wrong with boys? I thought you loved your *Aba*. I'm a boy." Cyrus huffed in playful dismay.

"I'll show you what boys are good for." He laid the knife down on the cutting board and pounced on Cerise, tickling her until her giggles rang out.

"Daddy, stop tickling me. You're the only boy I like."

"I see," he brushed her wayward curls out of her eyes. "And what about the boy at preschool? What's his name?"

Cerise's dimple in her chin, so much like his, deepened with her smile. "Jacob—his name is Jacob. I forgot he's a boy." She shrugged one delicate shoulder.

"You forgot because he's your friend. That's what matters anyway." Cyrus tapped her nose. "I think you'll make a wonderful big sister to a baby brother. Think of all the things you'll be able to teach him, like the Rubik's cube."

"Daddy, he'll be a baby, too little for a puzzle."

Cyrus returned to the salad and threw in a pinch of salt and ground a healthy dose of pepper onto the salad, tossed it, and set it on the table. He smiled at his daughter's adorable face, scrunched up in deep concentration as she worked on completing the white side. When had this child of his heart grown up? That thought was scarier to him than going into battle. He tucked the wayward curl behind her ear, only to have it fall forward again.

"There's a butterfly clip in that little glass bowl beside the microwave," Layla commented as she watched Cyrus try to tame his daughter's curly locks into submission.

"She has your hair." He chuckled as he grabbed the clip and gathered Cerise's hair on top of her head. Cerise gave a triumphant yell when she finished the white side.

"Maybe, but she has your ability to tune everything out when she's working on something." Layla threw over her shoulder, making her thick auburn ponytail swing back and forth in its high ponytail. She winced, her hand dropping to her lower back. She was in the last bloom of her pregnancy, and her back had begun to trouble her.

Cyrus joined Layla at the stove, encircling her waist, he rubbed her back with one hand and caressed her belly with the other. When he kissed her neck, she leaned back into his shoulder and sighed.

I'm the luckiest man in the world to be so blessed. Somehow, this damaged spy has found true happiness.

The man who'd never wanted or aspired to marriage and children had somehow found both. Layla looked up at him with those incredible turquoise eyes that never failed to send a tremor through his body.

In his estimation, he was married to the most beautiful woman he'd ever known. Proof enough for him, there was a God. He continued to massage Layla's aching back as she explained to their four-year-old that she needed to be patient. He almost chuckled at that. His daughter was also like him in that way. Patience was certainly not one of his virtues, nor was it hers.

Cyrus's phone vibrated in his pocket. He took it out and frowned at the caller ID, then slipped it back into his pocket.

Layla waddled to the table with the frying pan and set it down.

"Mommy, what will we name him?" Cerise set the Rubik's cube down, her attention now on the eggs, her mother was dishing onto a plate for her.

Layla set the plate in front of Cerise, sat beside her, and caressed her hair. "Maybe we'll call him Rubik if he's a boy."

Cerise giggled as she picked up her spoon and scooped up a bite of egg.

Cyrus's phone hummed once again. He ignored it as he sat across from his wife and child. He dished a heaping amount of eggs onto his plate and beside it an equal amount of salad.

Layla lifted a delicate brow at him as she sipped her coffee.

"It's the office." Cyrus frowned at the screen once more, weighing whether or not to answer.

He could always say he'd been in the shower and missed the call.

"It could be important," Layla said.

"Everything's important to them."

"You have to answer it, Daddy."

Cyrus traced Cerise's delicate furrowed brows and tried to keep a straight face at his daughter's admonishment. Looking into her Nile, green eyes was like staring into a mirror.

Yes, she certainly is my daughter.

The phone stopped buzzing. "Too late," he said. "If it's important, they'll call back."

A second later, it vibrated a third time. Cyrus sighed, knowing the caller would just keep calling until he answered. "I'd better take this." He slipped out the sliding glass doors to the patio as he swiped the phone. "Hassani here."

Layla's conversation with Cerise faded into the background as he concentrated on what the man was saying.

"Aryeh disappeared a few days ago in Beirut," his supervisor on the Iran desk growled.

"Newsflash, Saul. That's what spies do. They go off the radar when necessary."

"Not with fifty million in diamonds belonging to Mossad," Saul countered. "The Ramsad wants to see you. Now."

"He promised me this leave of absence. He knows damn well what Layla and I have been through, how close we came to losing everything. Fuck, I nearly lost my child."

"Things change. Cyrus, this isn't a request; it's an order. He's waiting for you at headquarters."

Cyrus hung up and scratched at the stubble on his face. *Dammit, Aryeh, what the hell have you gotten yourself into?*

He returned to the kitchen and sat back down. Layla reached across the table and covered his hand with hers.

"You have to go, don't you?" she whispered.

He sighed as he watched his daughter. Cerise was munching on a slice of toast with her tablet in front of her and watching her favorite Disney movie, Frozen, for the tenth time, at least.

"Yes."

Layla set his hand on her belly. "I thought we had another week before you had to go back."

"I did too… but something's come up." He gently rubbed circles on her abdomen.

"Can you talk about it?"

"Aryeh's gone missing in Beirut."

Layla shrugged. "That seems pretty ordinary to me. I mean, he's an intelligence agent. Disappearing is par for the course, isn't it?"

"Normally, I'd say yes, but this might be a little more complicated." He leaned back and scraped his fingers through his black hair in frustration. "The Ramsad wants to talk to me. I have to go."

"The Ramsad? Will you be gone long?"

Cerise's laughter rang out, and he smiled, distracted.

"Do you think you'll be home for dinner?" Layla smiled, tantalizingly at him. "I'm making your favorite."

He chuckled. "My favorite, eh?"

She nodded, her eyes gleaming with sensuous promise.

"I'll call you and let you know if the meeting goes long." He pulled her into his arms and brushed his lips over hers. "I can hardly stand leaving you. You know that, don't you?"

The call couldn't have come at a more unwelcome time. He and Layla had just reconciled, and things were still fragile between them. Whatever it was, it better not take him away from Layla and Cerise.

She gazed into his eyes. "Yes, I know," she said softly, "I can't bear to be without you, either, but you have to go."

Like what you've read so far? You can get RANSOM (Tip of the Spear Series Book 3) on Amazon in 2020. Or visit belleamiauthor.com to find out more.

ABOUT THE AUTHOR

Belle Ami writes breathtaking international thrillers and compelling romantic suspense with a touch of sensual heat. A self-confessed news junky, Belle loves to create cutting-edge stories weaving world issues, espionage, fast-paced action, and of course, redemptive love.

Belle is the author of the international espionage thriller series *TIP OF THE SPEAR*, which includes the highly acclaimed *Escape*, *Vengeance*, and *Ransom*. She is planning more books for the future.

She is also the author of the bestselling *OUT OF TIME* thriller series, which includes the #1 Amazon bestseller—*The Girl Who Knew da Vinci* and #1 Amazon bestseller—*The Girl Who Loved Caravaggio* and the upcoming *The Girl Who Adored Rembrandt*.

Belle is also the author of the romantic suspense series *THE ONLY ONE*, which includes *The One*, *The One & More*, and *One More Time is Not Enough*.

Recently, she was honored to be included in the RWA-LARA Christmas Anthology *Holiday Ever After*, featuring her short story, *The Christmas Encounter*.

A former Kathryn McBride scholar of Bryn Mawr College in Pennsylvania, Belle, is also thrilled to be a recipient of the *RONE*, *RAVEN*, and *Readers' Favorite Awards*.

Belle's passions include hiking, boxing, skiing, cooking, travel, and of course, writing. She lives in Southern California with her husband, two children, a horse named Cindy Crawford, and her brilliant Chihuahua, Giorgio Armani.

Belle loves to hear from readers—you can contact her at: belle@belleamiauthor.com

Connect with Belle Ami online:
belleamiauthor.com
BookBub
Amazon
Twitter: @BelleAmi5
Facebook
Instagram
Newsletter Signup